PRAISE FOR DIANE BENEFIEL

Solitary Man

NATIONAL READERS' CHOICE AWARD WINNING NOVEL

"I am in love with this story. I devoured this book and didn't want it to end. The chemistry between the characters and the plot kept me wanting to read late into the night. This is my first read from Diane Benefiel but definitely not my last. I can't wait to read more from this amazing author. Thank you Diane Benefiel for getting me hooked on your books!" ~ CJ's Book Corner

"Ryder was exactly who Brenna needed in her life, and trust me when I say you will love him because yeah he really is that good of a guy. Solitary Man is my first book by this author and it will not be the last. I really think you all will enjoy this one as much as I did it is one I do recommend." ~ I'm A Sweet And Sassy Book Whore

"I really enjoyed this book and there were a few twists and turns that kept me completely involved in the story. This is the first time I have read this author and it definitely won't be my last!" ~ Sassy Southern Book Blog

THE JAMESONS US MARSHALS SERIES

Hidden Betrayal

"As someone who never pre-orders ANYTHING, I put my order in a WEEK before it came out. Know why? Because I just didn't want to wait! And this was definitely the right move. I loved the dialogue between her and Linc--with her saying, "I didn't stay back because *I* was handling it." Yes, he's a hottie with a protective streak, but she's certainly no little woman. It really WORKS. In the end, 10/10. Can't wait to pre-order the next one too!" ~ Amelia

"An exciting, romantic read with a sexy hero and a determined heroine who is hell-bent on doing things her own way. The romance heats up as the plot thickens. Link and Mikayla need to work together to survive, but along the way, the sparks start flying. You need to read this!" ~ Danube Eichinger

HIGH SIERRAS SERIES

Flash Point

"Diane Benefiel takes us on a story filled with mystery, suspense, and action as we try to solve what is going on in the small town of Hangman's Loss. Flash Point is a story that will have you flipping the pages and wondering who is the behind the attacks against Hangman's newest resident and why." ~ Sarah Reads

"*Flash Point* really surprised me. It's not what I was expecting but I really enjoyed reading it. It's a fun easy read that captured me from the start." ~ Coffee Chat

Dead Giveaway

"Diane has written yet another winner in her High Sierra series. Murder witness and 'person of interest' Gwen flees with her godson to Cameron's uncle Eli. Gwen and Eli have no use for one another but come together for Cameron's sake and to find the true murderer...and in the process find their way to one another. My evening with Gwen and Eli couldn't have been more delightful, and I look forward to the next installment of the High Sierras." ~seniorphotog

"I loved this second book in the High Sierras series. This is a story of two people who are attracted to each other, but reconnecting under the worst of circumstances. I discovered Ms. Benefiel's books and have loved the careful way she draws you in to the story with characters that make you feel as if you are reading about friends. I am really looking forward to the next High Sierras book, *Already Gone*." ~paytonpuppy

Already Gone

"This series has only gotten better and better! Seriously, there's something that really speaks to my heart about Maddy and Logan, and Hangman's Loss FEELS like a small California town tucked away in the Sierras. They're such a power couple! I read this book in just a couple of days--totally sucked me in. It's that perfect blend of fun, sizzle, and suspense! I just want to live in Maddy's life forever but since I can't--I can't wait for the next book!" ~Katharine Montgomery

"A wonderful story about second chances. The minute you start reading, you will be instantly hooked. The author weaves a tale of drama and romance that keeps you enthralled and turning the pages. Maddie is feisty and Logan is her brooding and over protective suffering hero. The sparks fly every time they see each other. Eventually they give in and realize that they are perfect for each other and have always been. This is a great story right up to the last word." ~Simatsu

Burnover in **Rescued Anthology**

"Sweet, Sexy stories featuring furbabies and helping to save lives, it's a win win for all." ~Kara's Books

"8 stories by 8 outstanding authors. In these stories, there is a tattoo artist, two firefighters, two sheriff deputies, a famous furniture maker, a veterinarian, and a country music singer, and I loved them all. Then add in that each story has a dog or puppy that is rescued, along with a story of love and romance, it is a winning combination." ~Susan D

Deadly Purpose

I loved everything about this book, and it made me want to check out the other books in the series! The immediate suspense drew me in, and the High Sierras setting was perfect, as was the mysterious stranger Meg finds in her cabin. This novel had a well-written, exciting, and descriptive narrative that kept me glued from start to finish. Without giving away spoilers, the author has crafted one exciting, romantic ride, full of twists and turns. I highly recommend this book and can't wait to see what the author comes up with next. ~Sebastian Moran

This book took me by surprise. I didn't expect to get so caught up in this book that my whole day was spent captured in its pages. It has been a long time since I couldn't put a book down but Deadly Purpose did this to me. I loved every page. ~WildfireJane

Clear Intent

"I'd been waiting on this one awhile!! I truly loved the story! I laughed, cried and got so frustrated I couldn't see straight! I'm now hoping there will be more from Hangman's Loss, I don't want to see this series end! Thank you for a very wonderful getaway!! I highly recommend this complete series!!!! Wow! Just Wow!!" ~Linda Helms

"I've looked forward to every book in this series and have enjoyed each one, loving the characters as it feels you walk with them through exciting, scary situations and sigh as relationships become beautiful. This was an exciting story with almost nonstop action and heart stopping dangers. All of my favorite people in Hangman's Loss are together to help Jack, Dory, Adrian and the town through crisis." ~JLocke

HIDDEN JUDGMENT

The Jamesons, US Marshals – Book Two

Diane Benefiel

www.BOROUGHSPUBLISHINGGROUP.com

ISBN 978-1-951055-71-4

This book was being finished when the C-19 quarantine was put in place, and is dedicated to the medical professionals, grocery workers, truck drivers, sewer facilities workers, garbage collectors, police officers, and many others who allowed the rest of us to stay home and stay safe. As much as the spread of the disease has been controlled, it's because of you.

Thank you.

ACKNOWLEDGMENTS

Thank you to the *real* US Marshals who have written about their profession and made their knowledge available through books and online sources. You've made a writer's job much easier. Of course, any mistakes are my own.

HIDDEN JUDGMENT

Chapter One

Ellie strode from the restroom to the bank of elevators then jabbed her finger on the up button. She didn't usually pay much attention to her appearance, but she'd slipped into the bathroom to check her makeup. That morning she'd been compelled to put on her game face, which meant brushing on mascara and applying lipstick she normally didn't wear. Neither had been smudged, and her hair had stayed back in its tortoiseshell clip. Her marshal's star hung securely from the lanyard around her neck, and her Glock was safe in its shoulder holster. If she was honest, she'd also made the stop to take a breath and force herself to relax. Whatever happened in this meeting, she would rein in her hair-trigger reaction, and listen before forming an opinion.

She tapped her foot. Waiting sucked, and only served to make her more nervous. She caught herself before she could chew off her lipstick. *I can do this.* Two other people joined her at the elevator bank, looking up at the progress of each car: a balding man who needed to cut back on the carbs, and a petite Asian woman with stiletto heels. Both, like her, wore professional attire.

The elevator binged and they entered the car. Ellie chose her floor, then waited through stops on lower floors before getting to hers. She'd tried to get information about this meeting, but all she'd been able to learn was that it involved protection for a federal judge. Samuel Creed.

Everyone knew about Judge Creed. Four months ago, a defendant had somehow smuggled a knife into his courtroom and the video of him all but flying over the bench to help take down the guy had been played and replayed on social media and news programs around the world. He'd refused interviews and downplayed his role, but that had only sharpened curiosity about him. It didn't hurt that there was *something* about him—his looks, his presence, his steely gray eyes—that made everyone sit up and pay attention.

For over a decade, she'd been able to tuck memories of the man into a corner of her brain labeled "best forgotten." Hard to do now with social media being what it was.

After his superhero maneuver, other aspects of his judicial career began gaining attention, like the unconventional sentences and statements from the bench that had led one fan to create a blog titled "Creed's Law," which had garnered tens of thousands of followers.

At thirty-seven, Samuel Creed was the youngest federal judge in the country, and there was that forceful *something* about him that had memes speculating about what lay hidden under the judge's black robes. Not that she paid any attention except in her capacity as a US Marshal, whose responsibilities included the protection of federal judges.

She was counting on him not remembering her.

She exited the elevator, went through the frosted glass doors stenciled with "US Marshals Service, District of Oregon," waved to the receptionist, and walked briskly to the door of the conference room. Another steadying breath and she opened the door.

The whole team was present. Seth, her eldest brother, was Chief Deputy in charge of the unorthodox group assembled to locate their father, fugitive Richard Jameson, as well as other members of his right-wing extremist group.

Seth stood at the counter with the coffeepot that filled the air with its life-giving aroma, sipping from a cup while her other brother Linc poured coffee into a travel mug. They'd both shed their suit jackets, and wore their holsters under their shoulders and marshal's stars on their belts. When Linc saw her, he raised a brow and held up the pot, and at her nod filled another cup. Rounding out the team was Marshal Isabella Nikolaev.

There'd been some major pushback from the higher-ups in Marshals Service when the three offspring of Richard Jameson had been assigned to hunt him down. But Seth had argued their case and used every ounce of influence he had, and finally, the brass approved.

Which didn't explain the presence of the man standing with his back to her, gazing out the window. He stood separate and alone. Outside was a dazzling example of perfect Portland fall weather, but she wondered if Sam Creed even saw the view. He hadn't turned when she'd come into the room, and she was glad for the momentary reprieve.

Taking the steaming cup from Linc, she sat next to Bella. Ellie and the other female marshal had become fast friends. They needed to stick together to make their voices heard over the two men on the team who thought they were right about every damn thing.

"Let's get started," Seth spoke with firm authority.

Creed turned and Ellie braced herself. His gaze rested briefly on her before moving on to the others.

So far so good.

Seth sat at the head of the conference table. "Let's get the introductions over with." He indicated the man who sat to his left. "This is Judge Samuel Creed of the US District Court in Pendleton." Seth gave the team members' names.

Ellie watched Sam's face carefully when Seth said her name. Nothing changed in the judge's expression. No flash of recognition, no confusion over trying to place her. Relief brought a slight easing of her tension. Apparently, thirteen years was long enough to erase any memory of her.

"Here's the background," Seth continued. "Judge Creed is the recipient of anonymous threats with a commonality that says they're from the same or similar sender. We believe the threats are linked to right-wing militias active in eastern Oregon. Our investigation has turned up evidence connecting some of those groups with the larger American Freedom Confederation we've been after."

"What do they want?" Linc asked.

"Primarily, someone freed from prison who we suspect is affiliated with their organization. They've included general warnings against US government facilities, then more specific threats against the judge for decisions he's made that they consider attacks on Second Amendment rights. They claim the country would be better off without traitors who refuse to defend the Constitution, and the judge has been warned to watch his back. You know, typical shit." Seth sipped his coffee before continuing. "We've offered a protection detail, which His Honor turned down."

Ellie glanced at Sam, whose gaze remained fixed on Seth.

"He's made a somewhat irregular proposition to deal with the threats." Seth tipped his head to Sam. "Judge, you want to explain?"

Sam nodded at Seth before running his gaze over the group. "Thank you for agreeing to this meeting." He spoke in a low, clear voice Ellie thought likely helped him maintain control of his courtroom. "Protection is reactionary. It won't find whoever's threatening me. My plan is to lure in those involved, open myself to action on their part, and hopefully trap the bastards before they can harm me or anyone else."

Seth commented, "The Marshals Service sees value in this plan, but is unwilling to leave him undefended, so Judge Creed's girlfriend is moving in with him. That will be you, Ellie."

Ellie could almost hear the click as Sam's gaze locked on her. Panic had her sitting up straight. "Ah, I'd make a terrible girlfriend. Bella's a much better choice."

Ellie shifted when Bella's heel came down on Ellie's toe. *Way to throw a friend under the bus.* Moving her foot out of range, she continued, "I'd like to follow up on the leads I've uncovered on the AFC."

Seth never gave much away, but over thirty years of knowing her brother allowed her to read the slightly raised brow to mean *What the hell, Ellie?* as clearly as if he'd said the words out loud.

His voice held cool authority. "Sam and I discussed the options, and we agreed you're the best choice to act as the girlfriend, in part because you both attended University of Oregon at roughly the same time so it's plausible you could have met there. Bonus, you have a law degree, so you come from the same background."

Damn. Seth was right. No way out of this without giving herself away. Ellie forced a nod of agreement. "Okay. What about the rest of the team?"

"Bella, Linc, and I will relocate to Pendleton for as long as you're providing the judge's protection. In addition to adding to the judge's security, we'll continue working on our ongoing investigation of the anti-government movement in eastern Oregon and Idaho. We think the threats against Sam are connected."

"Four marshals in Pendleton, Oregon?" Bella's brow furrowed over her exotic eyes. "Something else must have happened to justify that level of protection."

"Correct. You want to tell the team what you found on your car, Sam?"

A flash of some emotion crossed his expression, but his tone remained dispassionate. "C-four attached to an inside wheel well of my vehicle."

Linc leaned forward in his seat. "No shit? How'd you find it?"

Sam shrugged. "This was two weeks ago. I was parked on dirt. It'd rained, and I noticed fresh boot prints around my car. There were indications someone had knelt by the rear passenger tire. I took a look and saw a brick of plastic explosive, complete with a detonator, attached with duct tape."

His voice had deepened, become richer in the years since he'd been in law school. Ellie ignored the shiver snaking down her spine. Focus was the word of the day. "Where was your car parked? Were there any witnesses?"

"I was parked along the River Parkway. The chief deputy can better answer your question about witnesses."

"The investigation is ongoing, but as of now we have no witnesses," Seth affirmed. "The C-four had a motion-activated detonator. We're looking into possible sources for the bomb materials, but it appears likely the C-four is from a batch stolen from a military base near Portland. Part of our investigation is determining whether there was inside help at the base."

Someone attempting to blow up a federal judge was serious business and added a layer of urgency and danger to the job of protecting Judge Creed. "What are the details of my cover?"

"We're keeping it simple. You and Sam were long-distance boyfriend and girlfriend, and decided to take your relationship up a notch. You've come to Oregon to live together. You'll use the name Rachel Sinclair. Cover documents are being made. You're a lawyer and have been working for a firm in San Diego. Your plan is to spend your time studying for the Oregon bar exam."

"And what will you be doing while I'm moving in with my boyfriend?"

"We've procured a short-term rental, a residence not far from the judge's house. Linc will be the marshal assigned to the courthouse, and since a marshal's job is to protect federal judges, that won't be remarkable. To keep anyone from being tipped off by the large number of marshals assigned, Bella and I will pose as lawyers representing a client. Our cover will allow us access to the courthouse and keep our investigation under wraps."

Bella set down the mug she'd been sipping from, the string from the teabag trailing over the side. "Why keep our mission to protect Judge Creed secret? As federal marshals, it shouldn't be so unusual to see us at the courthouse."

"True," Seth replied. "But we're going to maintain cover so we don't tip off the court staff about what's going on. We can't assume the threat is only from the outside."

"You think the messages could be a misdirection," Ellie surmised.

"Actually, I don't think they are, but we can't ignore the possibility."

"Wouldn't locals, court staff included, already know about the threats to the judge? People tend to pay attention when a bomb is found attached to a judge's car." This question came from Linc.

Seth shook his head. "You'd think, but Sam did us a favor. Instead of calling local law enforcement, he called ATF to deal with the bomb. They defused it and the locals are none the wiser."

"Except for the bomber, who must have wondered why his toy didn't work," Ellie pointed out.

Seth nodded. "We control what we can control. Here's our immediate plan. Bella, Linc, and I will travel separate from you and the judge so no one sees us together and connects us." Seth turned to the judge. "Sam, you flew here?" At Sam's nod, Seth said, "We'll arrange a rental car so you and Ellie can drive back to Pendleton."

A woman wearing a marshal's star came in and passed an envelope to Seth. He opened it and tipped out the contents. "Here's your new identity, Ellie. You're now Rachel Sinclair, so give me everything for Eleanor Jameson. You can keep your weapon, but don't wear it."

Ellie transferred her new identity into her wallet and couldn't help feeling that she was being stripped bare as she handed over her badge and ID.

"I need to go back to the hotel to pack."

Sam spoke directly to Ellie for the first time. "Did you drive here today?"

She shook her head. "I took a rideshare."

He nodded. "We'll pick up the rental and stop at the hotel to get your things, then we'll get on the road."

They had a good, sensible plan, but she couldn't help feeling she needed a little alone time to fortify her defenses before she and Sam Creed were thrown together as lovers.

Chapter Two

Ellie stared out the window of the rental sedan as they drove through the outskirts of Portland, Mount Hood looking austere and imposing in the distance. Kind of like Judge Creed. They hadn't spoken much since leaving the Marshals Office. He'd been distant and preoccupied, except for the couple times when she'd caught his hawk-like gaze on her, making her feel like a novice defense lawyer arguing her first case before the bench. In fact, the whole situation made her uncomfortable. She resented feeling like she had as a young undergrad, dazzled by the attention of the hot law student. She reminded herself she wasn't that naïve sophomore any longer. She could handle herself with Judge Creed.

It didn't help that Sam had grown into his looks. As a law student he'd been thin to the point of gawkiness. Thirteen years and he'd filled out some, though he was still lean. The hair he wore combed back from his forehead now had threads of silver that matched the slate gray of his eyes. Combined with the slashing cheekbones, he had the look of a seasoned warrior.

She stifled a sigh. Their shared history made the current situation a messy business. That history was like a block wall between them that only she could see. Which made it her problem to deal with. She and Sam had had sex, that was all. Despite the distance of time, she remembered that night in crisp detail.

From the moment she'd arrived at the party, she'd been aware of the longhaired law student with the fast grin. He'd caught her attention on campus before then, and she'd even made a point of going by the coffee shop where she'd once seen him on the off chance he'd be there. She'd been thrilled when a friend had introduced them.

They'd ended up talking, flirting back and forth, and drinking more than they should. He'd been cool and sexy, and so much more mature than the other guys at the party. They'd gone up the back stairs to his bedroom.

Later, he'd asked her to go out with him, and promised to call to set up a date. She'd never heard from him again. The man sitting beside her gave no indication he remembered any of that. She'd never completely forgiven or forgotten him, and when he'd appeared on the news with his takedown heroics, the memories had planted themselves once again firmly in her psyche, a distraction she worked hard to ignore.

Acting as his fake girlfriend was *not* the way to get past the stupidest of college mistakes.

He put on the turn signal and glanced over his shoulder before changing lanes, his mirrored sunglasses hiding his eyes. "We should fill in our story." His voice rolled over her like warm chocolate, smooth and sensuous.

Judge Creed and warm chocolate did not belong in the same thought. "Right."

He'd pulled off his tie and unbuttoned the top button on his shirt, turning back his sleeves to above his elbows. His suit jacket lay across the backseat. A few locks of thick black hair had fallen over his forehead, softening his rather severe image. The intelligence and intense personality that had drawn her all those years ago hadn't abated. Okay, that was an understatement. The added maturity pegged the needle on the hot meter all the way over to the bonfire zone.

"We should keep it simple, like your brother suggested. When I was in law school, you would have been an undergrad. Let's say we met at a party, then again years later at a conference, and have kept in touch since."

Ellie didn't allow anything in her demeanor to give away that what he'd described was exactly how they had met. "Fine. Where was the conference?"

"You've been to Las Vegas?" At her nod, he said, "I attended a conference there last year. Let's say we met there, hooked up, and kept in touch."

"Wow, super romantic. If you plan on telling people this story, you better inject some emotion."

The corner of his mouth lifted a fraction. "I'll assure anyone who asks that you're the love of my life."

Only sheer force of will kept her gaze steady on his. "Let's not go overboard, Creed. But there's a problem. Rachel Sinclair is a smart, confident, modern woman, and she wouldn't be willing to take all the risk in this relationship. She's given up a position at her firm—where she was on track to make partner, by the way—to move to the wilderness to see if it'll work out with her judge boyfriend. I think she'd want more of a commitment than that."

"You want me to ask you to marry me?"

Ellie couldn't hold back the laugh. He didn't give much away, but the flash of panic on his face was gratifying.

"Take it easy. I don't think the bent knee thing would suit you. But yeah. Rachel Sinclair is in love, but not stupid kind of love. I'll talk with Seth and get him to approve the purchase of an engagement ring."

Another long look, then he said, "I'll take care of it."

She shrugged. "Fine, you talk to him."

He drummed long, squared-off fingers on the steering wheel. "Pendleton is not the wilderness."

"I'm from Southern California where wilderness is a prized commodity, so my observation is no insult. Regardless, I looked at a map. Pendleton is a remote outpost in the wilderness."

He opened his mouth like he would argue the point, but shook his head and said, "Give me a rundown of what I need to know about you."

She so didn't want to do this. Any of it. She didn't want to have a cozy chat with Sam Creed on a long drive to his home in Pendleton. She didn't want to pretend she was engaged to him. She didn't want to share her life story. All of it made her feel vulnerable, which she simply needed to get over.

"Right. I'm thirty-two. I was born and raised in San Diego where my mom and stepfather still live. For the most part, my brothers and I had a typical suburban childhood. I attended college at the University of Oregon, then law school at Hastings."

He waited a beat. "That's all you've got? There's not more to Eleanor Jameson?"

"I'm telling you about Rachel Sinclair. Granted, I'm keeping close to my own story, but all you need to know are the basics."

"We want this to work, don't we? If people are going to believe we have a soul connection, you'll have to go deeper, get past the superficial. Tell me more about Eleanor Jameson."

It took all her self-control not to lean away from him with arms folded over her chest in a defensive posture. "Like what?"

"Like why Oregon for college?"

The question was the same a much younger Sam Creed had asked her sophomore self. She kept her tone level. "University of Oregon offered me a full ride with a sports scholarship."

"What sport?"

She lifted a brow. "What do you think?"

"Since you're all leg and have to be nearly six feet tall, I'd guess basketball."

"You'd guess right. And I'm five eleven, damn it."

"Damn it?"

"Another inch and I could make Linc stop calling me Shorty. There's respect in my family if you hit six feet."

"Ah, understood. So you played basketball for the Ducks. Major?"

"History. You?"

"History as well, but at Cal."

"You went to Berkeley?"

He nodded. "But I only played intramural basketball."

She narrowed her gaze. "You'd have had to pay out-of-state tuition, which would have made Berkeley expensive in addition to the cost of living in the Bay area. Either your family is wealthy, you have a boatload of student debt, or you earned a scholarship."

He gave a wry laugh. "My family was not wealthy. I got an academic scholarship along with some debt."

"Then you went to University of Oregon for law school."

"Right."

The questions went back and forth. He told her he'd clerked for a federal judge, but she'd had to pry out of him that the judge had been on the Ninth Circuit Court of Appeals and was now a Supreme Court justice. Obviously, a prestigious appointment he wanted to downplay.

After his clerkship, he'd been with the US Attorney's office while teaching classes at the University of Oregon. Then had come the federal bench appointment. Ellie knew his was an amazing upward trajectory. But while he answered her questions about his career, he was reticent about his personal life. Sam hadn't revealed much about himself that couldn't be learned in a quick web search.

"Were you raised in Pendleton?"

"Thereabouts."

"What's that supposed to mean? Either you were or you weren't."

He shrugged. "My dad owned a ranch about thirty miles south of Pendleton until he died. That's where I grew up."

"Was it a real ranch with cows and horses, or a hobby ranch with a nine-hole golf course?"

"Rock Creek is a real ranch with cattle, not cows." Something shifted in his expression. "My brother is running it now."

"You have a brother? Sisters?"

"No."

"Do you have a girlfriend who'll wonder why you're suddenly engaged and not to her?"

"No girlfriend. How about you? Any ghosts from the past who'll show up to beat me bloody for grabbing you from under their noses?"

He was the only ghost from her past. "Nope. No guy for me."

He fell silent, and Ellie turned to look out the window, glad for the reprieve. She tamped down the ember of resentment that had flared to life. It was stupid. She *knew* it was stupid to let that one night affect her so hard. They'd had a hookup. Not a big deal in and of itself, but his careless and soon forgotten promise to contact her after had been a blow to her confidence. What she thought would be the beginning of something had turned into a one-night stand she'd never intended. Add that to her father's abandonment: no wonder she was distrustful of relationships.

They arrived at the Pendleton airport where they were to turn in the rental car and pick up Sam's vehicle. After parking, they approached the airport's double glass doors when an older woman stopped suddenly in front of Ellie. She stepped back and found herself against Sam's solid chest. His warmth radiated in the cool afternoon and she found the sudden closeness uncomfortable.

"Excuse me, sorry for being so scattered." The woman gave a flustered laugh. "My son and daughter-in-law are arriving with my new grandson and I'm so excited to see him that I completely forgot my phone in the car."

"A new grandson is exciting. Congratulations." Ellie pasted a smile on her face as she struggled to ignore the blazing heat where her body connected with Sam's. Layers of clothing didn't seem to have any effect on the intensity generated by their proximity.

She filed that knowledge away for future use: physical distance must be maintained if equilibrium is desired when dealing with Sam Creed.

They were crossing to the car rental kiosk when Sam caught her hand in his. She glanced at him in surprise and he kept a firm hold when she tried to tug free. "I think we need to establish some boundaries, pal."

"We'll establish boundaries later. Go with it," he muttered.

"Sammy, my man. How's it going?" A short, florid-faced man zoomed toward them like a heat-seeking missile, his voice booming in greeting. He slapped Sam on the shoulder and Ellie wanted to kick the guy when his gaze traveled over her, making a prolonged stop at her breasts before rising to her face. She felt the sudden need to take a shower.

Sam pulled her closer to his side.

"Didn't know you were out of town. Where you been?" While his tone was overly jovial and on the surface he appeared affable, Ellie detected calculation in his eyes.

"Finster." If he noticed Sam hadn't answered his question, he didn't acknowledge the fact.

"Who's your gorgeous friend, Sammy?"

"Gordon Finster, Rachel Sinclair." Sam's introduction was abrupt to the point of rudeness.

Ellie nodded her head. "Mr. Finster."

"Call me Gordy, sweetheart, everyone does." His gaze headed south once more. Once past her breasts, he seemed to focus on their clasped hands. "Here I am, gone for a couple days and it looks like things happen."

"Looks like," Sam agreed as he nudged Ellie so they could move around the unpleasant man.

"See you at work on Monday, then," Gordon spoke to their backs as they resumed walking.

It wasn't until they'd picked up Sam's vehicle and were on their way to his home that Ellie felt they could talk without the danger of being overheard. "Tell me about Gordon Finster."

"Besides being an obnoxious asshole, he's case administrator for the federal court in Pendleton." Sam glanced at her, then back at the road as he steered his Land Cruiser onto the highway on ramp. "He's also under investigation for sexual harassment after two female clerks made complaints against him."

"Are you involved in the investigation?"

"Peripherally. Gordon is looking for allies, hence the bro act. You'd think he wouldn't leer at my girlfriend, but he's an idiot as well as an asshole."

"Any motive for him to send you threatening messages?"

Sam shrugged. "I supported the complainants, plus my interview didn't go well for him and maybe he got wind of that, but I don't think he has the balls to retaliate. I also don't think he knows shit about C-four."

Ellie considered his response as she took in the landscape of rolling hills and farmland as they drove from the airport. She was a little surprised at Sam's vehicle choice. The Land Cruiser had to be at least twenty years old and appeared well cared for. If she'd given it any thought, she'd have pegged him as driving a cool Audi or BMW.

A semi ahead of them forced them to slow. She watched Sam step on the clutch and shift the manual transmission into a lower gear. She'd always wanted to learn how to drive a stick. Linc had promised to teach her, but after one lesson he'd banned her from ever touching his Jeep again, claiming she'd likely stripped the gears in his transmission.

She couldn't really blame him after the horrible grinding sound it'd made. She eyed Sam. Maybe he'd teach her. Not that he was exactly approachable, but maybe he'd be friendlier once they were more comfortable with each other.

Ellie had been on plenty of witness protection assignments that sometimes had involved working closely with interesting men. While the number of female marshals was larger than it'd ever been, the Marshals Service was still dominated by men who tended to be take-charge, I'm-the-coolest, alpha-male kind of guys. But she'd *never* had trouble separating personal feelings from her job.

She was starting to wonder if that would become a problem with Sam. Maybe she should have shared their previous connection with Seth. But she already knew how that conversation would've gone. He and Linc would've turned all protective big brother and pummeled Sam to a pulp, which wouldn't bode well for their careers.

She'd had a hookup with Sam, and in college that had been normal for so many young women, though not normal for her. She'd never engaged in casual sex before or after that event. But then, at the time, she hadn't thought what had happened with Sam had been casual. She'd thought he'd shared that instant connection.

She'd given him her phone number but hadn't gotten his, and when he'd failed to contact her, she'd been hurt. It had taken a stern talk from a girlfriend to discourage her from going to Sam's house and asking him what was up.

After their one-night stand, she'd avoided the campus coffee shop. In the end, she'd had to chalk it up to a lesson learned. Being with him now, she couldn't help thinking about it. But that was her problem. She was ninety-nine percent certain that if she asked him why he'd never called her, he'd have no recollection of that evening, which had been so significant to her.

Chapter Three

Ellie tried to appreciate the scenery, but the reality of living with Sam was drawing ever closer. She needed to put a lid on her emotions before they got her in trouble.

How exactly she and Sam would figure out their living arrangements had yet to be determined. As much as she could, she'd rely on the normal procedures for witness protection. Out in public they had be a couple, but in his home she was a marshal protecting a judge. She'd be friendly but professional, remain clear-headed and logical, and she'd get through this assignment. Pulls of attraction would have to be ignored.

They crossed a bridge, and the river below swirled with deep currents.

"That's the Umatilla River."

"It's beautiful."

"You ever kayaked?"

"Sure, down in Baja and in the Sierras. I kayaked in Morro Bay once."

"I've got a couple of kayaks. We could take them out." She caught his speculative look and her heart gave a heavy thud. "All in the interest of doing couples activities, of course."

"Of course."

Being engaged to Sam was going to be tougher than she'd anticipated.

He slowed the Cruiser as he drove through an old, established neighborhood with houses on large lots separated by wooded areas. He turned into a driveway that ran along one edge of a sloping lawn bordered on the far side by groupings of tall pines before circling to the back of the house.

The house was a surprisingly appealing two-story colonial with clapboard siding painted a weathered gray with white trim. A wide porch framed a door painted deep red that matched the shutters on the dormer windows on the upper story. Sam clicked a device on his visor and the door on the detached garage rolled up.

Two kayaks hung suspended from overhead beams and he parked beneath them. Along one wall was a rack doubling as a stand for skis as well as fishing poles. He appeared to enjoy his outdoor activities.

Ellie stepped out of the garage and did a slow survey of the property, stuffing her hands deep in her coat pockets against the cool temperature. An area around the back door of the house was enclosed with a wire fence, but the rest of the property was open. While the garage matched the house, it appeared to be a more recent construction.

Behind it the land sloped up a hillside dotted with shrubs, rounded granite boulders, and clumps of tall trees. A short border wall of moss-covered rocks delineated the property and the weathered look of it made her think it had been around for most of the past century. She loved the rustic atmosphere that gave the property a homey appeal.

Nice as it was, she wasn't moving into Sam Creed's home for the environment. Rock walls, trees, boulders—all were nice for a person living a comfortable life without enemies. But that wasn't the case here, and the yard offered too much cover for someone interested in hanging out with a rifle and scope and taking shots at Judge Creed.

She tipped back her head to take in the gorgeous early-November leaves of red, yellow, and orange on a huge tree that spread wide branches over the lawn near the enclosed pen.

"This is the most beautiful tree I've ever seen. What is it?" The not-so-keep-it-professional words were out of her mouth before she could think to hold them back.

Sam stood at the back of the SUV. She glanced over when she felt him staring at her and caught an expression that made her think she'd surprised him. Then he was opening the rear door and pulling out her luggage. "Oregon white oak. Pretty common around here."

Right. *Pull it in, Ellie.* Most Southern California trees never wore fall colors like Sam's Oregon white oak. She didn't need to make a fool of herself about it. Good thing she hadn't gushed about the rock wall or he'd think she was really a nut. She fully intended to get a closer look at that wall, but later without Sam's unsettling presence.

Sam took the larger of her two suitcases, and Ellie didn't bother objecting. It was exactly what her brothers would do regardless that she was perfectly capable of managing her own luggage. She grabbed the remaining suitcase and they went through the gate to the fenced area. Wild barking echoed from inside.

"What kind of security do you have for your house?" She eyed the eaves and spied cameras and security lights at both rear corners.

He pulled a ring of keys from his pocket. "Besides the dogs, I had an alarm system installed when I moved in." He pointed. "The security lights are motion-activated."

"Are there cameras throughout the property or only around the house?"

"Around the house."

"Who does the system alert when there's been a breach?"

"There's no alert for the outside cameras—they only record. With the alarm system, I get a text if there's a breach, and the local police are notified. We good to go in or do you want to search the house first?"

"Doing my job, Creed. We'll want to put cameras up that slope." She indicated the hill at the back of the house.

He didn't say anything, and carried her suitcase as he climbed the steps and pushed open the door. Ellie followed him into a mudroom lined with hooks holding hats, jackets, and dog leashes, and a bench with shoe bins beneath it. There was a scrambling clatter of nails on the wood floor followed by a firm command to "sit." A matching pair of tri-colored beagles quivered with their butts planted on a mat that ran the length of the mudroom's hardwood floor. Sam deactivated the house alarm.

"Oh, you have beagles." Ellie's heart melted.

As far as she was concerned, beagles were the most adorable of all dogs, and she'd promised herself she'd adopt one once her job wasn't constantly taking her away from home.

Setting her suitcase onto the bench, she went down to her knees and offered a hand for the dogs to sniff. "Hey, guys. Aren't you gorgeous?" She turned her face up to Sam. "What are their names?"

"Tony and Cleo."

Tony and Cleo took hearing their names as a sign they were free to move. They rushed her with wagging tails, sniffing noisily at her feet as she stroked sleek coats.

"Let me guess, Marc Antony and Cleopatra. Am I right?"

"You win the cookie." Sam indicated hooks. "You can hang your coat here. I'll show you the house, then we'll take your suitcases up."

"Okay."

After coaxing the dogs outside, Sam took her from room to room, his tone not unwelcoming, but not exactly hospitable. He was doing his duty as her host, all without revealing much of what he was thinking.

She didn't want to be curious about Sam Creed, but being in his house only made her wonder about him more.

If she'd had to guess the type of home he'd live in, she'd have thought a low-maintenance town house with a minimum of fuss and clutter. But as with his vehicle, the opposite of that guess couldn't have been more extreme.

His home was richly decorated with solid furniture, and colors and textures that combined to make it inviting. The house's décor made up for his lack of welcome.

The history nerd in her loved the antique pieces, especially because they weren't confined to a specific period. The desk in his office looked like it dated from the antebellum era, while the drop leaf table in the living room with its gorgeous slag glass lamp looked late Victorian. The mix gave the home a comfortable, settled feel, one she could see herself happily living in.

Making mental notes of points of entry, as well as views from various windows, helped her to store the insights Sam's home gave into his personality. But the fat gray and white cat who lay curled at one end of a couch and the finely crocheted doilies under some of the knickknacks seemed so incongruous they made her frown.

Sam did not look like a fat cat or doily kind of guy. She reached out to stroke the cat, which stretched under her hand, extending needle-like claws.

"Her name is Gumbie."

Ellie couldn't hold back a laugh. "Someone's read their T. S. Eliot." She straightened and caught the considering look. "What?"

"Nothing."

She gave Gumbie a final rub. "How long have you lived here?"

"Year and a half."

"What did you do, buy out an antiques store to furnish it?"

"I inherited the house fully furnished from my aunt, and it came with the dogs and cat. She was a middle school English teacher, hence the animals' literary names. I haven't changed much of anything." He turned to the stairs. "I'll show you your room."

She wondered if he hadn't changed anything out of sentimentality or lack of interest. If she had to guess, the latter seemed more likely.

The upstairs landing led to a long hallway with doors on either side. He pointed to a door directly across the landing. "That opens to the back stairway that goes to the kitchen." At the end of the hall, he indicated a room on the left that faced the front of the house. "That's my room."

The open door revealed a room with a sloped ceiling and west-facing dormer windows that showed the sun setting through the trees and cast the room in a half-light. A wide bed with four posters of what looked like polished mahogany was covered with a gorgeous quilt in a traditional wedding ring pattern. The colors of deep burgundy and cream were a beautiful contrast to the golden wood floor and the painted white walls.

"Oh wow, I love your bed." She felt him check his movement, and her gaze flew to his. His expression remained unchanged, except for the minute lift of the corner of his mouth. "Don't get any ideas, Creed. I appreciate antiques, and you've got some beautiful pieces."

"Then you'll like your room." He motioned across the hall.

Ellie stepped through the door and all thoughts of focusing simply on her job fled. "Oh my god. Is that a pewter bed frame?" She brushed past him to run her fingers over the burnished metal. The head- and footboards had a classic curved design and she guessed it had to be over a hundred years old. "And look at the quilt. Oh, I love the colors. This is a broken star pattern. Did your aunt make the quilts?"

She looked up. His expression had lost that distant look and her heart gave an uncomfortable thud in her chest. "You keep looking at me like I'm a weirdo."

Sam shook his head. "Not a weirdo, and yes, my aunt made the quilts. I'll bring up your suitcases."

He moved down the hall and she let out a careful breath, trying to find her mental balance. The man stirred her up, and she had no idea how he felt about her. Not that it mattered. She was here to protect him and that was it. No way was she opening herself to hurt like she'd experienced from his disinterest when she was young and foolish. She was neither now, and she reminded herself that she avoided the love 'em and leave 'em types like snakes in the grass.

Sam brought in her suitcase and smaller tote and deposited them at the foot of the bed. "We'll have to share the bathroom next door, unless you'd rather use the three-quarter bath downstairs. Put what you want in whichever you choose. I'll leave you to settle in." He pulled her bedroom door closed behind him.

Ellie sat on the edge of the bed, fingering the classically patterned quilt. She needed to build up her defenses because whatever had drawn her to a much younger Sam Creed was still there, waiting for those moments when all she could think about was that he was the most intriguing man she'd ever known.

He wasn't the most handsome, and he certainly wasn't the most charming, but he was hands-down the most *compelling*.

Maybe she should try viewing him as she did her brothers. They were both great guys, and women certainly found them attractive, but to her they were simply her brothers, sometimes dorks, sometimes annoying, but always decent humans.

The temperature in the house was on the cool side so she changed into leggings and a warm sweater that fell below her hips, and dug out the fleece-lined boots she was glad she'd ordered online when their assignment had sent the team away from sunny Southern California. She paused at the top of the stairs when her phone chimed with an incoming text.

Bella: *How's it going with Judge Hottie?*

Ellie rolled her eyes and texted back: *Really?*

Bella sent a meme that had Ellie choking back a laugh. It showed Sam in black judge's robes with a sexy scowl. The caption read "Spank me, please."

Bella: *Definitely. So?*

Ellie: *Fine, so far. We're figuring it out. He's working under the assumption that I'm a little deranged. I like his house. He has BEAGLES!*

Bella knew Ellie was obsessed with beagles, and had even taken her to a beagle rescue farm on her last birthday. Ellie had been able to play with beagle puppies to her heart's delight.

Bella: *Don't let them sleep in your bed. It's a bad precedent.*

Ellie: *I don't think their daddy would allow that, it seems a bit warm and cuddly for him. I get frostbite if I get within five feet of him.*

Bella: *Harsh. We'll be at Judge Hottie's house as soon as your brother gets over himself and lets me navigate.*

Ellie didn't have to ask which brother Bella was referring to. If Sam gave Ellie frostbite, Seth and Bella shared a deep freeze as frigid as a Siberian winter.

Ellie texted a thumbs up.

Tucking her phone under the waistband of her leggings and telling herself she was a coward for being nervous, she made her way downstairs.

She passed through the living room where a gas fire burned in the fireplace. The room felt so cozy she could easily spend the evening curled on the couch with a good book. Sam must've started the fire. Maybe she'd been too quick to judge the judge when she'd been texting Bella.

Framed photos on a shelf caught her attention. One showed a young Sam standing with an older woman with a self-conscious smile who had her hand on his shoulder. The image appeared to have been taken in front of this house. His aunt?

Ellie made her way to the kitchen to find Sam standing at the sink peeling sweet potatoes. He too had changed and wore a dark gray Henley with the sleeves pushed to his elbows and loose-fitting athletic pants. The hair that had earlier been combed back now fell over his forehead, softening his appearance. Damn. He was way too appealing.

"Bella texted. The team's on their way here. We weren't that far ahead of them, but I'm glad they're arriving under cover of night. We can't be seen with them. We're not supposed to know them."

He nodded. "Agreed." He set the potatoes on a cutting board. "They probably hit rush hour traffic. Lots of people who work in Portland live in the country." He toweled off his hands. "Tell Bella I'll feed you all. You a picky eater?"

"No. Especially if I don't have to cook what I'm eating."

She texted Bella about dinner.

"You don't cook?"

"I cook, but I don't particularly enjoy figuring out meals."

"How are you with prep work?"

"Excellent. What can I help with?" They were having a normal conversation. Normal was good. Normal would keep the one-sided erotic thoughts at bay.

Chapter Four

Sam pulled a knife from a drawer and set it next to the sweet potatoes. "Cut these in one-inch chunks."

She did as directed, chopping the sweet potatoes, then the onions he handed her, and finally brussels sprouts, all while listening to the local NPR station playing through a Bluetooth speaker.

Every moment they worked quietly together she was uncomfortably aware of him. How he looked, how he moved, and when he reached in front of her for the pepper grinder, how he smelled of what made her think of the outdoors on a crisp fall day.

He lined a baking pan with foil and arranged the veggies on the tray, his movements competent. He drizzled them with olive oil, then sprinkled herbs and sea salt. He took filleted chicken breasts from the bag where they'd been marinating and arranged them in another pan, then put both chicken and veggies in the oven. A bottle of wine sat uncorked on the counter.

"You want a glass?"

"Hmm?"

"Wine, Eleanor. Would you like a glass of wine?"

Head in the game, Ellie. Head in the game. "That would be nice. Do you mind if I make a pot of coffee? My brothers will want some."

"Sure." He opened a cupboard over the coffee \maker and pulled down a canister. When she was filling the carafe with water, she said, "Do you have copies of the threats you received? I'd like to see them."

"I emailed them to Seth. He didn't share them with you?"

"No. I only know what was said at the meeting today. I haven't seen the actual emails."

"Right." He poured wine for them and set her glass on the counter where she was standing. "I'll get them."

Once the coffeemaker was glugging away, she took her wine to a table recessed in a corner nook of the kitchen. A cozy spot with windows in both walls showing the back and side yard of the house and the driveway, she imagined a pancake breakfast here would be fabulous.

A formal dining area lay between the living room and the kitchen. With the local newspaper folded next to her, she guessed that this more casual space was where Sam ate his meals.

He returned with a sheaf of papers and set them in front of her. He'd printed the emails and gave them to her in chronological order. All of them had been sent to Sam's official email address at the courthouse. The sender's email handle was "Freedom Defender." The first message, dated mid-September, was short and to the point.

Traitor Judge, prepare your own defense. Come for our guns and we come for you. Heed the warning. Those who violate our rights die. Protect the real America. Free Frank Bannister.

The next email, also from Freedom Defender, had been sent a week later.

Judge Asshole, want to see your world burn? The sword of righteousness will destroy the symbols of tyranny. The defenders of America will prevail.

Five days later, a third email was sent.

We know where you live. We know what you drive. We know where you shop. Read the Constitution, traitor. Free Frank Bannister.

She flipped through the pages. The emails had come nearly every week and the messages were along the same theme. A couple contained lengthier diatribes against restrictions on the Second Amendment, while most were brief and increasingly threatening. She glanced up to find Sam leaning against the counter, arms crossed over his chest, serious gray gaze on her.

"Who's Frank Bannister?"

"Member of a Constitutional militia group based east of here. ATF arrested him on weapons violations after he was pulled over and found to have a half dozen semiautomatic weapons and a couple of grenade launchers in his possession. They'd been stolen from a military base. I presided over his conviction and sentencing earlier this year. He's incarcerated at the federal penitentiary in Lompoc, California."

The dogs made a racket outside and Sam gave a half smile. "Early warning system." He tapped on an iPad and opened an app before handing it to her. "Here's what my security cameras show."

The cameras provided a wide angle, and the images they captured remarkably clear. Linc drove a large SUV that pulled up in front of the garage.

Setting down the iPad, she followed Sam through the mudroom to the back door. The beagles were at the fence, barking and howling. Ellie stood at the steps while Sam went to open the gate. Linc, Seth, and Bella approached the house. Bella had her huge purse slung over her shoulder and her arms crossed in front of her. Seth wore what as a teenager Ellie had dubbed his butt face, meaning completely expressionless, a look that meant he wanted to hide what he was thinking. Linc gave Ellie an eyeroll that she easily interpreted to mean that Seth and Bella had been in their usual prickly standoff, likely for the entire drive. It made Ellie feel a little better about travelling alone with Sam.

A few moments later, the kitchen was full of people and animals. Even the cat ventured in to investigate the commotion.

Seth gave Ellie a portable gun safe so she could safely store her weapon. She ran upstairs with it, and when she came down, Sam was offering beverages. As she expected, both Seth and Linc opted for coffee.

Sam took down mugs and Ellie began filling them. She felt more than saw her brother behind her back. Linc loomed over her shoulder in a way he knew she found annoying. Some things never changed.

He spoke in a low voice. "How are the new digs? Creed treating you right?"

She poured coffee and handed him the mug. "Back off, big brother." She leveled a look. "I can take care of myself."

"I know you can, but I'm still your brother."

"Then give me some respect." There was nothing new in this argument. Seth approached and she handed him a full mug. "At least you could be like Seth and not verbalize the big brother crap."

"Doesn't mean I don't think it," Seth muttered as he walked by.

She made a shooing motion. "You're crowding me."

Her brothers moved away as Sam approached. "What about Bella?"

Bella had left the room after being directed to the bathroom. "She'll want tea. Point me in the direction of a tea kettle and I'll put it on."

He shook his head even as he was reaching over her into an overhead cupboard. Before she could move out of his way, he'd brought down a little red kettle.

"I'll rinse it out and put the water on." He pointed to another cabinet. "Look in there for teabags."

She rummaged around and found a box in the back. She hoped tea didn't go bad. With the kettle on a cooktop burner, Sam found another mug. He nodded to Seth. "Why don't you all go in the living room. We'll eat in about half an hour."

The aroma of baking chicken vied with the stronger smell of full-bodied coffee. While the others trooped out of the kitchen, Ellie stayed behind, sipping her wine while waiting for the water in the kettle to boil. The slightly smaller of the beagles sat next to Sam, staring longingly into his face.

"Is that Tony or Cleo?"

"Cleo. Besides being a girl, she has more brown than black on her coat. She's reminding me it's time for their dinner."

"Show me what they're fed and I'll do it."

***

Sam studied the people sitting around his living room. He was always interested in family dynamics, maybe because growing up in his own family had been so atypical, and watching his father had been key to survival. As a judge, he paid attention to the defendants in his courtroom—if they fidgeted, how they talked to their lawyers, whether they acknowledged any friends or family among the spectators. The habit often gained him valuable insight into their character.

While he figured any of the Jameson siblings could easily take on the group leader job, they seemed satisfied leaving that role to Seth.

The four-member team appeared tight, the Jamesons tighter still, and while he detected tension between Bella and Seth, they appeared able to work around it. Bella sat next to Linc, who currently had his eyes glued to his phone, a grin on his face as he tapped out a message. Seth sat in the recliner, and instead of opting for the second single seat, Sam sat on the loveseat next to Ellie. He caught her surprised look. Too bad. If they were going to pull this thing off, she'd have to get used to being close to him.

He hadn't been kidding when he'd said she was all leg. She was wearing some sort of tights that showed off those long, toned legs perfectly. When they'd talked on the drive, he'd had a moment of déjà vu. That bugged him, because he generally had an excellent memory for names and faces. They'd barely scratched the surface of learning about each other. At some point she'd say something that would jog his memory and he'd figure out where they'd met before.

When the emailed threats had started coming in, he'd contacted the US Marshals Service and spoken to Chief Deputy Seth Jameson. Seth had started the investigation and wanted to assign a two-deputy security detail. Before that could happen, Sam had discovered the C-4 attached to his car. There'd been enough explosive power that if that bomb had detonated, he'd have been dead, and anyone in a thirty-yard radius would have been as well.

He'd been so pissed he'd come up with the plan to leave himself open and flush out whoever was targeting him. Seth hadn't liked the idea so the compromise was Sam's "fiancée" would be an undercover marshal. He didn't want a babysitter, but he acknowledged his safety was compromised.

Of all people to play the part he had to get a woman who wound him up. That reality had to do with more than her looks. Ellie made observations and asked questions that revealed an inquisitive mind, and he knew for damn sure that if he'd met her under different circumstances he'd have asked her out.

The plan was for them to live in the same house, sleep across the hall from each other, and, in public, behave like an engaged couple. That instant punch-in-the-gut attraction he'd felt when he'd first laid eyes on her? He'd have to ignore that. Hell, he hadn't even had to lay eyes on her. His back had been turned when she'd walked into the conference room, but he'd felt the air suddenly charge like a lightning storm was imminent. and had turned to find she'd been the cause.

He wondered if she felt the connection, and if that was why she seemed to be trying to rein in what he guessed was her naturally open behavior when she was around him. Maybe she wanted to maintain a professional distance between them. She appeared comfortable in his home, willing to help out, and at least with her brothers and Bella, had a ready smile or laugh. She only held back around him.

Ellie reached out her booted foot and nudged Linc. "You texting Mikayla heart emojis, lover boy?"

"Maybe."

"How's she doing with you being gone?"

"Looking forward to our assignment being done, but she gets that being away from home is part of my job."

"Well, tell her smoochie-smoochie bye-bye. We've got work to do."

"My wife misses me. What can I say?" He was still smiling when he stuffed the phone into the front pocket of his jeans. He jerked his chin toward the papers his sister held. "What do you have there?"

"These are the threats emailed to Sam." She handed the sheaf of papers to Linc, then turned to Seth. "Judge Creed filled me in on his connection with Frank Bannister. What else do we know?"

"Bannister was raised in a small town east of here. His father was suspected in the bombing of a BLM office in eastern Oregon three years ago. While ATF was looking into that, the elder Bannister and another son blew themselves up in their barn in what appears to be an accident. Our guess is they were constructing a bomb and likely would have targeted some other federal facility. That was a little over two years ago. We found they were members of an anti-government group calling themselves 'SecAm,' short for Second Amendment, that appears supported by the American Freedom Confederation."

"Any similarities to the bomb found on Sam's car?" Linc asked.

Seth shook his head. "Not that we've been able to verify other than it's the same type of explosive. When the Bannister father and son blew themselves to hell, they also destroyed physical evidence that might have connected the two devices, so right now we've got nothing."

Ellie arranged a cushion so she could lean against it. "I'm calling Freedom Defender FD, and he feels like a guy to me. I'm sticking with that unless I learn differently. Any ideas who FD is or where his emails are coming from?"

39

"No. The emails were sent from a public library in a small town east of here. We requested and received video surveillance footage, but the only cameras are on the outside of the building and weren't helpful. We're focusing on known associates of Bannister, but FD could simply be an admirer and not know Bannister personally."

"Are Bannister's visitors and mail being monitored, and has anyone else received emails from FD?" The questions came from Bella. She spoke with a hint of an accent. Given the surname Nikolaev, Sam guessed if not Russian, then something close to it.

Seth nodded. "There are no reports of other judges or federal officials receiving communications from Freedom Defender. All contact with Bannister is being scrutinized. Our investigation has focused on members of SecAm. Their primary ideology is that the US government is illegitimate because it isn't upholding the Constitution, in particular by allowing restrictions on gun ownership. While their primary goal is what they consider defense of the Second Amendment, there is an underpinning of white supremacism, and some members espouse neo-Nazi bullshit. They believe in a version of Social Darwinism, arguing that Americans of northern European descent are naturally superior, and their job is to defend the country from the invasion by people of 'inferior' races." Seth turned to Sam. "Anything you can add to that?"

Sam nodded. "SecAm has held or participated in rallies in various locations in the northwest. Videos have surfaced definitively credited to them showing bonfires where people give the Nazi salute as books and brown-skinned dolls are thrown onto the flames. There's a case coming up on my docket involving four members of SecAm accused of kidnapping three migrant workers from Guatemala. The arrest records state the workers were taken from a farm in Oregon to a cabin across the state line in Idaho where they were beaten and held. One of the three hostages, the only woman, escaped and notified authorities."

"Fucking bastards," Linc muttered. He turned to Seth. "Have you interviewed these four about SecAm?"

Seth nodded. "We tried, but they sat mute next to their lawyers." He shrugged when Linc scowled. "We have their records, which go back a few years, and we've been trying to make connections to other members through their former cellmates or known associates. The group is careful and insular. Nailing these four is the first break we've had, but SecAm is cagey. They haven't gone back to that farm or anywhere near that area. We're keeping a close watch on a few places where there are clusters of migrant workers, but I'm sure they're not going to repeat that mistake."

Ellie turned to Sam. "How can you be impartial when you're being threatened by that group?" She scrunched her brows. "I'd want to kick their asses."

"There's nothing to indicate these four had anything to do with the emails or the explosive strapped to my Cruiser. In and of itself, group affiliation, no matter how distasteful the group, is a liberty protected by the Fourteenth Amendment. They're entitled to a fair trial based on the evidence that's presented. Besides, most of what we've talked about is circumstantial. You've inferred that the bomb is connected to the person sending the emails, and that the person sending the emails is connected to cases I've tried, or to the SecAm group. You went to law school, you know you'd need a hell of a lot more hard evidence if you want to draw a solid line between your suppositions."

"I'd still want to kick their circumstantial asses."

Sam smothered a smile as Bella and Linc both laughed.

"But seriously," Ellie persisted, "couldn't they claim that you're biased because of the threats?"

"Their lawyers might try to have me recused, and the case might be given to a different judge, but so far that hasn't happened. We'll have to see how it plays out."

A timer chimed and Ellie rose when Sam did and followed him into the kitchen. "What can I do?"

He pointed. "Get plates from that cabinet. Dining room table is bigger so we'll eat in there. Utensils are in the drawer by the dishwasher."

Sam opened the oven and used a fork to test the food, then took the trays out to set on the cooktop to cool. Ellie gathered plates, stacked them with knives and forks, and took them to the table. When she returned, he handed her cutting boards. "Put these on the table and I'll bring out the food."

"You're serving dinner in what you cooked the food in? Your aunt must have had serving dishes."

"What's wrong with serving in the pans?"

"Nothing, if you're eating by yourself. You're not, and nice tableware makes a difference."

"And a lot more dirty dishes. Let's keep it simple."

"Nope." She began opening cupboard doors. "Don't worry about cleanup, we'll make Linc and Seth do it. I love doing that. Here we are." She reached to an upper shelf, her sweater hitching up to give him a view of an enticingly cupped ass. She brought down a platter and oval-shaped bowl he wasn't even sure he knew he owned.

She examined the blue and white pattern, then turned over the bowl to look at the mark on the bottom. "Ooh, made in England. I love English pottery."

She set the serving pieces now laden with the chicken and veggies on the table, and Sam had to admit the table looked nice using the old dishes. They took their seats, Linc again busy texting.

"Pardon my brother, Sam," Ellie told him. "Linc's been married only six weeks and is still in the stupid-love stage of being a newlywed."

Linc looked up with a wry grin and pocketed his phone.

"I think it's sweet," Bella commented. "Mikayla is lucky Linc is so devoted to her."

Sam caught the heated glance Seth shot Bella. From what he could see, the two marshals seemed to avoid speaking directly to each other, but there were little things that gave away what he was beginning to suspect was a keen attraction they both appeared to be fighting.

It didn't go unnoticed that Seth had nudged his brother aside so he could sit next to Bella, or that when their hands brushed, they both froze before jerking back. He caught a look of amusement pass between Ellie and Linc after they also witnessed the exchange.

Sitting beside him, Ellie turned to Sam. "Tomorrow's Saturday. What do you usually do on weekends?"

"It varies." He nudged the platter of chicken toward her. "I catch up on reading for upcoming cases, and I get outside, try to do something physical. Take the dogs out, spend time with friends." He paused to sip wine. "Be ready for questions when I introduce you. People will wonder how I've suddenly acquired a fiancée." He reached into his pocket. "Here."

He set a jeweler's box on the table between them.

"What's that?" She eyed the box with suspicion.

"Engagement ring. You said you wanted one."

"That was quick." She looked at the box like it was going to bite her. "Did a previous girlfriend return it?"

With a sigh of frustration he opened it himself. "Give me your hand." He held out his, palm up.

"I'll put it on."

"Eleanor, give me your hand."

"Don't be bossy. Besides, it won't fit."

He waited until she laid her hand in his with a huff of breath.

He slipped the ring onto her finger and their gazes locked like puzzle pieces fitting perfectly together. Looking away was impossible, her deep blue gaze pulling him in.

"Aw, that's sweet." The comment broke the tension. Across the table Bella held her phone up in front of her. "Let me know if you want the pictures to post. It would make your cover story more believable."

Ellie tugged on her hand and Sam realized he still held it gripped in his. He loosened his hold as Seth raised his brows.

"You two are acting engaged?"

Ellie gave a definitive nod, as Bella said, "It's an excellent idea. Rachel Sinclair wouldn't move in with her boyfriend unless she had a commitment."

"Exactly," Ellie stated. She held her hand up to the light. "Classic ring, Creed, and bonus that it fits. Either you or your previous girlfriend had excellent taste."

Sam figured it was time to change the subject. "Where exactly are you all staying?"

Chapter Five

Ellie's eyes popped open and she groaned. Nope, sleep would not be returning. She pushed back the quilt and swung her legs out of bed. No matter how late she stayed up the night before, when five a.m. rolled around, she was awake and there was no getting back to sleep. She pulled on her shearling boots, and after a quick trip to the bathroom, crept down the back stairs, trying to make as little noise as possible. She thought of returning to her room to get her phone to use as a flashlight, but a dim light from the kitchen allowed her to see the outline of the steps.

She'd made it to the bottom tread when a dark shadow moved toward her. She had a split second to think how stupid she'd been to leave her gun in her room before a light blazed on and she let out a wheezy breath. "Jesus Christ, Sam. Are you trying to scare a year off my life?"

"Why didn't you turn on the light instead of creeping down the stairs in the dark?"

"Because I thought you were sleeping and I didn't want to wake you."

"My bedroom door is closed. How would the light have woken me?"

"I don't know. I was trying to be considerate. Next time I won't be."

Now that she no longer felt like her life was in danger, her brain was catching up with what she was seeing, which was Sam with tousled hair, low-slung flannel pants, and no shirt. She wondered fleetingly how someone with such a full head of thick dark hair could be hairless on his chest.

She bit her tongue before she could ask if he waxed.

Of one thing she was certain: she could now tell the many women who'd panted over social media posts speculating about what Judge Creed had hidden under his robes that they wouldn't be disappointed if they ever scored a peek. Ripped, cut, however you wanted to describe the muscular perfection, this guy had it.

She cleared her throat. "Aren't you cold? Shouldn't you put on a shirt or something to cover all that," she waved her hand up and down the length of his body as her gaze traveled over him, "um, skin?" She gripped her hands together before she gave in to the urge to trace her fingers over the fascinating ridges of muscle from his chest to abdomen.

He cocked his head and the corner of his mouth turned up. He was standing far too close and she could feel heat radiating off him. His gaze traveled over her. "I could say the same about you. That's a lot of leg you've got there, marshal."

He had a point. While her top was a waffle-knit thermal, her sleeping shorts barely covered her butt, and with her feet in the clunky boots, she probably looked more like a surfer chick than a federal marshal. She gave the shorts a quick tug down in what she hoped was a casual move. "I didn't pack thinking I'd be going on a sleepover."

"It might be contrary to my own interests, but I could offer you sleep pants to borrow."

"Ah, no. I'm good." He didn't reveal his thoughts much, but there was no doubt the gleam in his eyes indicated appreciation. That plus the implied compliment was making her more than a little jittery.

"What are you doing up so early?" His voice was early-morning rough and for some reason made her salivate.

She swallowed. "Curse of a morning person. I can't sleep past five. I was going to make coffee."

"Already made."

If she hadn't been so focused on the male specimen in front of her, she would've smelled the rich aroma of coffee. "Right. What about you? You an early riser, too?" Did she sound as overly chipper to him as she did to herself?

He nodded. "You better change into exercise gear."

"Why? It's five a.m. No one needs to exercise at five a.m. I'm having coffee."

"You're my bodyguard. I run every morning. How can you protect me if you don't go running with me?"

"I'm not your bodyguard. I'm a Deputy US Marshal assigned to protect a judge, and every morning, really? Don't you have a treadmill or elliptical machine? You could stay inside and exercise. That would be much safer than running around your neighborhood."

"I'm leaving in ten minutes. That should be enough time to inhale a cup of coffee and change into workout gear."

"You're mean."

There was that upturned corner of his mouth again, and she thought a mere glimpse of it was like holding a winning lottery ticket. That she was starting to think her life wouldn't be complete until she saw him give a full-throated, all-in laugh alarmed her more than a little.

He moved past her to climb the stairs, taking his body heat with him.

***

Sam wasn't kidding about ten minutes. He was waiting when she descended the stairs wearing her black running pants, a long-sleeved athletic top in neon green, and her favorite running shoes. She'd pulled her hair back in a ponytail and wore a wide band around her head that went over her ears to keep them warm.

She stood with gloved hands on her hips as he went through a series of high knees and heel kicks.

"You should warm up. Warm your muscles, loosen the joints."

"The sun's not even up."

"Your point?"

Seeing no alternative, she groaned only a little bit as she did a few heel kicks and leg swings.

"Did you get coffee?"

She shot him a dirty look. "A measly half cup."

"Then you're good to go."

"You're all heart, Creed." She did a few more halfhearted leg swings then followed him to the front door. "Don't you take the dogs?"

"No. There are two of them and they're a pain in the ass when you're running. Cleo gives me about two miles before she decides she's gone far enough and wants to be carried, and Tony tries to follow every damn scent he comes across. They're in their pen in the backyard. They're fine."

She followed him out the front door, which he locked, and then set off at an easy lope down the driveway and onto the street. Ellie followed a few paces behind. His shirt and pants had reflector panels, and he wore blinking red lights around his biceps and carried a flashlight. All good for warning drivers that he was on the road, but also a beacon to someone with nefarious intent.

She matched his pace, her gaze constantly scanning the area around them for potential threats. Tall trees bordered the street in front of his house for about fifty yards, then opened to reveal a farm-style home set back from the street.

Farther on, more houses sat on smaller lots. Other than a dog barking in the distance, the only sound was the slapping of their feet on the pavement and their breathing. Well, Ellie's breathing. Sam wasn't breathing heavily at all.

Overhead, an incredible blaze of stars swept across the sky, the payoff for getting out the door so early. In the east, a thin layer of pink had begun to push against the darkness. Reminding herself to focus on her job and pay attention to their surroundings, she caught up to Sam, matching his warm-up pace as they jogged side by side.

"How far do you usually run?"

"Five or six miles. I'm not training for anything, so I only run to maintain."

"Do you go at the same time every day, and run the same route?"

"Unless the weather is really bad, I run daily about this time, and I generally run the same route along the river."

"Then you need to vary your routine, break up the pattern."

"Right. Today we'll run through town. We'll go by the address of the rental house so you can see where your team is staying, and I can point out the courthouse."

Despite her complaining, Ellie found herself enjoying the run. She'd gotten into the habit of using a gym and realized that she missed being outdoors as the sun rose and the world was still quiet. Following Sam's gesture, she caught the quick movement of an animal as it disappeared into the brush.

"What was that?"

"Wild turkey. We have a few around here."

They turned onto another street where the houses sat on small lots and the road sloped downward. They ran through pools of light cast by the occasional streetlamp. The sound of an engine starting some distance away broke the peace. Through a gap between two houses she saw the headlights of a large vehicle on a parallel street as it pulled a U-turn in the middle of the block.

"That's where your brothers and Bella are staying." Sam pointed to a small house with the SUV Linc had driven parked under a carport. "It's been a short-term rental for about a year."

Given that the residence was not far from Sam's house, Ellie thought it a good choice. They reached the bottom of the street where lights illuminated the wide expanse of a bridge over the Umatilla River.

While she would have liked to take a minute to look at the river, Sam continued across. On the other side, businesses started to edge out residences, and within a few blocks they were in the downtown area. The rising sun, still hidden behind the mountains to the east, had turned the sky lavender and the underside of the puffy clouds glowed golden. They passed a church with a domed steeple, and Sam indicated a three-story building with a brick façade. "There's the courthouse."

"Oh, I love the architecture. It's beautiful. That's what a courthouse should look like."

"Agreed."

Ellie was puffing, but she refused to ask Mr. Fitness to slow down. He maintained the pace as they turned back toward the river. The bridge had a pedestrian walkway bordered by a short concrete guardrail, but with no traffic they ran side by side on the narrow road.

She was going to suggest they stop and view the swirling waters below when a vehicle with high beams appeared coming the opposite direction, fog lights glowing amber. Since the sun had now risen over the horizon, the lights were overkill. Sam moved ahead so they were single file. They were less than halfway across the bridge when the vehicle started over the span. The engine revved and the car picked up speed. She didn't second-guess the instinct that had her racing forward to grab Sam's arm. She saw now that it was a truck, its engine roaring, high beams blinding as it approached, crossing the center dividing line and barreling straight at them.

"Over the guardrail!"

The shout was barely past her lips when Sam grabbed her arm and they both vaulted over the concrete rail. Without slowing, the truck careened over the pavement where they'd been running only moments before, scraping the barrier in front of them before it sped away.

Ellie whipped out her phone, concentrating on controlling her breathing as she called nine-one-one. In clipped tones, she gave the description of the truck, an older model Dodge Ram, dark gray with a white shell over the bed, aftermarket fog lights in front, the driver a heavyset male whose ethnicity or race she hadn't been able to determine.

She tucked the phone back in her pocket and looked at Sam, who appeared amazingly calm for having just avoided being flattened like roadkill. "The dispatcher said to stay here and she'd send over a patrol car."

"I'd rather the patrol car be out looking for that truck." His gaze blazed over her, and she realized he wasn't as unaffected as she'd assumed. "Those are pretty good reflexes, Marshal Jameson. Thanks." He reached for her hand again.

A patrol car approached with its light bar flashing red and blue, but no siren. Ellie tried to pull her hand free but Sam wasn't letting go. She scowled at him.

"You'll have to control that 'fuck off' look whenever I touch you. Engaged couples surviving a near-death experience would likely hold on to each other." The recollection that she was playing the part of his fiancée came rushing back. She'd been in marshal mode, and had forgotten she was undercover.

With her hand still in his, they stepped back over the concrete guardrail and onto the roadway. "And that report to the dispatcher," he muttered. "It sounded like how a cop would speak."

So noted, Your Honor.

The officer, a tall Hispanic woman with stripes on the sleeve of her coat, stepped out of the cruiser and settled a wide-brimmed campaign hat securely on her head. She nodded in their direction. "Judge Creed."

"Barb. This is Rachel Sinclair, my fiancée. Rachel, this is Officer Barbara Herrera."

Ellie nodded at the other woman.

"Fiancée?" The comment was directed at Sam, and the officer didn't bother hiding her surprise. "I didn't know you were getting married. Congratulations."

"Thanks, it's a new development."

She nodded, then got down to business. "Tell me what happened."

When Ellie would have opened her mouth, Sam tightened his grip on her fingers. "Dodge Ram came straight at us," he said. "Would have hit us if we hadn't jumped over the barrier."

"Is there any chance the driver might have drifted over the center divider line, that maybe he was distracted or DUI?"

"He may have been DUI, but he wasn't drifting. It felt intentional. He was accelerating and steering straight at us." Sam pointed at the dark scrape on the guardrail. "He left some paint there so you're looking for a vehicle with some front driver-side damage."

"I'll add that to the description we got over the radio. Did you recognize the vehicle?"

When Sam shook his head, she asked, "How about the driver, did you get a look at him?"

"No."

Officer Herrera turned her attention to Ellie. "Same questions, Ms. Sinclair. Did you recognize the vehicle?"

"No. I've only been in town since yesterday, so I wouldn't have. I did get a glimpse of the driver through the side window as he sped away. I think medium height, and maybe heavy, though that impression might have been due to him wearing a bulky coat."

The officer continued to ask questions, making notes in a little booklet. After a few minutes, she tucked the booklet into the cargo pocket on her pants. "There's a BOLO out for the vehicle. Judge Creed, you want me to give you two a ride back to your place?"

"No, but thanks, Barb."

"Okay. Be careful." With a half salute, Officer Herrera returned to her cruiser.

***

Sam listened as Ellie spoke on her phone, filling Seth in on what had happened. They were walking back to his house, and turned onto Sam's street as she disconnected. He caught her hand.

"Geez, you sure like holding hands, Creed."

"Get with the program, Eleanor," he muttered.

Earlier, when she'd called her brother, she'd put her gloves in her pocket. Now, he rubbed his thumb over her finger where the engagement ring should have been.

Two women, both bundled in brightly colored parkas, came down a driveway to the street being led by equally bundled dogs on leashes. He and Ellie were about to get their first real test.

"Hey there, Sam." Yvonne wore a yellow parka and had tightly coiled gray hair peeking from under a matching beanie. Her skin was a shade lighter than that of her ebony-skinned friend, Francie. Yvonne waved as her dachshund in a matching yellow sweater strutted on the end of his leash. Francie's color choice was red and her small poodle looked like he was dressed for a party in his red sweater and black bowtie.

Sam nodded. "Morning, Yvonne, Francie."

Francie eyed his and Ellie's joined hands. "Who's your friend?"

"This is my fiancée, Rachel Sinclair." He wasn't surprised at his neighbors' matching shocked expressions. He turned to Ellie. "This is Yvonne Jackson and Francie Hogan. In addition to being neighbors, Yvonne works at the post office and Francie is the city's librarian."

Ellie dipped her chin. "Nice to meet you both."

Francie's eyebrows had disappeared under her beanie. She ignored her poodle tugging on the leash. "Well, aren't you a sly one, Sam Creed. We never even knew you were seeing someone."

"It's been a long-distance relationship. Rachel is moving here from California."

Francie finally let the little dog pull her to a bush where he lifted his leg.

"Well, isn't that something." Yvonne smiled as she spoke. "Welcome to Pendleton, Rachel."

"Thank you. You have a beautiful community."

"That we do. We're proud of what we have here."

Neighborly pleasantries over, the women and dogs continued their walk on the other side of the street. Sam could all but feel their speculative looks. He and Ellie reached his driveway and he stopped, tugging her closer so he could speak in a quiet voice. "Listen, we need to make our cover story work."

He brought her hand to his lips, gaze riveted on hers. She went stock-still, and he had the thought that the flush on her cheeks wasn't all from the cold. He found flustering her didn't bother him one bit.

She licked her lips. "Okay."

"Part of that is you wearing your ring. Where is it?"

"It's your ring, and I left it on my nightstand. I don't want to lose it."

"You won't lose it. You need to wear it. People will notice if you don't have an engagement ring."

"Right."

"And the least engaged couples do is hold hands." He leaned forward. "Unless we're in the house, we act the part, and that means keeping up the pretense so that anyone looking gets the message. You can't act like I'm about to assault you every time I take your hand."

"You're right." She seemed to make a herculean effort to recover herself. "But honestly? I'm operating on that measly half cup of coffee, and we were almost run down by a crazy person."

"Excuses, marshal. Get in the game."

His skin prickled as Yvonne and Francie walked past.

"Go with it," he muttered, not for the first time. He dipped his head and pressed his lips to hers. A brief kiss that lasted no more than a heartbeat, but sent a jolt through his body that struck all the way to the soles of his feet.

He pulled back, the raw heat on her face hard to miss. "What the hell, Creed?" Her voice was pitched low, and any observer might have thought she was vowing everlasting love.

"My name is Sam, and it's all part of the cover." The impulse for the kiss, he told himself, had at least started out that way. The problem was he was finding too many things about Eleanor Jameson that appealed to him.

Like the fact that she was nearly as tall as he was, and with only a slight duck of his head they were matched lip to lip. Like the suspicion in those deep blue eyes that was incredibly sexy. Like her quick brain, which kept him on his toes.

He leaned forward, his breath frosting the air between them. "Those two women have lived in Pendleton their entire lives, and between them they know everyone in town. You can bet that within the hour news that Judge Creed has a fiancée will be spreading like wildfire. Seeing us kissing makes it more believable. It'll go a long way to countering anything that comes from your marshal-like nine-one-one call."

Her gaze dropped to his lips. "Fine, then. Let's make it a good one."

She gripped the front of his shirt and yanked him down, all but fusing her lips with his. This time he expected the jolt, but not the explosion of heat that seared his blood. He wouldn't be surprised if steam was billowing from the top of his head into the chilly morning air.

She pressed that long, lithe body against his, and it took all his willpower to keep from pulling her hips into his where all the heat in his body was pooling.

Judges were supposed to maintain a certain level of decorum when in public, and it was a hard-fought contest to keep control when her mouth was avid on his, their tongues mating in a way that promised incineration if they ever ended up in bed.

She eased her grip and broke the kiss, but not before giving his bottom lip a nip that had a groan rumbling from low in his throat. "They gone?"

"Ah…" He was supposed to be able to think?

"Yvonne and Francie and their dogs. Are they gone?" Her expression was entirely too smug.

"Jesus." He rubbed a hand over his face. "Yeah, long gone."

Her smirk turned into a laugh. "This was all for show, right?"

"Yeah, for show. Let's get inside."

He had the uncomfortable feeling their situation had just gotten a lot more complicated.

Chapter Six

Ellie sat on the couch, the gas fire in the fireplace making the room warm and homey. Since their morning run, clouds had blown in and the temperature had dropped. A glance out the window showed a blustery wind stripping trees of their fall foliage. She guessed there'd be rain within the hour.

Gumbie stretched her paws out in front of her, yawning in the way only cats could manage, then settled again on the back of the couch. Ellie glanced at the door to Sam's office, ajar by about half a foot. Wide enough for her to hear him over the past hour, on the phone, tapping on a keyboard, or shuffling papers.

Thank god he'd disappeared into his office after his shower and breakfast. She needed to be alone to gather her thoughts without him distracting her. What had she been thinking to kiss him like that? Sure, she'd been curious, and he wore his maleness like a banner, but they had a history she shouldn't forget.

She'd gotten over him pretending to be interested in her when all he'd really wanted was a hookup. That didn't mean she trusted him now. The man who'd acted like that as a young law student wasn't likely to have changed who he was at heart.

So she'd been caught up in the moment and kissed him. It didn't mean anything other than proof that whatever pheromones he possessed worked extra well on her. She'd take it as a cautionary lesson not to get too invested in the role of fiancée. She settled back against the cushions with her computer on her lap.

A search found plenty of newspaper articles on Frank Bannister, as well as his father, and the groups they were affiliated with. She read through those, then dug deeper, using her security clearance to find more detailed information in government databases.

It didn't surprise her at all to find her father's name came up in conjunction with some of the same groups as the Bannisters dabbled in. Richard Jameson was linked to not only the American Freedom Confederation, but also to SecAm.

Next, she scoured social media platforms, following threads down the rabbit holes of right-wing conspiracy theories. There was an entire world of craziness once you dug beneath the surface of groups who self-identified as patriot militias.

Some simply wanted a platform to spout off their anti-government, often racist, warped worldviews. She figured they'd always been present to a degree in American society, but the Internet had given them an avenue to crawl out from under the rocks that had hidden them to reach like-minded people.

Others held ideologies that had evolved to the point where they'd become radicalized and fit the definition of domestic terrorists. Her father matched that profile, which made finding him more urgent before he caused greater destruction and pain than he'd already done.

She opened her secure memo app to note the names and handles of those posting manifestos, delving into databases of known right-wing domestic terrorists, and found numerous references to the bombing of a federal courthouse in east Texas attributed to Richard Jameson. Not for the first time did she wonder what had turned her father down that path.

Shaking off the mood that always accompanied evidence of her father's betrayal, she continued working, noting her observations and research in files she saved on secure servers.

A flash caught her attention and had her glancing out the window. The sky had darkened to a half-light and another bolt of lightning gave a strobe-like burst, followed by a crack of thunder echoing through the valley. The muffled patter of rain sounded against the roof as it began to pelt from the sky. Ellie set her laptop aside and rose to her feet to stand at the front-facing window and watch the show through the semi-sheer curtains.

Treetops swayed, leaves caught a gust of wind and skittered across the road, and the darkened sky let loose with a deluge. Maybe it was because Southern California got so little real weather that she found the storm exciting. Lighting forked across the sky, and the thunder rolled through her. There was a click of nails on the hardwood floor and Cleo came to stand beside her, whimpering.

"It's okay, baby. You're safe inside." Ellie reached down to soothe the scared dog.

Movement outside had her looking out the window again. A battered pickup turned onto the driveway, its headlights slicing the gloom. She watched until it passed out of sight as it drove around the house.

With Cleo following close on her heels, Ellie crossed the room, stopping to rap her knuckles on the doorframe of Sam's office. She pushed open the door. He sat at his desk, his hair fell across his forehead and retro horn-rimmed glasses were perched on his nose.

She'd always been a sucker for the sexy nerd. Hot and brainy did it for her. If they were really engaged, she could see herself moving across the room to slide onto his lap, then taking off those glasses to see if she could distract him.

Sam looked up from the papers in front of him at the same time as a chime sounded from his phone. He ignored the phone as his gaze snagged hers.

She tried to will away the heat coming up her neck and cleared her throat. "We've got company."

He looked away to retrieve his phone and she let out her breath with a faint whistle. Fantasies like climbing onto his lap were going to get her in trouble. She should remember if that scenario ever played out, he'd likely finish it off by dumping her.

He tapped the screen, then threw it down on the desk. "Damn. I'll be right back."

When he would have brushed past her, she caught his arm. "Hold it, Creed. Tell me who it is."

"My brother. I'll get rid of him."

"You have to introduce us."

"Not today."

"Now who's not playing the part of the fiancé? And why wouldn't you introduce me to your brother?"

"Because he's got nothing to do with this, and I don't want to lie to him."

"A little while ago you were claiming that the women we met this morning would tell everyone in town we're engaged. Plus, I'm *living* here. The first person you should have told about our engagement is your brother."

He sighed. "It's not like that." He held up a hand when she opened her mouth. "But you're right."

"Of course I'm right."

The corner of his mouth twitched. "Come meet my brother."

While Sam moved to the kitchen, Ellie slipped up the stairs and grabbed the engagement ring off her nightstand. She returned to the kitchen as Sam ushered in a dark-haired man from the mudroom. Cleo and Tony pranced around, sniffing the visitor's shoes and pants as he bent to scratch heads.

"Drew, I want you to meet someone." He beckoned her and Ellie stepped forward into the curve of his arm.

Sam's brother was not what she expected. Physically, the differences weren't so great. Both men were tall, but while Sam had a rangy build that spoke of sinewy strength, Drew looked thin to the point of gauntness. Sam was clean-shaven, his hair long on top while neatly trimmed on the sides. Drew grew his lank and unkempt hair past his collar, a black baseball hat with yellow stitching that read *Cattlemen's Association* on his head. She wondered if this was the brother Sam had mentioned on the drive, the one who ran the ranch where Sam had been raised.

"This is Rachel. I've asked her to marry me, and she's accepted."

Drew's eyebrows rose in unison. "No shit, you're getting married?"

"Yeah. The long-distance thing wasn't working for either of us. We were ready to get married, so I proposed."

Ellie gave an internal grimace. Sam explained their engagement with all the romance of a practical and advantageous business merger.

Drew didn't appear surprised to learn that his brother had been involved in a long-distance thing. If she ever popped a surprise engagement on her brothers, she couldn't see their reaction being anywhere near subdued. Explosive was more like it. If she'd been seeing someone long distance and hadn't told them, they'd be all up in her business about it, grilling her like she was a murder suspect.

Drew's pale blue gaze traveled over her. His expression looked puzzled, which she could understand, but what she didn't understand was the flash of anger.

Sam offered coffee, and Drew nodded, gaze still on Ellie. She was usually good at reading people, but none of his reactions were what she'd consider typical of a man meeting his brother's fiancée for the first time.

"You pregnant?"

"Drew." Sam's tone slapped out a warning.

"Ah, no," Ellie said. "We didn't get engaged because I'm pregnant."

He grunted, then turned to his brother. "We've got trouble again out at the ranch."

Sam opened a cupboard and retrieved three mugs before turning to face Drew. "What trouble?"

"Damn fucking wolf killed a bull calf. Pete won't go after it."

"Why do you think it was a wolf? Wolves are rare around here."

"Animal was gutted, chewed to shit. What else could it have been? Damn environmental liberation bastards brought the wolves back when we'd gotten rid of them a hundred years ago. They want to drive ranchers out so wolves and grizzlies can have the land to themselves." He took the coffee Sam poured for him. "Good thing we've got our guns. You've got to talk to Pete, get him to track it down."

"Pete doesn't do anything he doesn't want to do."

"He'll listen to you."

"Could be he doesn't think it's a wolf."

"I'm telling you, it was a wolf. You track nearly as good as Pete. You could go after it."

Sam passed Ellie a steaming mug. There was an odd dynamic between Sam and Drew she found puzzling. Drew clearly deferred to his brother, but she sensed that he felt Sam owed him. She wondered for what.

Sam sipped his coffee. "That why you drove into town, to tell me about a dead bull calf?"

Drew shrugged. "Shouldn't need a reason to visit my brother." He glanced at Ellie. "Wouldn't know you were engaged if I hadn't. Not like you called to tell me."

"Phone goes both ways, brother."

Drew slid his gaze to Ellie before giving Sam a long look. "She know about us?"

Sam paused, mug halfway to his mouth.

Drew gave a wheezy laugh before turning to Ellie. "Make sure he tells you about our screwed-up family before you walk down the aisle, sweet thing, because you'll likely want to hightail it in the other direction."

"Everybody's family is screwed up in one way or another. Whatever it is won't change how I feel about Sam." She looked at Drew over the rim of her own mug, her gaze cool. "And 'sweet thing' doesn't work for me. You can call me Rachel."

Drew gave a bark of laughter. "Now I know what Sam sees in you." He finished his coffee and turned to his brother. "You coming to the ranch?"

"I'll call Pete. If he says it's a wolf, I'll make the appropriate call."

"Then you'll go hunting with me."

Sam shook his head. "I'm not hunting wolf. They're needed to balance the ecosystem."

"That's bullshit."

"No, that's science."

***

Drew left and the muted ticking of a wall clock could be heard in the quiet of the kitchen. Tony sighed as he lay down on a large, flat cushion in one corner of the floor. Next to him, Cleo lay with her nose on her paws, big brown eyes following the movements of the humans in the room.

"What do I need to know about your family?"

Sam remained standing at the sink, staring out the window. When he finally spoke, she thought he sounded tired. "Drew's last name is Martin. His mother married my father when Drew was four."

"So he's your stepbrother. How old were you when they got married?"

"Ten." He finally turned to face her. "Drew was this skinny little kid. He'd never say boo, but followed me around like a damn shadow."

"What happened to your mother?"

"Died." He looked down. "I was eight. We weren't earning enough with the ranch so she worked in town as a waitress. She was coming home from a late shift and got hit head on by a pickup. Drunk driver crossed the double yellow."

"Jesus, Sam. I'm so sorry." Her own father had disappeared from her life when she was about that age so she understood some of what Sam was feeling. She wondered if Richard Jameson choosing to abandon his family made it better or worse.

"It was a long time ago."

"What about your dad?"

He shrugged. "Joss Creed was a tough man. His way of dealing with grief was to take it out on his son. My aunt, Mom's sister, found out he was beating the shit out of me and called the authorities. I was placed with her for a while, but eventually ended up back at the ranch."

"You were just a boy."

"It doesn't feel like I was just a boy. But I'd learned things were better if I could stay out of my dad's way. Anything I could do to get away from the house and him, I did. Went hunting for days on end, hiked all over the mountains, worked the ranch. Spent most of my time with the foreman's family. Then Dad married Jane, Drew's mom. After that, things got better."

"Did your dad mistreat Drew?"

"He ignored Drew, for the most part. I guess that's its own form of mistreatment." He shrugged. "He was strict, and certainly not a loving father, but he didn't beat him. I don't know that Jane ever loved Dad, but marrying him got her out of a bad situation and she seemed content with that. She took care of us, made the house a home."

Sam arranged the mugs in the dishwasher. When he didn't continue his narrative, she said, "That doesn't explain Drew's comment about your family being screwed up. It seems like your family came together."

"Sounds pretty screwed up to me."

There was more there, she was sure of it, but his tone said that avenue was closed. She made a mental note to look into Drew Martin's background. "What was your aunt like?"

"How is she relevant to the investigation?"

His question was a good reminder that her interest shouldn't be personal.

"The more I know, the better I can fit together the pieces of the puzzle. Plus, we could be in a social situation where someone would expect that I know something about you."

"Right." He shut the dishwasher and leaned back against the counter, arms crossed over his chest. "Her name was Nan Beauchamp. She was my mom's older sister. They were close. They'd been raised on the reservation until their dad died, then my grandmother moved them to town."

"You're Native American?"

"Part, from her side. Nan was engaged to her high school sweetheart. He proposed before being shipped off to Vietnam. He was killed in the Battle of Khe Sanh a week after getting off the troop transport. She never married or had kids of her own, but she made a good life for herself. I told you she taught English, and she loved to learn. I owe her for where I am today."

Ellie wasn't so sure about that. Even all those years ago, she'd recognized in Sam an inner drive and intensity that she was confident would have taken him as far as he wanted, even without support from his aunt.

Sam caught her gaze. "What about you? Won't I need to know something about Ellie Jameson for social situations?"

"Rachel Sinclair."

"I want to know about Ellie Jameson. It's got to be hard on a kid when her dad abandons her family and eventually becomes a fugitive."

"How'd you know about that?"

He gave her a look. "Really? Three siblings, all with the Marshals Service, and all on the same team assigned to investigate extremist groups in Oregon? You don't think I'd do a little investigating of my own?"

"I guess you would." She could talk about the crimes her father had committed, about his activities with right-wing terrorist groups, but she was never comfortable opening up about how her father's abandonment had affected her family. "I don't want to talk about him."

"Ellie—"

The dogs sprung to their feet to scramble across the floor a moment before a knock sounded at the front door. Ellie heaved a mental sigh of relief for the reprieve.

"Who do you know that uses the front door?"

"There's a few people."

"Let me check it out."

He raised a brow. "You putting yourself between me and danger, Eleanor?"

"That *is* my job."

"The hell with that." He strode to the front of the house, and when he would have reached for the doorknob, she stopped him with a hand on his arm.

"Hold on a minute. We need to have a serious discussion about our roles, Creed, but for now, at least slow down enough to look through the peephole."

"Fine." He put his eye up to the hole, and a moment later yanked open the door.

The man standing in the other side had jet-black hair pulled back in a ponytail and facial features that looked carved from granite. He also had a baby on his shoulder and dark brows pulled into a frown as he glared at Sam.

What looked like a daypack hung from one shoulder, a capped baby bottle sat in a side pouch. "What the hell, man?"

His gaze shifted to focus on Ellie and he brushed past Sam to step inside.

Chapter Seven

"You must be Rachel. I'm Ben Montoya." Ben shifted the baby so he could hold out a hand. Ellie shook it cautiously.

"Nice to meet you."

"This is my daughter, Georgie." He turned so she could see the tiny face with infant-blue eyes open to the world. "I hear you've gotten engaged to my best friend." He gave Sam a hard look. "And I didn't even know you existed."

"Ah, yes."

Sam shut the door. "Come in and I'll explain."

Ben settled on the couch, laying the baby on his lap. A little foot in a pink and green striped sock stuck out from under a fluffy blanket.

Ellie caught an enigmatic look from Sam before he said, "We're not engaged."

"Sam!"

He turned to her. "Ben isn't threatening me."

"We don't know who's threatening you, and if you tell one person, you can't control where it goes. He tells his wife, she tells her sister, who then tells a coworker, and it spreads."

"That would be husband," Ben cut in.

"What?"

"I have a husband," he stated. "Not that it matters given your concerns. Are you law enforcement?"

"Ben, this is Deputy US Marshal Eleanor Jameson. Using the name Rachel Sinclair, she's posing as my fiancée while the threats against me are investigated."

Ellie threw up her hands. "Great, just great. Why don't you write me a list of all the people you think aren't threats and we'll gather them all together at the same time to tell them our engagement is fake?"

"Ben is the only person I told about the emails. He's the one who urged me to contact the Marshals Service."

"Which, being a federal judge, you should have done immediately."

"I planned to contact the marshals, but I talked to Ben first. A few things had happened out at the ranch and I wanted Ben's take on whether he thought they were related to the threats."

Ellie had to restrain herself from pulling her hair out by the roots. "You mean things happening at the ranch that you failed to mention before now?"

"Yeah. Ben and I grew up together at Rock Creek. His father is the foreman, Pete Montoya. Drew mentioned him."

"You talked to Drew?" The baby made little squeaky noises while she sucked on a pacifier and Ben stroked her cheek with a long finger. "Did he complain that Dad hasn't grabbed a rifle and gone wolf hunting?"

"Yeah. Was it wolf?"

"No. Dad thinks human, but Drew's not buying it. He's already posted shit online blaming environmentalists and insisting defending gun rights is the only thing that will keep us safe from marauding carnivores."

"Hang on, Creed. Can we get back to the point at hand?" Ellie tried to keep the anger out of her voice. "You've jeopardized our mission, and since this is the first I've heard about events at your ranch, it's apparent you haven't been forthcoming. Me posing as your fiancée to provide protection and doing the investigation this way was your idea, and the team agreed because it had merit. But if you can't maintain our cover story and aren't willing to bring the Marshals Service all the way in, you should have told us up front and we could have done this differently."

"I haven't jeopardized our cover story. Ben's a vault. He won't tell anyone."

His assertion only irritated her more, but while her words might have been biting, she worked to keep her tone even so as not to disturb the baby. "You should have told us about the ranch at the beginning, and giving away our cover to even one person is irresponsible." She glanced at Ben. "No offense, but that's how it is." She pulled her phone from her pocket. "I need to call Seth and let him know."

With the phone to her ear listening to it ring, she watched Sam reach down to scoop up the little girl. Ben rose to his feet and headed to the kitchen with the baby bottle.

Seth picked up, and Ellie explained the situation. A few minutes later, she tucked her phone back in her pocket.

"Your brother pissed?" Sam held the baby with ease. Judge Hottie holding a baby should look incongruous, but he looked perfectly natural and at ease.

Georgie stretched out a little hand. Ellie couldn't resist and held out a finger for the tiny girl to grip. Ellie matched Sam's quiet tone. "Not as pissed as I am. He seems to trust your judgment, but says to get a promise from Ben that he won't tell anyone, including his husband." She frowned. "Tell me what's going on at your ranch."

"Five weeks ago someone started a brushfire. It scorched a couple acres but would have been a hell of a lot worse if the guys hadn't jumped on it. There's been some vandalism. Rocks through windows on a couple trucks, and some fences pulled down. Drew wants to hire armed militia. A dead calf raises the stakes."

The baby cooed and Ellie smiled. "Hey there, sweet pea." She glanced up to find Sam looking at her with his usual hard-to-read expression, and realized they were standing close enough that she could see silver glints in his dark gray eyes.

Ben returned, shaking the bottle, and Ellie took a quick step back. He took Georgie and settled back on the couch, where the baby immediately latched onto the bottle.

"How'd you hear about my engagement?" Sam sat in the recliner.

"Went to the grocery store for formula and ran into two different people who asked me what I thought of your fiancée. If you'd wanted me to put on a good show, you should have given me a heads-up. As it is, I told them I had yet to meet your intended but meant to soon. So here I am."

Figuring she had to make do with the cards she'd been dealt, Ellie decided to pick Ben's brain. "What's your take on the threats Sam's been receiving? Do you have any thoughts on who might have sent them?"

"Not specifically, but I can guess. I'm sure you know Eastern Oregon has been plagued by right-wing, anti-government groups. Many of their members think owning a gun is the basis of all political freedom. They've built their entire identity around the use and ownership of firearms. Sam has handed down a few decisions that they perceive as restricting their Second Amendment rights. Some of them are batshit enough to go after a federal judge. That's where I'd start looking."

"We have been. Any other ideas?"

He looked thoughtful. "There are also people who harbor resentment against Indians, particularly Indians who have done well for themselves. Sam is Umatilla. My people are Nez Percé. Sam's a federal judge. I'm a doctor. Some folks don't like when people like us don't stay where they think we belong."

"How has that resentment manifested itself?"

"Comments." Sam shrugged. "I've been called 'chief,' been told to go back to the rez, had my impartiality doubted. It's infrequent, but it happens. More people than I can count are dumbfounded that I don't practice tribal law, like that's the only choice for native lawyers."

"Me, I've had my credentials questioned. Comments like 'I didn't know Indians went to med school.' Shit like that."

Sam's phone rang and he crossed to his office to answer it. Georgie was making good progress with her bottle. "How old is Georgie?"

"Six weeks. She was two days old when Justin and I got her. It's been a crash course on being dads. Thank god for our parents." He gave Ellie a look that made her understand she was being assessed. "This goes against Sam's core makeup, you know."

Ellie raised her brows. "What does?"

"You two posing as an engaged couple. Intellectually, he gets it, but Sam's the most honest person I know. He has a basic, bone-deep integrity that's unshakable, and lying will weird him out."

"Having a fake fiancée was his idea. The Marshals Service wanted to provide a security detail. Sam's plan was to try to draw out whoever is making threats against him."

"It might work, but that doesn't mean it'll be easy for him. I don't think he planned on telling me the truth about you, but when I showed up at the door, he couldn't lie."

Sam came back into the room. "That was Officer Herrera. They found the truck that nearly ran us down. It had been abandoned on a dirt road out near the quarry."

"Abandoned? Who's it registered to?"

"The woman who reported it stolen last night."

"They recover any prints?"

"They're still processing the vehicle, but the steering wheel was clean so whoever was driving this morning wiped it down or was wearing gloves."

"Damn."

Ben put Georgie to his shoulder and gently patted her back, despite the fire that leapt in his eyes. "What the hell do you mean you were nearly run over?"

"Hey, can I burp her?"

"Sure." Ben handed Ellie a cloth. "Put this on your shoulder." He shifted his daughter over.

Ellie settled her and sniffed the dark little head. "She smells so sweet."

She looked up to find Sam's gaze on hers, the corner of his mouth lifting in his not-quite-a-smile smile. He reached out to run a hand over the baby's head, the back of his hand brushing Ellie's cheek.

"Sorry to interrupt the moment, but the being-almost-run-over thing? I'd like an explanation."

"Right." Sam recounted the incident, bringing back for Ellie the vivid memory of the roar of the engine and the blinding high beams as the truck barreled straight at them. "Good thing we were where we were. The guardrail offered good protection."

"You're positive it was intentional?"

"Given what else is going on and the fact that the truck was reported stolen? Yeah, I do."

"If the driver is known to you, he took a risk of being identified."

Ellie patted Georgie's back. "The sun wasn't all the way up and he had his high beams on, surely to intentionally blind us. Maybe he counted on that minimizing the risk."

"You two be careful." Ben stowed the empty bottle in the daypack. "I need to get going. Georgie naps about this time, and hopefully Justin will have put together the baby swing."

Sam shook his head. "Used to be you and Justin would be planning your next rock-climbing goal. Times sure have changed."

"For the better, brother. Still love rock climbing, but nothing beats being a dad."

***

Sam ran along the dirt road on the outskirts of town, Ellie keeping pace, their footfalls beating a steady rhythm. To vary his routine, they'd delayed the morning run by forty-five minutes and chosen a route he rarely followed. He hated having to change his life because of some assholes. But one of the reasons he'd opted for this type of operation was because he wanted those assholes caught. It wasn't good enough to simply keep himself safe. If the investigation could produce enough evidence, they might be able to imprison individuals who posed a fundamental threat to law and order, and hopefully cripple their organization and its ability to radicalize. That made the risk to himself worth it.

The best thing to come out of the situation for him personally was the woman running at his side. Eleanor Jameson presented an intriguing package, one that hit about all the marks for him. She might be frustrated with her struggle to keep things professional, to rein in her emotions as she tried to remain analytical, but he found that tension fascinating.

Case in point? That kiss yesterday morning.

She'd gone with the impulse, and maybe it had started as a show for his neighbors, but her lips had landed on his and she'd taken him under until all he could think about was having more. The conflict was that she was a professional doing her job, and he respected that. Plus, she had two brothers who would likely beat him to a pulp if he made a move in that direction. Not that that would stop him if that's where he wanted to go, but it was a consideration.

The sun rising over the eastern mountains colored the thin layers of clouds pink and gold. They passed a house with smoke wafting from its chimney and the smell of wood smoke tinged the crisp air.

Wide fields already harvested of their wheat flanked one side of the road, the other dotted with pastures for grazing cattle and horses. He liked Pendleton's small-town vibe, with the added bonus of being surrounded by the charm of farms and pockets of land left wild. Ellie seemed to appreciate it, but that might be more because it was different from San Diego, but not as a place where she'd like to settle.

And why was his mind going there?

"You talked to Ben's father last evening." Her breath came in frosty puffs of vapor. She caught his look. "The office door wasn't all the way closed. Besides, it's my job to be nosy."

"I wasn't thinking you were nosy. My life's an open book."

She made a "pfft" sound.

"You don't think I've been open?"

"Honestly? I think you've been open about what you deem valid areas for our investigation, but the rest you hold back. I get that. It's human nature, but not helpful in allowing my team to get the full picture."

She had a point.

"Pete says someone killed the calf. Sheriff said no other ranchers have reported problems like we've had."

"Did he take pictures?"

They crested a hill, their strides getting longer as they took the downhill slope toward town.

"No. I asked, but Pete doesn't even own a cell phone. Reception is crap out there so he and Drew carry walkie-talkies, and they don't carry cameras."

"How many people work on the ranch?"

"Pete and Drew, plus a guy who comes in when needed."

"I'll talk to the team, but we may need to go out there."

"That's where I thought you were heading. I have a full schedule this week so it's not likely to be before next weekend."

"What's wrong with today?"

He glanced at her. Things were moving a little faster than he'd anticipated, but he could adjust. "Nothing."

They transitioned to a cool-down pace as they took the last half-mile uphill to his street.

They returned to the house and Ellie's phone chimed as they stepped inside. She read the text, then said, "Linc says to come by their place. He's cooking breakfast, and Seth wants to go over the plan for tomorrow."

That worked for him. The less time he spent alone with Ellie, the less opportunity he had to do something stupid, like following up on that kiss.

Chapter Eight

Forty minutes later, after they took a circuitous route to the rental, they parked behind the house and went up a small stoop to knock on the back door. Bella opened the door dressed in the type of professional attire women often wore in his courtroom. She grabbed Ellie's arm and pulled her inside. "Good, you're here. Your brother is giving orders like he's the last tsar of Russia. He should remember how things ended for that autocrat."

Seth came up behind her. "I wasn't giving orders. I only made a simple suggestion."

Sam followed Ellie into the house.

Bella's expression remained frigid enough that he was surprised Seth wasn't suffering from frostbite. "It's a suggestion that I change how I dress while I'm at work? That I adopt a hairstyle that is not professional? I have read the US Marshals rules and regulations. I am dressed appropriately for my profession."

Seth rubbed a hand over his face. "I merely suggested that since we're hanging out here this morning, you might be more comfortable wearing something, you know, looser. And 'letting your hair down' is an American idiom meaning to relax, but since your hair is in a bun as tight as your—"

"Time out. C'mon, clueless brother." Ellie caught Seth's arm, giving him a sunny smile as she asked, "What's for breakfast?"

Sam's sympathy was with Seth, but he thought it wise to keep his mouth shut. He closed the door behind them and followed the others across a small living room that opened to the kitchen, the spaces separated by an island lined with stools.

Linc stood at the stove using a fork to lift bacon from a pan onto paper towels laid out on a plate. "Hey there. Everything's keeping warm in the oven. Get it on the table and we're ready to eat. There's coffee, tea, and OJ so get your own drinks."

Since breakfast for Sam usually ran to coffee and cold cereal or toast, he appreciated the bounty before him as he took his seat, placing his steaming mug of coffee next to his plate. Bacon, eggs, hash browns, toast, and sliced melon all looked pretty damn good. Ellie sat across from him. He guessed it wasn't by accident that she placed herself between Seth and Bella.

"This looks great, Linc."

"I am master of the breakfast." He grinned at his sister. "You're on cleanup detail."

Ellie nodded as if she expected no less. "Any new developments since yesterday?"

Seth shook his head. "Nothing new." He pointed to Sam. "We've got a team installing security cameras around your property. We'll cover the front down to the street and the slope behind your house. The company that's doing the installation will be there Tuesday morning. Next, the Marshals Service has taken possession of the stolen truck that was recovered yesterday. We're also looking for footage from any traffic or commercial surveillance cameras that might show the movement of the truck before and after the driver tried to hit you. Hopefully we'll get a hit from that."

Ellie frowned. "When we were starting out on our run yesterday, we were about a block from Sam's house when a big truck started its engine the next street over. I could see it between the houses as it turned around. Did you see it?" Her gaze turned to Sam and he was struck again by the intense blue of her eyes. Something flickered, an impression of those eyes from somewhere in his past. He frowned to bring the image to mind but the memory was gone. He shook his head. "I didn't notice anything."

"I just remembered that. It was on that street one block farther down the hill from the first street we turned onto. Do you usually run that way?"

"Yeah. The trailhead for the river path I usually take is off that road. Did it look like the truck that tried to hit us?"

"It was the same general size. Since that's your usual route, the driver could have been waiting for you."

"At their own homes, people don't usually park in a way that they'll have to turn around, and that's early for folks to be up and around." Linc gestured with a crispy piece of bacon. "Maybe it was someone waiting for you. Would they have been able to see you on the street you were on?"

"There were streetlights, plus Sam has visibility arm bands that have blinking red lights. They're distinctive. If the driver had been waiting and noticed him a street over, he would have had time to adjust his plans."

"Perhaps there are homes on that street that have cameras."

Sam nodded at Bella's comment. "It's possible, though home security cameras are not that common in Pendleton. My current situation aside, there's not a lot of crime here."

"We'll look into it." Seth added ketchup to his hash browns.

Sam forked up excellent scrambled eggs cooked with peppers. "Explain something to me. The point of my plan is to draw out whoever has been threatening me. If that's the case, why aren't I running the same route, at the same time I normally do?"

"And then what?" Ellie asked. "Give him another chance to run you over?"

"We could be armed. The rest of your team could be in vehicles at a couple different places along the route, ready to catch the guy. It seems a reasonable way to draw out the perpetrator."

Ellie was already shaking her head. "I think it's too dangerous. We were lucky we could jump over the guardrail yesterday morning. Next time, there may not be anyplace to jump. I'm all for luring out our perpetrator, but I'd like it to be a situation where we have more control."

"Let's hold that idea back for now." Seth spread jam on a piece of toast. "It appears they already know you're varying your routine, so it may be too late anyway." He nodded to Sam. "Tell us about your relationship with Gordon Finster."

"I've known him for several years. He's case administrator at the courthouse. Our relationship is professional."

"The statements from the women who filed complaints against him indicate that you guided them through the process."

"True."

"Finster likely knows what you did."

"If he does, his behavior toward me hasn't changed. He's been acting like his usual sycophantic self, though it's possible he's putting on an act." He leveled his gaze at Seth. "You think he's behind the threats?"

"There's no evidence of that currently. We're looking for motivation. What's your opinion of his competence?"

Sam shrugged. "He's sloppy, doesn't pay attention to details, and gets by because staff has saved his ass more than once. Anyplace else, he'd have been fired. Because we're a court servicing a large geographical area, but we're in a small community with a low population, I think there's a fear we wouldn't be able to replace him if he was fired."

"Did you witness any instances of the harassment he's been charged with?"

"No. He's careful not to pull shit in front of the judges, but I'd heard rumors so I asked around. Both complaints were made by members of the custodial staff. One confided in me, introduced me to her friend who had a similar experience with Gordon, and they both asked for my help. I walked them through the grievance process."

"Are you aware that Gordon Finster has a side business buying and selling firearms?"

Sam set down his fork. "You're shitting me."

Seth shook his head. "That's what put him on our radar. He attends gun shows and is active in a couple of pro-Second Amendment organizations. Nothing real extreme. Has he ever talked with you about his political views?"

"No. I avoid conversations with him."

"Do you see him socially?"

"We run into each other occasionally, like Ellie and I did at the airport Friday, but that's about it. I know he's divorced and has a teenage son. I think the kid recently graduated from high school."

"I can corroborate Sam's assessment of Finster's attitude," Ellie cut in. "At the airport, their encounter seemed like the high school loser trying to ingratiate himself with the star quarterback. There's definitely a power dynamic at play."

"I'll be at the courthouse tomorrow," Linc said, "as a marshal providing the usual court security. I'll find Finster and work up a conversation with him, bring up guns, make him think I'm a fellow traveler. Could be he'll volunteer some information."

Seth nodded. "That's solid."

"I think Sam and I should drive out to his ranch this afternoon. Someone killed a calf."

That announcement resulted in a series of questions and required that Sam reiterate what he'd told Ellie about his family issues. It frustrated the hell out of him because he didn't think it had anything to do with the threats emailed to him, or the explosive taped to his vehicle. "I think you all are getting off on the wrong track. You're better off spending your time investigating right-wing militias."

"You don't want your family involved. I understand that." Bella spoke softly, which brought the conversation ping-ponging around the table to a stop. He'd noticed that before. She tended to listen quietly and not interject much when the Jameson siblings got going, but when she did speak, her words carried weight. "But," she continued, "that doesn't mean we can ignore the possibility that what's happened at your ranch is related to the threats against you."

Seth nodded. "We need a marshal there to ask questions, so visiting the ranch today is a good plan."

"What about tomorrow? Linc will tackle Finster, but what will the rest of us be doing?" Ellie asked.

"I think Ellie should drop Sam off at work because he wouldn't want to leave her without a car," Seth said.

"They should meet for lunch someplace where a lot of people eat. We want the newly engaged couple to draw attention and perhaps push FD into acting."

"Thanks, Bella. That's an excellent idea." Ellie's wide smile had Sam checking his movement, his fork halfway to his mouth.

"Why the hell does that make you so happy?" Linc asked.

"Because Sam's Land Cruiser is a stick shift and he'll have to teach me to drive it since my *brother*," she shot Linc a dirty look, "won't teach me."

"Oh, shit. Sorry, Sam."

"Wait, what am I in for?"

"She about stripped the gears on my Jeep transmission." Linc's face took on a pained expression.

"That wasn't my fault. You weren't teaching me right, and only gave me one chance before banning me forever from the driver's seat."

"Got that right."

"Learning to drive stick aside, dropping Sam off at work's not a bad idea," Seth broke in. "And when she's not with him, El can keep following the leads online she's been working on. Linc will show up tomorrow as the new marshal assigned to court security. He'll conduct sweeps of the courtroom and Sam's chambers and be present during court proceedings."

"What will you and Bella be doing?" Ellie asked.

"We've adapted our role to the current situation. We're posing as the lawyers for the complainants against Gordon Finster. We've already cleared it with the agency handling the complaint. That will give us the cover we need to question courthouse staff."

***

After they said their good-byes, Ellie followed Sam to his Land Cruiser. "I should drive."

"Ah, maybe later."

"No time like the present. C'mon, Creed. Driving to the ranch will be good practice, which I'll need if I'm driving on my own tomorrow." She patted the hood of the car. "It'll be fun."

He snorted. "Like getting a tooth pulled is fun."

"You're exaggerating.

"I'm terrified."

"You are not. It would have been no big deal if Linc hadn't been a baby about his Jeep."

"The Land Cruiser was my first car. I worked my ass off to buy it."

"Which means it has to be well over twenty years old, so it's about time to get a new transmission anyway." She laughed at his expression. "You actually went pale. I'm kidding. Really, don't worry. I'm a good driver. It's the shifting part I need practice on. C'mon, be a sport." She held out her hand, palm up.

He fished the keys from his pocket with obvious reluctance, then drew them away when she reached for them. "You have to promise to listen to me, and to be gentle."

"Of course." She reached out and rolled her eyes when he pulled the keys back again.

"And you have to step all the way down on the clutch before you shift or the tranny won't disengage. That's what causes the grinding."

"Yeah, yeah." She snagged the keys before he could make any more conditions and crossed to the driver's door. "Lighten up, Creed. Where's your sense of adventure?"

He was still grumbling when they were both belted in. "Look, step on the brake with one foot, and the clutch with the other, then you can start the engine."

"Yes, Dad."

"I'm not joking, Eleanor. You need to take this seriously or you'll damage my car."

"I am taking it seriously. You're worse than Linc, and that's saying something."

That brought more grumbling, and he kept an eagle eye on her as she did as directed, then turned the key in the ignition.

"Okay, look." She thought he was sounding a little panicked. "Every standard transmission has a different feel. Put the clutch in and move the selector to get a sense of where the gears are."

She did as directed. She struggled with finding reverse and he put his hand over hers, wide palm covering her knuckles. Ignoring the shot of hormones she got whenever he touched her was becoming routine, and she didn't like it.

He let go of her hand. "Now you're in reverse. Do you understand the mechanics of what the clutch does?" At her nod, he continued. "Ease out the clutch until you feel it start to engage, then give it some gas."

She followed his instructions and stalled the engine. She cast a glance at the house. "If Linc comes out to laugh at me, I'm going to flip him off. You might want to cover your eyes."

"I'll flip him off for you. Don't worry about your brother. Focus. You want me to turn it around so you don't have to start out in reverse?"

"No, I'll do it."

It took two more tries before she succeeded in getting the vehicle to move in the direction she wanted. She backed out of the driveway.

"Clutch in when you come to a stop."

She managed to stop without stalling and accomplish a rough shift into first. The shift to second was smoother, and into third, smoother still. "Ha, look at that. I'm doing fine." She glanced at Sam. "You can let go of the armrest now. I think your fingernails have left grooves in the upholstery."

"Just drive, Eleanor."

He really was a patient teacher. The scariest moment was when she came to a stop sign on an incline and a car pulled up behind her. He talked her through it and after only one stall, she got the Cruiser moving again. She was feeling quite accomplished by the time they reached the highway that took them south.

The day was spectacular with the sun shining brightly in a deep blue sky. The highway wound through small towns scattered through rolling hills dotted with cattle, and wide-open stretches of grassland that made her feel glad not every inch of land had been developed. "Are those deer?" She pointed to brown and white animals grazing in an area of scrub brush along the highway.

"Pronghorn antelope. We usually don't see them this close to the highway."

"Antelope, really? That's awesome." Something must have spooked the animals because in a split second they were a blur racing across the land. "Wow, they're fast."

"Outrunning predators is how they survive." Sam pointed to a highway sign. "Our turn is coming up."

She slowed the Land Cruiser, downshifting easily into third to take a curve. She was getting the hang of the standard transmission.

Following Sam's directions on a road that had them traveling due west, about fifteen minutes after leaving the highway she saw a sign for Rock Creek Ranch and turned onto a gravel road.

Chapter Nine

"Park beside that truck next to the barn."

She did as directed. A tall man with long white hair strode out of the barn, a pair of dogs running ahead of him. With their identical features, Ellie could see what Ben would look like in thirty years.

Sam and Ellie got out of the SUV, the dogs busily sniffing their legs and shoes. The man caught Sam in a one-armed hug before turning to face Ellie, sharp brows lowered over black eyes giving him the look of a hawk on the hunt. Sam's face was tight as he introduced her as Rachel Sinclair. She remembered Ben's words and understood that lying to Pete Montoya cost Sam.

"If you meant to see your brother, you've wasted your time. He's off somewhere."

"I came to see you. Wanted you to meet Rachel."

Pete stared at her hard, then gave a quick nod. "You ride, girl?"

"Not recently. I took lessons when I was a teenager." She wondered if she was being tested.

"Come see my mare."

Ellie glanced at Sam, then they followed Pete into the barn. He led the way past a row of stalls, most empty, until they got to the last and largest one. A sorrel horse with a white star on her face stuck her head over the door and gave a soft whickering sound in welcome.

"Oh, she's beautiful." Ellie stroked the mare's neck, and a glance inside the stable had her commenting, "And very, very pregnant."

The door was on rails and Sam slid it back to step inside. A thick layer of straw covered the floor. He ran his hands over the mare's side, talking softly. "Hey there, Minnie. How's it going, girl?"

The mare responded by nibbling on his sleeve. "She's due any day now, isn't she?" he asked Pete.

"I'm guessing tonight or tomorrow. She's not in labor, though she's been restless for the last hour or so." Pete held Minnie's head and gazed into her velvety brown eyes. "I don't see pain yet."

Ellie could only have sympathy for the pretty mare and what she would endure to have her baby. Sam stepped out of the stall, sliding the door shut. He leaned back against the half wall, arms crossed over his chest. "You going to tell me what's going on?"

Pete gave a dry laugh. "What the hell you think is going on? We got someone who's got a bug up their ass about Rock Creek and is making their displeasure known."

"In a serious way."

"God damn serious when they start a fire. Even more serious when they butcher a calf."

"It wasn't wolf."

"It wasn't wolf," Pete agreed. "Had its neck slit, then was cut open. Guts strewn all over the place. His poor mama was crying her heart out." He glanced at Ellie. "Sorry, miss. But that's the way it is."

"Don't worry about me," Ellie told him. "I'm sorry to hear you lost a calf in that manner. It has to hurt."

"It does. Damn shame. Whoever would do a thing like that is sick."

"Guts strewn about will attract other animals," Sam said.

Ellie could read behind the disgust on Sam's face to see that killing the calf hurt him.

"Probably that was the idea." Pete spread his hands in front of him. "Coyotes got to it, made it harder to tell that it was killed by human hand. But the sheriff saw it for what it was."

"Drew's convinced it was wolf." A look passed between the two men that made Ellie think there was more about Drew that they were holding back on.

Pete shook his head. "It wasn't."

***

The Gator bumped along the road back to the barn, Sam steering the utility vehicle around ruts. The ranch roads needed grading before winter hit. He glanced at the woman sitting beside him. Ellie had listened attentively as he'd driven around the property. She'd asked good questions that showed she was giving thought to the operation. He couldn't help finding satisfaction in sharing with her something that was important to him. That thought alone should give him pause, but he found he didn't give a damn. He liked her, and if he was honest, he'd given her a tour of the ranch because he wanted her to see where he came from. There was nothing to be gained from her seeing the land except an understanding of him.

He parked the Gator under the shed overhang. They went in search of Pete and found him in a small office in the barn, sitting at a desk piled with papers weighted down with a horseshoe. He looked up when they walked in.

"We're heading out." Sam paused. "Never thought I'd say it, but be careful. You're alone here until Drew gets back, and who knows when that will be. Whoever killed that calf might not be done messing with us."

Pete nodded to a gun cabinet on the far wall. "Figure I can still hit what I'm aiming at, if it comes to that. And god knows Drew likes his guns." His face took on a scowl. "I put that damn ad in the paper like you told me to. A guy's coming in tomorrow morning for a trial period. Likely won't know a pitchfork from a shovel."

"Don't make him pass on the job because you're a hardass."

"If he can't handle a hardass, he shouldn't take the job." He raised a weathered hand to stop a comeback. "But if he can work, I'll hire him. I'll keep my word."

"Make sure he knows what's going on so he can keep an eye out for anything unusual."

Pete nodded. "When Minnie goes into labor, they'll be more folks here. Ron Harder's daughters want to be here when she delivers. Told them I'd give them a call when the time comes. They'll liven up the place."

"They're kids, you sure they won't get in the way?"

Pete smiled, and the resemblance to Ben was stronger. "Lot you know. Those girls are thirteen and sixteen. The older one's bent on being a big animal vet and wants the experience, and the younger one's not about to be left out of anything her sister does. Ron hardly lets those girls out of his sight, so he'll be here, too."

"Thirteen and sixteen? When the hell did that happen?" Sam turned to Ellie. "The Harders are neighbors to the south."

Pete rose and walked with them out of the barn.

"Kids grow up and there's not a damn thing you can do about it. I got me a granddaughter now, and pretty soon she'll be big enough for her grandpa to take her out on a horse." He gave Sam a long look. "Don't worry about me."

***

"You're still worried about him."

"Yeah, of course I am. Pete's closer to seventy than sixty, but he won't slow down. It took both Ben and me leaning on him heavy before he agreed to hire another hand."

"I get why you're worried, but there's a serenity to that man that makes me think he's contented with his life. Makes me a little envious."

Sam glanced at her in question as she waited at a stoplight on the outskirts of Pendleton.

"You discontented with your life, Ellie?"

She shrugged and he caught her pensive expression. "Not really, but I've been thinking about the future a lot lately. I'm not sure the Marshals Service will be a lifelong career for me." She blew out a gusty breath. "Whew. I've never said that out loud before, much less told anyone that I've even thought it."

"Why not?"

"My singular goal since he left has been to find my father and bring him to justice for what he's done. We're getting closer, and it's made me wonder, what then? What will my goal be after Richard Jameson is behind bars?"

"There are plenty of fugitives who need to be brought to justice."

"True." She steered onto Sam's street, her expression still thoughtful.

They pulled in front of the garage. Sam gripped her arm when she went to open the car door.

"Hang on."

"What?" She went instantly alert.

"Someone's been here." He pointed to an area under the white oak where deep grooves gouged the sod, and dirt and grass had been churned into a muddy mess. Sam pulled his phone from his pocket.

"It looks like someone drove a vehicle and spun their wheels. Did you get a security alert?"

"Only the house alarm gives an alert, but I can access the camera recordings on my phone."

When the app opened, he held his phone so she could see the screen. The image was remarkably clear. An older model dark gray truck had turned onto the driveway from the street, then sped around the house to the back where it spun around a couple of times on the lawn under the tree. It sat idling for a moment, dark tinted windows making it impossible to see the driver. Then, with tires throwing up sprays of dirt, the vehicle spun in another tight circle before speeding back up the driveway.

Ellie frowned. "Do you recognize the vehicle?"

"No. But about everyone around here has a truck. It's not one I recognize, though. It has plastic covers over the license plates so they can't be read."

"This seems juvenile, like something a kid would do."

Sam considered her comment. "Yeah. An immature dumbass. How would they have known we weren't home? I park in the garage, so unless they saw us leave, they risked me coming out with my shotgun."

"Judge Creed has a shotgun?"

"Judge Creed protects what's his within the limits of the law."

What'd been a nice grassy area shaded by the big tree was now a gaping wound in the land with tree roots laid bare and mud sprayed in all directions. His aunt had spent hours tending that yard and it ate at him to see it laid waste.

They stepped out of the Land Cruiser. Ellie had her phone out, taking pictures of the muddy mess. The dogs barked from inside.

Sam touched her elbow. "I want to take a look around before we go in the house."

She nodded, walking with him around the garage, and up the back slope along a narrow path. "Anything look different?"

"Someone's been through here since it rained yesterday."

A bunch of grass and wet leaves may not look suspicious to her, but Pete had taught him to know when someone had tromped around his property. They reached the top of the hill and the posts that formed the boundary of his property, then followed the stone wall back down the slope. He pointed to a couple of clearly marked footprints.

"When's the last time you were up here?"

"Not sure. A couple of weeks at least."

"Do you have a gardener or neighbor who might come this way?"

He shook his head.

"Okay. Let's see if anything's been disturbed around the house. You should file a police report, and I'll call Seth to let the team know."

***

Ellie sat on the couch with her laptop, legs curled under her. Cleo and Tony lay on a rug in front of the fireplace, and Gumbie purred as she stretched. The cat had decided that the cushion next to Ellie was her current favorite spot. Ellie scratched under Gumbie's chin, making her purr louder. Sam sat in the recliner reading something on his iPad. They were one big happy family. It bugged her that she couldn't lock Sam away in a corner of her brain and focus on her work.

Seth had sent her a bulletin on a bank robbery that had occurred in southern Idaho the previous week. He'd also sent information that their father had been identified on surveillance footage at a gas station in the same town the day before the bank robbery. The three bank robbers wore bulky coats, and parking lot cameras showed them with ski masks on as they'd emerged from their vehicle, which, she noted, was not the same one Richard Jameson had filled up at the gas station.

The three had robbed the bank and returned to their vehicle with their haul, speeding away before police arrived. The robbers had to've spent the night somewhere and Ellie made a mental note to check short-term rentals. Investigators usually checked motels, but sometimes neglected other housing options.

Significant as the developments were, all the while she was reading through the email and viewing the attachments, she was cognizant of Sam in a way that was truly annoying. He breathed and she felt the air move, he tapped his fingers on the armrest and it sounded like a snare drum, he rubbed his hand over his chin and she could hear the rasp of the whiskers.

He was driving her crazy.

Maybe she should jump him, they'd have wild jungle sex, and he'd be purged from her system.

She tried watching him out of the corner of her eye without turning her head. Keen intelligence, integrity, and that long, lean body – yeah, her type of guy.

"You keep looking at me like that and there'll be trouble."

"Maybe I want trouble." She slapped a hand over her mouth.

He set aside his iPad and when she looked at him directly, his smoldering eyes told her he wasn't unaffected by whatever was simmering between them, but he was doing a better job of reining in any crazy impulses.

"I wouldn't mind some of that trouble myself, but I'm not scratching that itch for you, Eleanor. We get together, I want it to be for the right reasons, not because it's convenient."

"Jesus, there's irony for you."

"What's the hell's that supposed to mean?"

She could tell him what had happened all those years ago, expose the wall between them, but she didn't want to risk the complications. "Nothing. It means nothing." She stood up. "I'm going to bed."

***

The next morning she steered into the parking lot near the federal courthouse, Sam sitting in the passenger seat.

"I'll meet you at the diner at noon. You can park here and walk, it's a half block down that street." He pointed. "You okay to drive without me?"

"I'm fine. I didn't stall it once this morning. I've got this."

He cocked his head. "You should come in and see my chambers. That seems like an engaged couple kind of thing."

Her heart gave an extra-hard thud that she hid behind nonchalance. "Sure."

They walked to the courthouse hand in hand, and she realized she was getting used to the physical connection. They entered the building through a side entrance that led to a long, narrow hall lined with closed doors on either side.

A woman with glasses perched on top of a wild mass of salt-and-pepper hair gave a wide smile when she saw them. "Sam Creed, the rumors are true then."

"Liz, this is my fiancée, Rachel Sinclair. Rachel, this is Liz Potenciano, also a judge in this court."

"Nice to meet you, Liz." Ellie shook the other woman's hand.

"I'm pleased to meet *you*. I never thought I'd see this guy settle down. He's a sly one. No one even knew he had a girlfriend." Her phone chimed. "I've got to run, but I'll expect an invitation to the wedding."

Sam looked resigned as he took Ellie down another hallway. Ellie hoped his friends would forgive him when they "broke up." He stopped at a door with a nameplate that read "The Honorable Samuel D. Creed."

"What's the 'D' stand for?"

"David. My parents went for the conventional."

"It's a strong name."

"When I was a boy I wanted a name like Running Bear or White Eagle in the worst way."

"Who wouldn't?" she asked with a smile.

He unlocked the door and pushed it open. "Here are my chambers."

Ellie stepped into a paneled room with dark wood floors upon which sat a huge deep maroon rug with blue and white scrollwork throughout. In the right corner of the sizeable room was a large dark wood desk with a computer monitor on the left side, and an old-fashioned blotter with maroon edging in the middle of the desk. The chair behind the massive desk was a high-back executive chair in dark leather with brass studding around the edges. Behind the chair was a dark wood credenza, and several tall wood filing cabinets lined the wall opposite the desk.

"What, no bookcases full of law books?"

"That's what the Internet and my law clerk are for."

"How iconoclastic of you. When I was in law school, it seemed like a judge wasn't serious unless he had a wall of law books behind his desk."

"And I bet not one of those books was ever opened."

She approached the door on the opposite wall. "Do you mind?"

"Go ahead, but you're a US Marshal, you've seen dozens of courtrooms."

"But not yours." She stepped through the door and took in the space. The high wood-paneled judge's bench with the courtroom deputy clerk's lower attached desk dominated the room. In front of a half wall were two long tables for the defense and US attorneys, each with three chairs. Behind the half wall was a center aisle with seven rows of seats for the gallery on each side, and to the left of the bench was the jury box. In front of the bench was the court reporter's chair, and beside it was the judge's personal clerk's desk.

She liked courtrooms with their traditions and ceremony. They were emblematic of the rule of law that was the bedrock of a democratic society.

She returned to Sam's chambers and spied his black robe hanging from a hook. "You know, you're popular on social media."

"Huh?"

"Social media. You're popular."

"I don't know what you're talking about. I avoid social media like leprosy."

"It doesn't avoid you. The video of you taking down that guy with a knife went viral with over a million views. Women thought you were hot."

His expression held horror that could not be faked. "You're making that up."

She couldn't stifle her giggle. She pulled out her phone. "I'm not making it up. I can't believe people haven't shown you." She tapped out a search, then held up her screen. "Look."

First she showed the video of his heroics, then she shared a meme of a woman licking her lips and leering at an image of Sam, sexy in his judge's robes, the thought bubble over her head suggesting that she knew who she wanted delivering her punishment.

"What the hell?" Red stained his cheeks.

"Want to see others?"

"There are others? How do I take them down?"

"You don't. That's the price you pay for being a hot federal judge."

"You think this is funny," he said, accusation vibrating in his tone.

They stepped out of his chambers and she couldn't help laying her hands on the lapels of his suit jacket. She knew she shouldn't be enjoying his discomfort quite so much. "Maybe a little bit. No more heroic leaps over your bench and you'll fade into obscurity."

He was still scowling when she gave in to impulse and leaned forward to brush her lips against his. The warmth in his eyes turned flat when a loud "woohoo" echoing down the hall had them both turning their heads.

Gordon Finster flashed his toothy smile, wagging a finger like he'd caught them doing something naughty. Sam obviously thought she'd spied Finster and that her kiss had been for show. Better than the truth, Ellie assured herself.

"Christ, that man can't get a clue," Sam muttered.

"Let's give him something to gossip about." She went up on tiptoes for a kiss that was more than a simple brush of lips. Tension eased like a deep sigh. This was what she'd been missing since the last time they'd kissed, that rush of feeling from the top of her head to that hot curl of lust in her belly. It made her want to forget about being a marshal on the job and find a quiet place where they could explore that flare of heat that ignited whenever they touched.

"You're playing with fire, Ellie," he murmured against her lips. Then he was opening his mouth and his tongue swept across hers and she wasn't thinking at all.

Chapter Ten

Ellie parked the Land Cruiser on the driveway behind Sam's house. She eyed the mess left by the truck and found herself angry all over again. Someone had willfully violated the pretty and peaceful setting Sam and his aunt had created. Ellie was fairly certain that whoever had spun out their vehicle under the tree didn't have the same agenda as the person or persons threatening Sam. Tearing up a lawn didn't have the same impact as plastic explosives strapped to a judge's car.

With the bag of groceries in her hand, she dug out the house key Sam had given her. The wind had picked up to blow icy fingers down her collar, and the dome of the sky gleamed a hard and brittle blue. A honking sound above had her tipping back her head to witness a long V of geese flying overhead. She watched until they disappeared. While she loved San Diego with its diversity and quirky vibe, the wildness in this part of Oregon held an equally strong appeal.

Cleo and Tony rushed her with tails wagging as she went through their enclosure to the back door. They looked dapper in the plaid coats she and Sam had put on them that morning. Once inside, she disengaged the alarm, set the bag on the counter, and began putting away the milk, produce, and bread she'd bought.

Feeling unsettled, she filled the coffeemaker with water, measured out ground coffee, and set the machine to do its thing. Forty minutes after that sublime kiss she was still riding the high. She'd been an idiot going with impulse rather than control. Again. But she was done beating herself up about it.

Whatever had attracted her to Sam thirteen years ago still resonated. She liked his quick brain, the occasional flash of humor when he wasn't being so controlled, and while she didn't think him conventionally handsome, what he had did it for her in spades.

This whole fake engagement thing had definite disadvantages. Two healthy unattached adults, a lot of time spent together, and a few fake kisses to make it look good could turn into a recipe for disaster.

On an impulse, she returned to the mudroom for her coat, grabbed the dogs' leashes, and after snapping them on their collars, took them out the back door, through the gate, and out of the pen. With Cleo and Tony nosing and sniffing everywhere, she wandered Sam's property. She didn't find any fresh footprints on the slope but followed the rock wall past the posts marking his property line to the top of the ridge where a view of the valley spread out before her. The hill dropped steeply to a road below, and beyond that a stand of trees lined the swirling dark waters of the river.

Returning down the hill, she and the dogs circled to the front of the house. The deep red leaves of a Japanese maple gave a splash of color at the front corner of the house. Bright orange mums flowered next to the steps to the porch and Ellie made a mental note to bring some of the blooms inside. She couldn't imagine they would survive much longer given the cool temperatures.

She returned to the house, and after taking off the dogs' jackets, she opened a bag of treats. "Okay, babies, sit." They both went down on their haunches, quivering, staring fixedly at the little bone-shaped biscuits in her hand. They each took the treats politely, carrying them to their bed to enjoy.

Ellie poured herself coffee and made her way to the front room with her steaming mug to where she'd left her laptop on the coffee table. The dogs followed her, lying on the area rug beside the couch. Her phone chimed with a text from Linc.

L: *Met case admin Finster. He's an ass. He found out I'm assigned to Creed's court and about fell over himself to tell me he found the judge in a lip lock with hot fiancée. (I'll omit crude comment about fiancée, but what the hell, El?) Immediate impression – he's not our guy. Whatever he's thinking comes out his mouth. Still bears investigation, but don't think he has the self-control to plan anything beyond his next meal.*

As usual, Linc was able to cut through the bullshit and get right to the core. She ignored his reference to the kiss when she replied.

E: *Tend to agree. Finster's a cheap thrill kind of guy. Can't see him planning for a long game. Talk guns with him?*

L: *No. Will work it into conversation later.*

E: *Thx for update.*

While it was possible that there was more going on in Finster's head than they gave him credit for, and he did have connections with the gun rights community, she agreed with Linc that they needed to keep looking for the source of the threats against Sam. Computer humming, she searched for information on Drew Martin. Figuring Drew was short for Andrew, she went to work.

Sam may have been convinced his brother wasn't part of any plot, but Ellie wasn't so certain. She searched one database, then others without much luck. His name was fairly common, and she tried different search parameters to narrow the field.

It would help to know his middle name. That came up on census data, and with that information she was finally able to make some progress.

Drew hadn't served in the military and didn't turn up in any federal criminal databases. She dug deeper, even doing newspaper searches, until bingo, she found an incident from five months previous. A woman had filed a complaint that an intoxicated Andrew Martin had showed up at her home and threatened her. The woman claimed that the reported incident hadn't been the first time since she'd ended a romantic relationship with him that he'd come to her home uninvited. She'd obtained a restraining order. The reporter had mentioned that Andrew Martin was the stepbrother of Judge Samuel D. Creed. Drew's lawyer had managed to get the charges reduced to trespassing and Drew had been sentenced to thirty days in jail, less time served.

Ellie wondered if she could get a copy of the police report. She'd get Seth on that. Sam must know about his brother's brush with the law and had made a decision not to tell her about it. He'd been insistent that his brother wasn't involved with the threats, but Ellie thought Sam was being willfully blind. Family loyalty could cloud the judgment of the most rational and clear-thinking individuals.

Sunlight glinted off glass through the front window. Ellie rose to her feet to watch a truck turn onto the driveway. Speak of the devil. Barking wildly, the dogs rushed to the back door, nails clicking on the wood floor. Ellie shut the top of her laptop, then dashed up the stairs to grab her Glock from the gun safe. Down the back stairs, she slipped into the kitchen and stashed the gun in a drawer under neatly folded kitchen towels.

She opened the door to find Drew standing in the driveway, staring at the destruction under the white oak. Today he was hatless and wore a Sherpa-lined denim jacket open in front. He also wore a gun in a holster on his belt.

He glanced over as she crossed the dogs' enclosure to the wire fence, the beagles running ahead of her. "What happened here?"

"Someone with a pickup drove back here and spun donuts in the mud when Sam and I were out yesterday."

"Well, shit. Who'd do that?"

"Don't know." She pointed to the camera at the corner of the house. "Camera caught the truck, but we weren't able to make out the license plate or the driver."

He narrowed his eyes. "When did Sam put cameras in?"

She shrugged. "I didn't think to ask him."

He scanned the eaves, then the garage, before turning to face her. "You asking me in, future sister-in-law?"

She eyed the gun at his waist and gauged how to play the part. "I don't know, future brother-in-law. Seems weird that you showed up here when you know Sam would be in court, and with a gun on your belt."

"Oregon is an open-carry state, so it's legal."

"That may be, but my concern remains the same. Why did you come, Drew?"

Something flashed across his expression she couldn't decipher. "I thought you should know what you're getting into by marrying Sam. I don't think he's told you the truth, or at least the whole truth, about how fucked up our family is."

"And somehow you're concerned about me and want to correct that omission."

He hitched a shoulder in the jacket that hung loosely on his shoulders. "Sam gets every damn thing laid at his feet. He should at least be honest before he gets you, too."

She studied him. If she'd truly been Sam's fiancée, she'd tell Drew to get lost. But she was a marshal charged with protecting Sam, and his brother might have information that would benefit her team's investigation. "I'll invite you in, but the gun makes me uncomfortable. I'd like you to leave it in your truck."

"It's my right to carry a gun."

"Not on someone else's property, it's not."

He narrowed his gaze. "You a lawyer, too?"

"As a matter of fact, I am."

He looked at the house, then at her, and appeared to weigh his options. Whatever he wanted to tell her must have won out, because with a muttered oath he went to his truck and locked the gun inside.

"Thank you." Ellie held open the gate for Drew to pass through.

Once indoors, Drew paced the kitchen floor. He stopped at the window, stared out at the yard with a frown on his face, then paced again. The dogs sat on their cushion, eyes tracking the visitor.

"Would you like coffee?"

"Yeah." She moved to prepare it, and he said, "You know I'd never been in this house until my brother inherited it."

"No, I didn't know that."

"Sam's aunt thought he walked on water. She tolerated me, acted nice enough, but I wasn't kin so she didn't see me as part of her family. Had to have native blood for that. Left this place to Sam, and not a penny to me."

She handed him the mug.

"Got nothing to say to that, sister?"

"I've moved up from future sister-in-law to sister? That's quick. And no, I have nothing to say about that. Obviously, I never met Nan Beauchamp, and have no insight into her decision."

"You're a cool one, aren't you? No wonder Sam fell for you." When she didn't respond, he continued. "My mom married Sam's dad when I was a little kid. Sam tell you we aren't real brothers?"

"He refers to you as his brother, but did acknowledge that you're step-siblings."

"Mom worked like a slave for Joss Creed. Cooked for him, kept the house clean, even trucked feed to the cattle and mucked stalls if she had to. When I was old enough, I worked my tail off, too. Learned a lot, but got my ass whipped more times than I can count. Worked on that ranch more than Sam did. Sam didn't like the old man's discipline style so he'd take off every chance he got. He and Ben would go fishing, hiking, rock-climbing, whatever they wanted to do. Or he'd come here and stay with his aunt. Leave me behind."

Ellie wasn't even sure Drew remembered she was in the room. Once again he stood at the kitchen sink, sipping coffee as he stared out the window, seemingly lost in the past. Then he turned to face her and he was totally in the present, anger flaring hot behind pale eyes. "The old man let me call him Dad, said I was his son, and I stayed on at the ranch even after my mom died. He acted like I meant something. Then last year the fucker up and dies and he doesn't leave me shit. Left the ranch a hundred percent to Sam, because I don't have his blood coursing through my veins."

He pointed a finger at her, emphatic in his air jabs. "But you know what really burns? My holier-than-thou brother, the man who sits in judgment over others, didn't make it right. He didn't tell that lawyer to add my name to the deed. So now I'm working my ass off again, for nothing."

He set the mug on the counter with a snap. "That's what I got to say to you, sister. You should know who it is you're marrying. May seem to you that bagging a judge gives you a nice, secure future, but he'll screw you over like he does everyone else. Like he did me."

Once again, Drew began prowling the room, then jabbed a finger toward the window. "Must have pissed someone off big time to have them coming on his property to destroy shit. His line of work, he pisses off folks regular. He sends honest, hardworking men, men who are true patriots, to prison every day. No one should have that much power and privilege. You should consider that before you marry him." Drew's shoulders slumped and his anger seemed to have run its course. "You've been warned. That's all I got to say."

He slammed out the backdoor, and through the window she watched him tramp across the yard to his truck.

Ellie picked up her phone, and when Seth answered, she said, "We have a suspect."

***

Sam scanned the crowded diner and spotted Ellie sitting in a booth toward the back. His heart gave an unexpected lurch, and he rubbed the heel of his hand over his chest to ease the discomfort. He made his way across the floor, weaving between occupied tables. A few people said hello as he passed, or waved to acknowledge him, but he didn't stop.

Ellie looked up from the menu she'd been studying as he dropped onto the bench across from her. The smile she flashed him had to be for effect, but he couldn't ignore how it transformed her face. He leaned forward, cupped his hand behind her neck, and caught her lips with his, reining back the desire to take it deeper. Anyone looking would see Judge Creed greeting his fiancée.

He couldn't help the satisfaction at her flustered expression when he released her. She cleared her throat. "Sam."

"Eleanor. How was your morning?"

"Interesting. How was yours?" The mundane words belied the charged physical greeting he thought neither of them was ready to acknowledge.

"Routine, other than lots of congratulations on our engagement. Want to tell me about your interesting morning?" The group at the table nearest them left so there was little chance their conversation would be overheard as long as they spoke in quiet voices.

"Your brother came by this morning, guess he wanted to welcome me to the family."

He kept his expression relaxed even though a muscle jumped in his jaw. He was saved from having to respond by the arrival of the short, round woman holding a steaming coffeepot who rubbed a hand on his shoulder.

"Hey there, Judy."

Judy wasn't an inch over five feet and wore her bright red hair tied back in a frizzy poof behind her head. She carried menus tucked under her arm and had a pocketed apron tied around her waist that bulged with pens and straws, and wore more eye shadow than anyone he'd ever met. And she was hands-down one of his favorite people.

He rose from his seat to give her a hug. When he stepped back, she asked in her raspy voice, "How you doing, boy?"

"Better now that I've seen you. I want you to meet someone." He turned. "This is my fiancée, Rachel." Guilt gnawed another hole in his conscience as he considered how many people he was lying to.

"Wondering when you'd introduce me to your girl. Got wind of your engagement yesterday when Barb Herrera came in." She frowned. "You never told me you had a girlfriend, and now you've got yourself a fiancée."

Ellie stood, extending her hand. "Hello, Judy. It's nice to meet Sam's friends."

Judy shook her hand. "You're a tall one, aren't you? We'll be fine as long as you treat my boy right."

"I intend to."

"Good. Now you two sit and tell me what you want for lunch."

They gave their order, and Judy left after filling their mugs with coffee.

Sam bent forward, speaking softly. "Drew give you any trouble? He knew I'd be at work."

Ellie mimicked his posture and kept her voice pitched below the chatter around them. "Not really. He had a gun on his belt when he arrived. I met him outside and said I didn't feel comfortable with him coming in the house armed. He didn't like it but he left it in his truck." She gave Sam a considering look. "He didn't have a gun when he came by on Saturday."

"Because he knows better than to try that with me. I'm glad you called him on it." He picked up Ellie's hand and rubbed his thumb over her engagement ring, then brought it to his lips. He bit back a laugh at the scowl on her face. "Isn't this what an engaged guy would do when he meets his fiancée for lunch? He'd want to let her know he missed her. You should be smiling at me with little hearts in your eyes." He knew good and well that if they hadn't been in a dining room full of people, she'd bust his chops. "I'm new at this, so you'll have to tell me if I'm wrong."

"How should I know? I've never been engaged before." She tugged her hand and he let go. "But it feels over the top to me."

Sparring with her gave his mood a boost, and that after the heart-jolt when he'd spotted her. He felt a little like when he'd slid down an ice chute while hiking, unable to get traction. With effort, he reordered his thoughts. "What did Drew say?"

She tucked her hands under the table. "His basic implication was that you're a greedy bastard for inheriting the house from your aunt and the ranch from your dad when he didn't get a penny. He thinks you're privileged and that he's been treated like he's not part of the family."

The reminder of Drew's animosity had Sam's mood plummeting. He flattened his hands on the table when what he really wanted to do was hunt his brother down and give him a good kick in the ass.

"He shouldn't have dumped that shit on you. What he didn't tell you is that Dad did make provisions for him. It's not a lot because Dad's money was tied up in the ranch and he was cash poor, and Drew won't get that money until he turns thirty-five. Joss Creed was a strict son of a bitch and didn't suffer fools gladly. He didn't think

Drew had the maturity to handle the ranch or a chunk of cash. I tend to agree. I told Drew I plan to give him a share of the ranch, but he's resentful that I haven't done it on his timetable."

"Are you waiting until he's older?"

He leaned back against his seat. "That was my original plan, but I don't know anymore. I'm not sure age will make a difference. Some people never become responsible adults. He had a girlfriend who kept pushing him to come to me for money, fed him a line that he deserved more, that I should put him on the deed to the ranch immediately. They confronted me, and I told them there was no way in hell that was happening. Guess she decided to cut her losses when it was apparent Drew wasn't coming into quick cash. She broke things off with him, so there's another thing he blames me for."

"He left out a lot when he came to set me straight about your family."

Sam gave a disgusted sigh. "Of course he did. Drew also had a run-in with the law that makes me question his judgment even more. He tell you about that?"

"No, but I've been looking into his background." She held up a hand when Sam's eyes narrowed. "Doing my job. His case popped up."

"Then you'll understand why I'm in a wait-and-see mode with his inheritance. I'll see how he deals with his issues, drinking being one of them, before I give him anything."

Ellie sipped her coffee, blue eyes steady on his over the rim of her mug. "That's a crappy position to be in, isn't it?"

"Yep. Drew resents me, and I don't see that changing."

"You're doing what's best, Sam, even if Drew doesn't understand it."

Sam felt a knot of tension in his gut loosen. He wasn't used to confiding in anyone about his issues with his brother. Ben knew, and Pete, but somehow telling Ellie lessened the burden, made him think how it could be between them if they were truly engaged. Which they weren't. He needed to keep reminding himself of that fact.

"He doesn't. But he has a roof over his head and work when he cares to do it; he just needs to get his shit together."

Their order arrived with extra avocado heaped on Ellie's cobb salad, and a huge slab of corn bread on the plate beside his turkey chili.

Judy put a hand on his shoulder and nodded to Ellie. "Sam tell you he used to sit at this very booth and do his homework when he was a boy?"

Ellie smiled. "No, he didn't tell me that."

"When I stayed with my aunt, I'd come here after school until she could pick me up. My mom had worked here, and Judy was one of her best friends."

"So you're family," Ellie said to Judy.

"You bet I am." Judy sniffed, squeezed his shoulder, and pulled a handkerchief from her pocket to wipe her eyes as she walked away.

Sam shook his head at Ellie's distressed expression. "That was the perfect thing to say to her. She's never quite gotten over my mom's death. Mom had been covering a shift for Judy the night she was killed."

"Oh jeez. What a burden to carry."

"Yeah." He motioned to the plate in front of her. "Eat up, or Judy will be back to find out why you're picking at the food."

As always, the chili was excellent, and Ellie dug into her salad. He'd been on dates with women who acted afraid to enjoy their food. He was glad to see Ellie wasn't like that.

She speared a slice of avocado, brows lowering over her eyes in a way that made him think she was carefully choosing her words. Keeping her voice low, she said, "Sam, you need to consider that Drew could be behind the threats against you. He carries a gun and is aggressive in defending it as his right. That suggests affinity with pro-gun rights ideology espoused by FD."

"It's not a crime to support the Second Amendment."

"As long as that support isn't extreme. He made a comment that every day you send hardworking men to prison, called them 'true patriots.' That suggests anti-government beliefs that may come down on the wrong side of the law."

Sam set his butter knife against the plate with the corn bread. "It's not him. I've considered it, but it's not him."

"Is that an emotional assumption, or a logical one based on evidence?"

"Drew's my brother. Despite the current issues between us, he would never do anything to hurt me, and certainly wouldn't have taped a brick of C-four in the wheel well of my car."

Her expression was troubled, and he knew as clearly as if she'd said it out loud that she wasn't convinced of his brother's loyalty.

"What happened to Drew's mother?"

He sighed in relief at the change in subject. "She passed away when he was a teenager."

"Your family has had it rough."

"Yeah." He cut a piece of corn bread and slathered on butter, offering it to her. "He took it hard."

"Who wouldn't?" She took the corn bread, and when she bit into it, closed her eyes with a hum of appreciation. "Wow, that's good."

He moved the corn bread between them. "Have as much as you want."

"Thanks. I could make a meal of the corn bread alone."

"Tell me about your mother."

The quick flash of her eyes told him he'd surprised her. "Margaret Bollinger is the best mom in the world. She was a rock when my dad abandoned us."

"How old were you when he left?"

"Twelve."

"Vulnerable age for a girl."

"Yeah. Things hadn't been right before that. Dad would take off for these long weekends without us, so it felt like there was buildup to him leaving. He worked for the military as a civilian. We found out he'd been stealing weapons and explosives and selling most of it on the black market. Mom was shocked, and she was hopping mad, but maybe not as much as you'd think because she had an inkling something was up. But no matter what she felt, she kept it together for her kids. Made us all go to family therapy."

"That help?"

"I think so. My brothers were hurt and angry. I guess we all were. Seth tended to bottle things inside. Still does. I was more emotional and prone to rants, and Linc was somewhere in between. The therapist was good and we worked through it as best we could."

"How's your mom now?"

"Awesome. She married the marshal in charge of Dad's case. He's the best thing that could have happened to her."

"Betrayal like that from a family member is hard to overcome. Some people never do."

She wondered if he was talking about her family or his. "Arch Bollinger, that's my stepdad, he doesn't know the meaning of the word 'quit.' He told me that when he met my mom for the first time, his heart did this hard flip in his chest, and he thought 'there she is.' He said he'd been waiting for her his entire life. At first Mom brushed him aside, refused to go out with him. He'd step back, take a breath, and try again."

Sam frowned. "I know that name. Chief Deputy Archer Bollinger."

"You've met him?"

"Yeah, I've met him. He oversaw the Marshals Office assigned to the Ninth Circuit when I was clerking. He's a good guy."

"Yes, he is."

"And now you and your brothers are all marshals, and on the team to locate your father."

"We're getting closer. We'll find him and bring him to justice."

"I have no doubt." Sam pushed the empty chili bowl aside, thanking Judy when she warmed his coffee and cleared his dishes. He waited until she was out of earshot to speak. "You okay to be at home alone this afternoon?"

Ellie gave him that grin that warmed her eyes, the one that made him wish for an instant that the engagement wasn't fake.

"Who's the marshal here? I think I can handle your brother if he decides to show up again. Or anyone else, for that matter."

"We don't know what they're planning. Whoever made that threat may have moved onto plan B since running me over with a truck didn't work out."

"I'll be on the lookout. Don't worry about me."

"I don't think that's possible."

She gave him a sharp look as Judy slid the check across the table to Sam as she passed. Ellie held out her hand. "I'll pay. We can put it on my expense account."

"I got it." She scowled, and he said, "I pay when I take my fiancée to lunch, Eleanor. Deal with it."

Chapter Eleven

Ellie drove through the largest intersection in town and headed toward Sam's house. If something didn't break soon, she'd go crazy, as in running-down-the-street-naked crazy. She and Sam had settled into a rhythm and it'd been working for ten days. But she felt like she was a spring being wound tighter and tighter, and it was only a matter of time before she exploded. God knew where she'd end up when she finally sprung free.

There hadn't been any more disturbances at the house. No unexplained footprints, no trucks spinning out under the oak tree. Sam had hired a lawn crew to clean up the mess in the backyard and they'd evened out the soil and replaced sections of sod.

She and Sam went on outings together, took the dogs for walks and held hands for the neighbors, and even attended a social function where they'd acted the part of besotted lovers. Then they returned to the house where the barriers went up and they were roommates. Roommates whose mutual attraction was so palpable, it hung in the air.

Which resulted in her being on the brink of crazy.

Being around Sam meant being in a constant state of unrelenting lust.

Her perpetually aroused state wouldn't be so bad if she had an inkling that Sam reciprocated her feelings, but after the first weekend, the austere Judge Creed had returned. Now, he pretty much ignored her when they were home.

He no longer sat in the front room with her in the evenings, instead closing himself in his office until well after she'd gone upstairs. They still ran together in the mornings, taking a different route every day, but even then conversation was kept to a minimum.

She put on her blinker and glanced in her side mirror and saw the same work van that had followed her out of the grocery store parking lot was still behind her. The van turned left before the bridge. Could be nothing, but she recorded a voice memo on her phone noting the make, model, and time she thought its driver might have started to surveil her.

Once home, she brought the dogs in, set the alarm to "at home," and got to work on her laptop. Late in the afternoon, she tapped on the meeting app to join the team for a conference call.

Seth started with a general overview of their current status, then each team member gave an update of what they'd learned.

"I've interviewed more of the female staff about sexual harassment at the courthouse," Bella reported, her tone even and devoid of emotion. "The issue seems confined to Gordon Finster. An additional woman has sought to join the other complainants against him. Their case appears solid.

"Finster followed a pattern of staying late into the evening beyond his normal hours when the women were often working alone. He would use the opportunity to take advantage of them sexually. All the women feel indebted to Judge Creed, and believe his support provided them credibility and gave them the courage to make their cases. They are grateful to him."

Ellie made a conscious effort not to roll her eyes at the overly professional tone her friend adopted, particularly when she was around Seth, which was most of the time. Bella could be warm and fun, and interesting, but put her near authority and she projected all the emotion of a robot.

Ellie got Bella's reserve, and couldn't blame her given what she'd been through in her life, but Ellie couldn't seem to convince her that being a good marshal didn't mean she had to follow all rules and protocols to the letter. For Bella, rules brought security, though Ellie thought being constantly vigilant and afraid of making a mistake must be exhausting.

"I talked with other staff," Seth stated. "Not one claimed to be friends with Finster, and most find him obnoxious. He doesn't have much of a filter. He's the kind of guy who walks up to people and starts talking to them, but it's not a conversation. He simply disgorges whatever is on his mind, then moves on. He spewed out the details of his divorce, which apparently got nasty. Sympathy was with his kid for being the bone both parents were fighting over. The only topic he holds back on is his side business selling guns. Few people knew about that."

"Any rumors of someone on staff having a beef with Sam?" Ellie asked.

"No. He's well-liked and respected. I got the impression one of the women has a crush on him."

"Any talk of love interests?" Linc asked. "We haven't looked at Sam's romantic background. The threatening emails don't scream spurned lover, but could be there's an angry ex with an imagination messing with him. You'd have to be really pissed to duct tape C-four to your ex's car, but it's been done. He mention anyone to you, El?"

"No. He must have bought this engagement ring for someone, but he hasn't been exactly forthcoming."

Linc looked thoughtful. "I think a woman would be more personal, but a dude might go for explosives. El reported a visit from a close friend who is gay. Could be Creed is too."

"He's not," Ellie said, shaking her head.

"Have you asked him, or whether he has any angry exes?" Linc was sitting back in his chair, brow raised in a look of inquiry that for some reason always annoyed her.

"I haven't asked, but he's not gay."

She should have been more careful because Linc pounced. "And how do you know he's not gay?"

"Shut up, Linc. I know, okay?"

"Do you have anything for us today, Ellie?"

Grateful for Seth's rescue, Ellie mentioned the vehicle she thought had followed her. "Right now, I'd give it a fifty percent chance that it wasn't random and was following me."

"Anything more on Drew Martin?"

"Sam won't talk about him. My feeling is that Drew is angry and resentful because he hasn't made any economic advances in his life. He was counting on inheriting part of the ranch, and Sam is in the way of that. Losing his mother, not inheriting property he felt he deserved, and feeling overshadowed by his successful older brother are all adding up for him. The right-wing groups he identifies with reinforce this idea of injustice."

"Your analysis is on point," Seth said. "Joining a militia group would give him a sense of empowerment."

Ellie nodded. "The feeling that he never fully belonged to the Creed family has led to a nasty mix of anger and bitterness. One appeal of extremist groups is they make you feel like you've found your true home. They feed the anger and resentment to pull in the disaffected. If Drew found a place where he feels wanted within the right-wing militia movement, that could be our connection."

"Agreed," Seth said.

They concluded their meeting, and Ellie sat in the quiet house watching through the window as the last glow of daylight faded. A glance at her phone to check the time brought a frown. Every day, Sam was home from work shortly after five, and it was already six. She began to text him, then hesitated. Their engagement was fake and checking up on him felt too much like what a girlfriend would do. Which was stupid. She was a marshal, and her job was to protect her fiancé.

She tapped out a text, keeping it to a simple *You good?* before hitting send.

It took him a couple minutes, but his reply of *Fine, home soon* worked.

She went to the kitchen with Cleo and Tony following close behind. Getting the hint, she filled their dishes with kibble, then began gathering the ingredients for dinner that she'd purchased that morning at the grocery store.

Twenty minutes later she had a pot gently simmering on the stove. She was reaching for a wineglass when Tony and Cleo both sat up, ears perked. Her first thought was that Sam was home. Finally. But she hadn't heard the Land Cruiser or seen headlights of the vehicle driving to the back. The security lights on either end of the garage illuminated the area vacant of vehicles, so unless Sam had somehow already parked in the garage without her noticing, it wasn't him who had alerted the dogs.

Opting for caution, she ran up the back stairs and retrieved her Glock from the gun safe, tucking it into the back waistband of her jeans. Gumbie lay curled up and asleep on Ellie's bed so she shut the door rather than worrying about the cat getting out while she was looking for possible bad guys. She returned to the kitchen using the back stairs.

In the mudroom, she turned on the lights and opened the back door. The beagles bulleted out, barking furiously as they raced to the back fence. Movement, more of a shifting shadow at the side of the house than anything else, caught her attention. She dashed back inside, leaving the dogs out, flipping off lights as she went through the house so no one could see in.

From the side window of the library, she watched a dark figure leap from the rock wall to blend into the darkness under the low branches of a trio of trees.

Ellie stood still, waiting. After several minutes, she reached for the phone in her back pocket. The shadow moved, quick and furtive. Then the window exploded with a crash and she reeled back as shards of glass flew past her.

She dove for cover behind a couch and a thud sounded as something landed on the floor. Even with her eyelids squeezed shut and instinctively pressing her hands over her ears, she could detect the flash of light and explosive crack of sound.

The siren for the house alarm went off, sounding oddly muted. Ellie grabbed her Glock and rose cautiously to her feet. A quick look showed no fire. Slamming shut the door to the room, she ran for the front door, gun in hand.

The yard was empty, and the porch light on the neighbor's house came on. She tucked her gun back into the waistband of her jeans. Headlights gleamed through the trees as a vehicle raced up the street, barely slowing to take the turn into the driveway.

Sam's Land Cruiser skidded to a stop at the walkway and he jumped out of the car and raced toward her. The expression on his face as he ran his hands over her arms and shoulders had the breath backing up in her lungs.

Over the past week she'd decided he was indifferent to her, but now she realized he was a consummate actor. Silver glinted in his eyes as his wide palms reached up to frame her face as his thumbs brushed her cheeks.

"You okay? What the hell happened?"

His voice sounded like it was coming from deep in a well. She shook her head, trying to clear it, not sure if the feeling of disorientation was from the flashbang or the raw fear emanating from Sam.

"I think I'm fine, but I can't hear very well."

"Were you attacked?"

"No. Someone was outside by the wall. They threw a flashbang into the house. I ran outside but they were already gone."

"You could have been seriously hurt."

His grip tightened as his eyes blazed. This was the first time she'd seen Sam truly angry.

"But I wasn't."

"What room was it?"

"The library."

He nodded. Despite sounding muffled, she could hear the dogs in the back howling at the approaching sirens of three police cars, one arriving right after the other. They parked on the street, the fire truck following them coming up the driveway. The sirens were silenced, leaving circling blue and red lights slicing through the night.

As police officers approached, Sam took off his coat to drape around Ellie's shoulders. She sighed when he pulled her against his side, and she absorbed his heat like he was her own personal campfire.

"Be better if they didn't wonder why you're carrying."

Oh. Right. Sam's coat would hide her gun. At least he was thinking sensibly, while she'd been getting all warm and fuzzy feelings because of his apparent concern.

An officer, older than the others and with an extra stripe on the sleeve of his coat, asked them to follow him away from the house.

"Judge Creed." He nodded to Sam. "Are we looking for an intruder?"

"No. Whoever threw the device through the window took off. It sounds like it was a flashbang."

The officer relayed the information over his radio. "You in the house when all the fun started?"

Sam shook his head. "I was about two blocks from home when my phone alerted that the house alarm had gone off. Rachel was standing in front when I arrived."

The officer turned to Ellie. "Miss. I'm Officer Hickman. Had a bit of excitement, haven't you?" Officer Hickman was probably close to retirement age and had a pleasantly lined face and a comfortable paunch around his middle.

Ellie nodded. "Yes."

"Can you hear me all right? Flashbangs can cause temporary deafness."

"My ears are ringing, but I can hear you."

"Good, good. Are you hurt?"

She shook her head. "I'm okay."

"Our EMT is on another call, but someone with the fire crew will get you checked out. We can call an ambulance if you think you need a ride to the hospital."

"No ambulance."

Hickman nodded. "We'll get down to business, then." He licked a thumb to flip pages in a small notebook. "Let me get your name and whatnot."

While Ellie gave him the name Rachel Sinclair and other requested information, Sam released his hold on her and stepped away. The chilly breeze had her wrapping his coat more securely around her.

Officer Hickman finished writing her details. "Okay then, why don't you tell me what happened?"

"I was in the kitchen making dinner. Oh," she turned to find Sam on his phone. "I left soup cooking on the stove."

Hickman nodded toward the firefighters filing into the house. "They'll take care of that. Don't worry."

"All right." Ellie took a deep breath, then recounted how the dogs had alerted her, and when she'd let them outside, she'd seen someone by the rock wall. Skipping over how she'd run upstairs for her gun, she described the shattering glass, followed by the flash of light and loud noise.

Hickman nodded. "That's a flashbang. Good thing your instinct was to cover your ears as much as you did. Can you describe the person you saw?"

"My impression is male, medium height, average weight. He was wearing dark clothing, I think with a beanie low over his forehead and the hood on his sweatshirt pulled over that. I don't think that helps much."

"Everything helps," he assured her.

A firefighter came out of the house and approached them.

"What's the verdict, Lieutenant?" Hickman asked.

"There was no fire or scorching." The lieutenant looked at Ellie and Sam, who had returned to her side. "You folks are fortunate about that. Blew out some windows, and you've got a few broken knickknacks, but the damage is contained to that room."

"I left soup cooking on the stove. Did you turn it off?" Ellie asked.

"Yes, ma'am." He turned to Sam. "You have any plywood? We can board up the windows so you can secure your house until you get the glass replaced."

Sam dug keys out of his pocket, singling out one before handing it to the firefighter. "I appreciate it. The key is to the garage door, and there's plywood against the west wall. I want to stay with Rachel."

Ellie recognized a tall figure walking up from the street. Linc wore his marshal's star on his belt and no doubt his weapon in a shoulder holster under his leather jacket.

He nodded at Sam. "Judge Creed."

Sam introduced Linc as the US Marshal assigned to his court. Ellie found it more than a little weird to "meet" her brother as if they were strangers.

"Judge Creed called me to report the incident here at his house. I'll need to examine the scene."

Ellie waited for Hickman to put up the customary jurisdictional squabble, but the guy proved affable and waved Linc toward the house.

Once Hickman was done with his questions, he tucked his notebook into his pocket. "Guess you'll want to take a look at the damage. I'd like to have a look-see at your camera footage." He nodded to a camera under the eaves. "The deputy marshal will likely have the same request."

Hickman walked with them into the house now blazing with light. Linc came from the damaged room and met them inside the foyer, holding up two plastic bags so they could see the contents. "This one's your basic garden-variety rock." He held up the other bag. "This, however, is a military-grade flashbang device, which can cause a lot of property damage as well as physical harm that includes permanent hearing loss. Miss Sinclair will want to be checked out medically. The rock was thrown first to break the window, and then the flashbang was lobbed in."

Hickman was called outside, and the second they were alone, Linc's gaze drilled into Ellie's. "You good, El?"

"Yeah."

Sam bent at the waist and glared. "What the hell? Why didn't you tell me you were hurt?" Anger snapped through his words and he tugged her closer to a lamp.

"Sam, stop. I'm fine."

He held up his hand stained with drying blood. "Then where the fuck did this come from?"

Chapter Twelve

"Oh." She didn't know why until that moment she'd been unaware of any discomfort, but now a stinging sensation behind her left ear made itself known. In fact, there was stinging in several places. She held up her hand where her knuckles oozed blood. "I didn't realize. I had my hands over my ears. Seems like it was a good thing."

In a controlled movement, Sam held up her hair from her neck. "You're bleeding here, too. This is from flying glass. Damn it. We need to get you to the hospital."

"No, we don't," she insisted.

Linc walked to the door. "I'm going to find a first aid kit."

They were alone when Ellie took her gun from the waistband of her jeans. With the safety already set, she slipped it into the drawer of a drop-leaf table. She straightened and found herself pulled into a kiss that threatened to blister her with its heat before Sam released her.

"Sam, what—"

Hickman came in the open door, carrying a red plastic box.

"Oh. Good cover," she murmured.

"Look who I found." Hickman indicated the man following behind him. "Dr. Montoya just happened to be wandering around out front."

"Sam is a good friend. He left a message saying Rachel had a possible concussion, so here I am," Ben explained.

Sam exhaled sharply. "Thanks for coming. I wasn't sure you got my voicemail."

"I did. And your texts, so here I am." He turned to Ellie. "Let's take a look at you."

She followed Ben into the kitchen where she shed Sam's coat and sat in the chair Ben had pulled under the light. She glanced at the stove. The firefighter had not only turned off the burner under the pot of tortilla soup, he'd also found a lid for it. The sound of a power drill came from the library and Ellie thought the Pendleton Fire Department was awesome.

Sam washed his hands at the sink, and Ben followed suit, then donned gloves before scooting a chair to sit in front of her.

"First thing we'll check for are signs of a concussion. Did you lose consciousness or experience nausea?"

"No."

"How about blurry vision or feeling sluggish or groggy?"

"No again."

He looked in her eyes with a light, then took the ear device from the medical kit and checked both ears. "Eyes and ears look fine, but there can be damage I can't see. How's your hearing?"

"Seems normal now. The ringing has stopped."

"Good. I'm on duty in the ER at the hospital tomorrow. Come by and I'll get you in with someone for a more thorough check, including running a couple of tests." He gathered gloves, gauze pads, and various packets from the kit. "These cuts are shallow but will be sore for a couple days." He kept his voice quiet, explaining what he was doing, and launching into stories about Georgie. "That girl has us figured out. She won't fall asleep unless we're rocking her. Justin and I agree we can't get her accustomed to that, but then we're so exhausted that we end up rocking her to sleep anyway."

As a distraction, Ben's tactic worked. Ellie found herself paying more attention to his story than having her injuries tended to. "You have an excellent bedside manner, Dr. Montoya," she commented.

"You bet I do. Works better than tranquilizers to keep my patients calm." He cleaned the cut on the back of her left hand and the one on her neck behind her ear where he applied butterfly strips. Sam did a good impression of a worried fiancée, resolutely staying by her side with his arms crossed over his chest and a scowl on his face.

Ben tipped his head toward Sam. "This guy, however, could get a clue. If he looked at the defendants or lawyers in his courtroom with that face, he'd have them all asking that he recuse himself because of bias."

Ellie eyed Sam. "Women must like that look. Have you seen the social media posts about him? There are women who fantasize about whether he's wearing anything under his robes."

Ben gave a bark of laughter as Sam's frown deepened.

"Cut it out. You're blowing it out of proportion."

"Some of those posts have thousands of likes," she said. "But since Sam is kind of cute when he's not glowering, I get it."

He gave a disgusted sigh and dropped into the chair beside her. "Are we done messing with me?"

"Yep, all done," Ben affirmed, gaze travelling over Ellie. "Any cuts we missed?"

"Maybe on my back. I didn't notice at the time, but it hurts now."

"Adrenaline masks a lot of pain."

Ellie winced when Ben lifted her shirt that had dried to a cut on her lower back while Sam swore ripely under his breath.

"Little more blood on this one, but it still didn't get through the epidermis. Doesn't need stitches. Between the glass and the blood, your shirt's trashed." Ben cleaned the wound, applied butterflies, and taped a bandage in place. "You'll want to keep these dry." He produced a lollipop from the medical kit and handed it to her. "Your reward for being the perfect patient."

"Cool. I don't know when I last had a lollipop, and it's cherry, my favorite." She unwrapped the treat and stuck it in her mouth. She spoke around the candy. "Thanks for tending my wounds, Ben. I'm sorry Sam pulled you away from home, but not sorry to avoid a visit to the ER tonight, which is where I think he would have dragged me."

Chilled, Ellie rubbed her arms. Any warmth in the house had disappeared with the constant stream of people in and out the front door.

"Damn straight, I would have," Sam muttered. He disappeared up the back stairs as Officer Hickman stepped into the kitchen.

"Looks like Dr. Montoya got you patched up, Ms. Sinclair."

"Yes, he did an excellent job."

Sam returned with a charcoal gray sweatshirt that he helped pull over her head. It was too big, but she was glad for the enfolding warmth.

Hickman addressed Sam. "Officers are talking to your neighbors to see if anyone heard or saw anything. The marshal fellow says you've got someone sending you nasty emails, and you had that incident in your backyard a couple weeks ago. We'll be beefing up patrols in your neighborhood. Got a sec to show us the recording from your security cameras?"

Hickman took a seat at the table on Sam's on his other side as he accessed the footage on his iPad and brought up the recordings from different camera angles. Ellie moved closer to look over his shoulder. He tapped the camera that showed the south side of the house, then scrolled to before the time the alert had come on his phone. It'd been dark, and with no lights on that side of the house, the video showed only a shadowy image crouching under the trees. Then the figure straightened to heave an object at the house.

"He's throwing the rock through the window," Hickman said. "Ah, and there's the money shot."

The figure had run forward to heave the flashbang device through the broken window, and for a brief second his hooded face had turned to the camera.

"Not much of a money shot." Ellie drew in a sharp breath when she shifted and the injury on her back made its presence known. She caught Sam's frown. "About all you can tell is he's male and looks young."

"And that he's left-handed," Sam said.

"Good observation," Hickman noted. "And that's more than we had before. Judge Creed, can you send that to me? Here's my email." He handed Sam a business card and rose to his feet. "We're about done here. Our firefighting brothers and sisters are about to leave. Don't be bashful about calling us back if you have more trouble or think of anything that might be helpful in tracking down this yahoo."

Hickman left and Linc came back in. Sam went into the living room to speak to him, so Ellie let the dogs in, giving them both a good rub before retrieving their bowls to feed them. She turned the burner back on under the soup and was leaning against the counter when Sam returned.

Once again, he gave her that all-encompassing look that made her think he was assessing every nuance of her appearance. He picked up her hand with the bandaged knuckles, rubbing his thumb lightly over the white tape. When he released her, she recognized the remote, controlled look as the same one he'd possessed at the Marshals Office in Portland. That had been less than two weeks ago, but somehow her life had changed fundamentally since then.

He opened a cupboard and set a bottle of pain reliever on the counter. "Take two."

"I will after dinner."

"Don't wait and let the pain set in."

"It's not that bad, Sam. A few small cuts, that's all."

Her comment seemed to light a fuse. "Fuck that. A flashbang all but blew up in your face, and you're damned lucky if you come out of this with no hearing loss. You've been cut by flying glass, and you've lost blood. You were hurt because you're my fiancée."

"Fake fiancée."

His gaze flashed, and she suddenly realized that the remote look wasn't due to lack of emotion but was a means to mask that he was feeling too much. "The guy who hurt you sees you as my fiancée, so the distinction is irrelevant."

"Okay." She cleared her throat, not sure how to deal with him in this kind of mood. Add in that he was doing a good impression of truly caring about her, and heat began coursing through her from her cheeks to low in her belly, dispelling any chill she might have felt earlier. "Um, the soup shouldn't take too long to heat if you're hungry."

He stepped back and filled a glass with water, and then shook two tablets from the pain medication bottle. He handed her both.

"Thanks, Dad."

"Take them, Eleanor."

She rolled her eyes but swallowed the pills.

"There enough soup for your team?"

"Why? Are they coming over?"

"I've called a meeting."

"Oh, good idea. We should make sure everyone is working with the same information, such as it is." She lifted the lid on the pot to find the tortilla soup beginning to simmer. "I'll text Seth. He and Bella can pick up tacos or something to go with the soup. This won't stretch to five people."

Linc came in while Ellie was finishing her message to Seth. She dug up a cheese grater and a block of Monterey Jack cheese and handed them to her brother.

Sam set bowls on the counter and Ellie opened a bag of tortilla chips. About thirty minutes later the dogs alerted them that someone was at the back door. Sam let in Seth and Bella who carried bags of tacos and a six-pack of beer.

When she entered the kitchen, Bella wrapped Ellie in a hug. "Are you okay, friend?"

She returned the embrace. "I'm fine. Sam is more upset about all this than I am."

"Of course he is. A man wants to protect his fiancée, even if she's a temporary fiancée."

Bella released her and Ellie felt Seth behind her. She turned and he took a long minute to study her appearance before opening his arms. Ellie stepped into the embrace to rest her head on his shoulder and felt some of the tension drain from her body.

Her eldest brother had always been her rock, had always looked out for her, and had always understood her. He pressed a kiss to her temple before letting her go.

"I'm fine, Seth."

"You will be." He stepped back and addressed the group. "Let's take a breather. We need a minute to be glad we're all here and that the injuries Ellie sustained are minimal. Talk about the investigation can wait until after we've eaten."

Ellie caught the unguarded expression on Bella's face as she watched Seth, and not for the first time wished her friend wasn't so determined to keep her feelings for Seth to herself. Ellie had broached the subject once and the pain on Bella's face had forced her to back off.

Ellie ladled soup into bowls while Linc sprinkled on the shredded cheese, then took the bowls to the table. She found a big basket in a cupboard and filled it with tortilla chips. Tacos were distributed, beer passed out, and everyone sat around the table to dig in.

Conversation flowed, tacos and soup were consumed with compliments to the chef, and with Cleo settled at her feet under the table, Ellie finally let herself relax.

The man sitting beside her, however, emanated tension.

Sam's participation in the conversation was minimal, she'd caught him more than once drumming his fingers on the side of his beer bottle, and a glance at his face showed a muscle twitching in his jaw. Having someone attack your home had to elicit a range of emotions. She'd cut him some slack. This type of thing happened in her world, not his.

When everyone had finished eating, Ellie rose to gather dishes to take into the kitchen. Sam followed her carrying empty beer bottles.

"Ellie."

Bent over the dishwasher, she glanced up at the serious tone.

"I don't want to blindside you."

She straightened and braced herself. That could only mean bad news. "What are you talking about?"

"I called your team over because I'm asking Seth to reassign you. I no longer want to act like we're a couple."

"You can't do that."

"I can and I will. I'm sorry, but this isn't working out."

She jerked back as if he'd slapped her, and she wouldn't have been any less surprised if he had. "What about my assignment isn't working out? My job is to protect you while I keep my eyes open to find who's threatening you and I've been doing that."

He held himself stiffly, eyes hooded and his expression once again austere. "I'll explain myself to all of you together. I wanted to give you the courtesy of telling you before then."

"You know what you can do with your courtesy."

"Ellie." Seth stood in the open doorway.

"What? Did you know about this?"

"No, but I'm not surprised."

"Why? What do you know?"

"Let's hear what Sam has to say before we parse it out."

Furious, she stalked past her brother. She joined Linc on the loveseat, crossing her arms over her chest.

"What's going on?" Linc asked.

Seth came in to sit beside Bella, and Sam crossed to the cold fireplace, standing with his back to the room.

"I have no idea. Ask Judge Creed."

Sam turned to face them, dark brows lowered. "I want to change our arrangement. Presenting Ellie as my fiancée while we try to draw out the person threatening me isn't working."

"What the hell?" This came from Linc. "It is working. You've successfully established your cover. The two incidents here at the house are escalation."

"Escalation? I found enough C-four on my car to blow me to kingdom come weeks ago. How is making a mess in my yard and a flashbang an escalation?"

"Because we're dealing with two different people," Linc stated.

Sam frowned. "Explain."

"That's the conclusion we've come to. The emailed threats and the C-four are separate from the mess in your yard, which we think is connected to the flashbang."

"You're sure about this?"

Linc nodded. "While you were in here getting El bandaged up, I conferenced with Seth and Bella. Our conclusion is the only explanation that makes sense. The emails and the C-four? Those are cold and unemotional. The truck destroying your lawn, and then a guy breaking a window and lobbing in a flashbang device? That's in your face, and it's personal. The first person probably doesn't have a direct connection to you, the second likely does."

Sam shook his head. "Okay, fine. We're looking for two people. That doesn't change my decision."

Ellie put a hand on her stomach to quiet the jumping nerves. She hoped the feeling was contained to today's incident, and that it had nothing to do with memories of when a younger Sam Creed had also disappeared from her life.

She controlled her voice to keep her tone level. "I don't get it. As Linc said, we've established ourselves as a happily engaged couple to your family, neighbors, and the people at the courthouse. What's changed?"

"You were hurt," Bella observed.

Ellie rubbed her thumb between her brows, suddenly glad Sam had insisted she take the pain meds. Without them the headache she was sporting would be worse. "So? I'm not badly hurt."

"You could have been." Sam's quiet voice had her turning to stare at him.

"Is that what this is about, that I was hurt?"

"We didn't think through the risk you'd be taking. You were hurt because someone wants to get at me. What if they decide that the best way to do that is through you? I don't want you to be a target."

"You may not have thought it through, but the team has. I was aware of the risk when I took this assignment. I'm a Deputy US Marshal. I'm trained for exactly this type of situation. Have some respect. You can't pull me off the job because you don't want me hurt. It's not appropriate, and you don't have that authority."

"It's not a matter of respect, and, like it or not, you need my cooperation for our fake relationship to work."

"It's all about respect. If Linc had been assigned to protect you and was hurt, would you want him pulled off the job?"

"That's ridiculous and not the point."

"It's exactly the point. You feel guilty because I got a few scratches. You may not notice it, but I'm constantly monitoring your situation. You need a person close to you to be on guard. You're a federal judge and it's my job as a US Marshal to protect you. If you take me out or choose not to cooperate, you leave yourself wide open and vulnerable. Is that what you want?"

"If that's the only alternative, then yes."

She threw up her hands in frustration. "You're not only ridiculous, you're irrational."

Seth held up a warning hand to Ellie. "Sam, let's talk. Outside."

Ellie surged to her feet. "No way. You two aren't working it out between you. I have a right to defend my job. I haven't done a damned thing wrong."

Seth shook his head. "I'm talking with him alone."

She knew when Seth got his I'm-the-boss look. Even an edict from heaven wouldn't budge him.

"Don't you dare sell me out, Seth Jameson."

Chapter Thirteen

Seth and Sam went through the kitchen and mudroom, and out the back door, taking Cleo and Tony with them.

Ellie's anger vibrated through her body, looking for an outlet. She eyed Linc poking at his phone. He was probably texting Mikayla.

"Don't even think about it." He hadn't even looked at her.

"Too late." She kicked his foot from where it was resting on his knee.

"Is this you being a mature adult, Eleanor? You know it never ends well when you pick a fight with me."

"I can take you. I've done it before."

"You've never taken me." He held up his hand when she opened her mouth. "And the time when I had mono doesn't count, because I had *mono*."

She always hated it when Linc was right. But she didn't really want to fight with him when fighting with Sam would be so much more satisfying.

She wheeled around to stare out the window. Maybe she could sneak outside and spy on them. A glance at Bella had her checking the impulse.

"You're sitting there grinning like the damned Cheshire cat. I'd think you would be on my side about this."

"I am on your side. Sam should treat you as a professional, even if his personal feelings get in the way. You can trust Seth. He won't pull you from your assignment." She shrugged. "But still, I understand why Sam wants you off the case. I think it's sweet."

Before Ellie could ask Bella to explain, the back door opened and the dogs rushed in ahead of the two men, neither gave much away by their expressions.

Seth tipped his head to her. "Sam's agreed that we keep the situation as it is. The local PD will increase patrols in this area, and we'll check in with each other regularly. You're to take precautions to remain safe."

She nodded, relief flooding through her, Sam's blank expression telling her clearly the conversation hadn't gone the way he'd wanted.

***

Sam crossed the hall from the bathroom to his bedroom. He glanced at Ellie's closed door. Maybe she was still awake. He owed her an explanation for trying to get her assignment pulled, not that he was willing to go there. And he wasn't apologizing, either. Which led to the question of why he was standing outside her door with his fist raised to knock. Seth had figured out Sam's issue and that was bad enough. He lowered his hand. What he really wanted was to talk to her, make sure she was okay, get her to dial back on being pissed at him.

A thud sounded from the first floor. Sam's first instinct was to grab his shotgun and confront any new danger. But Ellie had called him out on respect for her job as a marshal, and she'd been right to do that. He knocked softly, then opened her door and flipped on the light. Her bed was empty.

He crept down the stairs, keeping to the outer edge of the treads to avoid the ones that squeaked. The dogs weren't barking, a good sign. But given everything that had happened, noises in the night made him more than a little cautious.

He cut through the living room. Light shone around the library door, which stood slightly ajar. He pushed it open. Ellie stood with her back to him, using a broom to sweep glass into a pile.

"Don't do that."

She ignored him in keeping with what she'd been doing for most of the evening since her team had left.

He brought a hand down on her shoulder. In a single, smooth movement she dropped the broom and whipped around with her elbow aiming for his face. He lurched back and she missed giving him a broken nose by a scant inch. Her eyes widened and she pulled wireless earbuds from her ears.

"Good way to find yourself flattened, Creed."

"What are you doing in here?"

She looked at the broom and back at him. "Sweeping?"

He tensed his jaw and felt his molars grinding. "You don't need to. I have a lady who cleans for me. I'll call her in the morning and she'll take care of it."

The room looked like a tornado had spun through it and had him clenching his jaw against the surge of anger. That Ellie had been through that tornado only magnified the anger.

Her hair was piled in a messy bun. She still wore his sweatshirt, which hung below her hips, and fatigue lined her eyes. Not for the first time did he wish things were different between them, that he had the right to pull her into his arms and simply hold her.

Seth had done that, and Sam had found himself jealous of the close bond between the siblings.

"So now she won't have to sweep up this glass."

"Neither should you. You should be in bed."

"What's with you acting like I'm a child who needs to be told to go to bed or to take her medicine?"

"Christ, Ellie. I don't think you're a child."

"Okay, then a woman who can't make her own decisions or do her job."

He pinched the bridge of his nose and wished he'd ignored the thud and gone to bed. "Let's focus on what's going on right now. Why are you cleaning in here instead of getting some sleep?"

"Because there's glass all over the floor. Because I'm too wound up to sleep and needed something to do. Why don't you go away and leave me alone?"

He should do exactly that, but he was an idiot. He bent to retrieve the broom, but she grabbed it before he could and held it out of reach. "Oh no you don't. I'm going to sweep and finish the podcast I was listening to."

"Why do you have to be so difficult?"

"Difficult? I'm being difficult? You bastard." The snarled words hung in the air as she tossed the broom back on the floor and stepped toward him, eyes blazing like blue lightning.

Okay, wrong thing to say. Again.

"You question my competence, my ability to do my job, and now you want to pat me on the head and tell me to go to bed? You act like a condescending chauvinist, and I'm the one being difficult?"

His own temper spiked. "I never questioned your ability to do your job. That was your assumption."

She waited a beat. "That's all you've got? No explanation, nothing other than to say I'm making assumptions and you expect me to walk away from my assignment because you've got a burr up your butt about it? That's the way you work, Creed, not me. I don't walk away from people. And I don't lie to them."

He narrowed his eyes. "What's that supposed to mean? When have I lied or walked away from you?"

She stepped back and he could see shutters slamming down over her eyes. "Never mind."

He caught her arm and pulled her toward him. "Tell me."

"Why? It's not like we've ever been honest with each other."

He stared at her as a shadow of memory surfaced. "We met before."

She pulled free of his hold. "Forget it, Creed. I'm done here. You can deal with the glass."

He didn't let go. "Tell me, Eleanor."

She rounded on him and hissed the words. "Get your hand off me, or you're going to find yourself on the floor."

She had moves, he was sure of it, but he didn't think she'd be able to take him down. Still, he released her and backed up a step. "Okay, I've let go. But I'd still like an explanation. Where did we meet before?"

She moved farther away from him like space would be enough of a barrier between them. Whatever was going on in her head played out on her face as a war of indecision. "Fine, I'll tell you." She crossed her arms across her stomach. "We met thirteen years ago at U of O, at a party at your place."

He shook his head. "At my place? We didn't have many parties."

"You had at least one. My friend talked me into going. I was a sophomore and you were a law student. You and I talked, got a little tipsy. Flirted."

The memory slammed into him. The music, the smart, funny girl, the instant connection, then… "Shit."

"Yeah, shit. After, you asked for my number, said you knew a great place to get Thai food. Made a big deal that you'd call. But I never heard from you again." She puffed out a breath. "Let's just say my first and last hookup was a good lesson for me."

"There was more going on than that."

"It doesn't matter anymore. You got what you wanted that evening, and I learned a lot."

She turned and walked out of the room.

***

After a night of tossing and turning, Ellie dragged herself out of bed to tug on her workout clothes. She'd do her job if it killed her. She descended the back stairs to the kitchen to find Sam leaning against the counter, not in exercise gear, but sipping from a steaming mug, his hair mussed like he'd rolled out of bed five minutes ago.

"I'm ready to go." Cleo sniffed her shoes and gave her a doggie grin while wagging her tail. Ellie crouched down to pet her. Tony remained on his cushion, nose on his paws. She gave Sam a side look and found him watching her.

Telling Sam of their shared past had been a mistake, mostly because he'd hurt her all those years ago, and that made her feel vulnerable now. Vulnerability was one of her least favorite emotions.

"I can see that. But you're not going running until you've had a doctor clear you."

"I really don't like you making decisions for me."

"I'm not making decisions for you. You've already been hurt because of me. I don't want to make it any worse."

"I wasn't hurt because of you. I was hurt because a horrible person threw a rock and a flashbang into the house."

Denial was written clearly on his face, but he shrugged. "I want to explain why I didn't call you."

"Really? After thirteen years, now you want to explain? You could have called me. You didn't. No big deal. Can we leave it?"

"No."

She rubbed a fist on her forehead, then held up a hand. This was too much before she was caffeinated. "Right, whatever. But not one more word until I've consumed at least a quarter cup of coffee. No, make that half."

He poured coffee into a mug and handed it to her, then set the dog dishes on the counter to feed them. Ellie wrapped her hands around her mug, closed her eyes and breathed in the coffee. It took almost a full ten minutes before she felt like her belly had warmed and the synapses were firing in her brain.

Sam leaned against the counter, arms crossed over his chest, gaze on her.

"You may speak."

"The morning after we met at that party, I got a call that Jane, Drew's mom, was back in the hospital. She'd been diagnosed with ovarian cancer two months before, but the disease had already spread to her liver and lungs. Surgery and radiation hadn't helped. She died that week."

"Oh, Sam, that's horrible. No wonder you didn't call back."

Back then, she'd imagined he'd been in a car crash and suffered from amnesia, or had lost her number and searched but been unable to find her. Eventually, she'd stopped fooling herself and accepted that he simply hadn't felt the connection, and acting interested had been all about getting in her pants.

To learn that his family had been in crisis gave her an entirely different perspective.

"I took almost a month's leave from law school to help at home. Drew was a wreck, and Dad wasn't much better. His way of coping was to work from sunup to sundown and make everyone else do the same. When I got back to the university, I was buried in work trying to make up for lost time, and I still drove home every weekend." His gaze held hers. "I'm sorry."

"Wow, that's a lot. I'm glad you told me. It stung at the time, but I moved on."

He held her gaze. "Another confession. I've got feelings for you."

"Huh?" She couldn't have heard him right. She bobbled her mug and set it on the counter before she dropped it.

"You heard me. You walked into that room at the Marshals Office and I felt like I'd taken a hit to the gut. Nothing that's happened since has diminished that sensation. These feelings have been totally unexpected and, honestly, unwanted. They've complicated things. I'm having a hard time negotiating that on top of you being assigned to protect me. The deal breaker was you getting hurt in the process."

She tapped a fist over her heart to get it beating again, and when it did, Ellie was sure Sam could hear it thudding heavily in her chest.

He gave a self-deprecating laugh. "I've shocked you. That's something at least." He checked the clock on the wall. "I need to shower and get going. I have a breakfast meeting with another judge this morning. Can you call your team if you need a ride anywhere?"

"Ah, sure."

"Good. I'll be out of here in twenty minutes."

She stared at his back as he climbed the stairs.

That was it? *I've got feelings for you. Not only that, but those feelings are annoying and they complicate things. And, by the way, I've got a breakfast meeting so find your own ride.*

He hadn't asked if those pesky feelings of his were reciprocated, and he didn't seem to care how she felt about any of what he'd told her.

She stabbed her fingers through her hair to hold on to her head so that when it exploded, she could keep the pieces together.

Pipes clanked as the water was turned on upstairs. Learning that he'd had a damn good reason not to call her all those years ago might ease the lingering resentment she'd held on to, but it also made one of the reasons she'd fought against her own feelings no longer valid. Talk about complicated.

She refilled her mug and forced herself to slow her coffee intake and try to settle herself. Why hadn't he kept that little tidbit to himself so she could go on thinking he was a jerk who'd tried to get her pulled from her assignment? He'd still wanted her reassigned, but his confession lowered him on the jerk scale.

Damn him. He had to go ahead and admit to *feelings* like she'd know what to do about them.

She stomped up the stairs, bringing her mug with her. She'd gained the landing when Sam opened the bathroom door and stepped out. With his black hair combed back from his forehead, he wore nothing but a low-slung pair of flannel pants that showcased the V-shaped muscles cradling ripped abs. That his body wound her up didn't help her situation one bit. She'd had enough.

"What the hell, Sam?"

"What the hell what?"

"You 'shared' you've got feelings for me, which, by the way, you're not happy about. You don't ask what I think about that, or if I have any feelings of my own. And now you're happy to walk around half naked?"

"I'm walking from the bathroom to my bedroom where I plan to get dressed. The important parts are covered." He narrowed his eyes. "But tell me about those feelings you have for me."

His step toward her could only be described as predatory.

A warning signal echoed in her brain and nerves were making her jittery. "Never mind. I've changed my mind. I don't want to tell you."

"Oh no you don't. You started it."

He reached out to take her mug and set it on the little Duncan Phyfe table against the wall. He checked her instinctive step back by catching her hands in his.

"What are you doing?"

"What do you think I'm doing? I'm keeping you from running away so you can tell me about those feelings you mentioned."

"I wasn't running. Implementing a little self-preservation."

"You can trust me, Ellie. I hurt you before, but not with intent, and I'm sorry about that."

"It doesn't matter," she muttered.

"It does." She couldn't look away from the intensity of his gaze. "What are your feelings for me?"

It took her a long time to respond, and she felt like her heart was lodged in her throat. If he could be honest about his emotions, so could she. She took a breath and pushed back against the anxiety that had panic tickling in the back of her throat.

"It's hard for me to admit, Sam, but I like you a lot, and I'm really worried that 'like' could turn into something more."

He nodded. "I get that, because it's the same for me. All I can see is you."

Her breath hitched. "Jesus. I don't know if I'm ready for this."

He flashed a wicked grin that had her sucking in a breath. Those little corner lifts of his mouth had whetted her appetite, and his full smile was worth the wait. "I'm not sure I'm ready, either. Only way to figure it out is to move forward."

Amusement vanished, and his gray eyes took on a smoky color as he closed the space between them. She was sure there were a dozen reasons why they shouldn't be standing this close together, but she couldn't think of one. He dipped his head and murmured against her lips, "No one's watching, Eleanor. This one's for us."

Their fingers entwined and his lips caught hers in a kiss that brought an instant wave of warmth, and a spike to her blood pressure. His mouth on hers, their breaths mingling, and the feeling that she could spend the next several hours happily doing this made her yearn for more. His tongue swept into her mouth and he tasted of mint toothpaste.

He released her hands to grip her hips and bring her snug against him, heat to heat. Ever since that first morning when she'd seen him shirtless, she'd wanted her hands on him. Now she gave in to the desire and laid her palms flat against his chest, and when she stroked, she felt the strong beat of his heart beneath her fingers.

At least she wasn't the only one affected. He speared his fingers through her hair, and when they brushed against the bandage behind her ear, he broke the kiss to lay his lips lightly over it. "It kills me that you were hurt." The soft words were barely audible.

He moved his mouth along the column of her throat and nudged her chin up to allow him better access. She shivered as her nervous system went on overload. She decided his kisses provided a better morning pickup than the strongest coffee.

She took her turn nuzzling his neck where warm skin smelled of soap from his shower. Trailing down, her tongue explored the hollow between his collarbone and neck, and his breath grew heavier.

They were locked against each other center to center, and it was hard to miss his arousal. She rubbed against his erection and murmured, "How badly do you want to go to your breakfast meeting?"

He groaned deep in his throat and she had to lock her knees to keep them holding her up. There were reasons she and Sam shouldn't do what they were thinking about doing, but she put a block on that part of her brain. Then with one last open-mouth kiss, he gripped her shoulders and took a step back.

She couldn't miss the regret on his face.

"I guess the answer to that is pretty badly." She tried to make her tone light, but it came out sounding hesitant.

He rested his forehead against hers and seemed to struggle to control his breathing until, with a sigh, he straightened. "It's not that simple, Ellie. You already think I don't value you as a marshal because you're female. I'm not reinforcing that belief by taking advantage of you living in my home."

"Is it taking advantage if I want it, too?"

"Right now, yes."

Chapter Fourteen

Despite feeling unsettled, Ellie spent a productive morning. Cleo and Tony kept her company while she finished the final report for an investigation she'd concluded the previous month. Next, she began whittling down a long list of emails, enjoying one from Mikayla with a picture of the mop-haired Labradoodle she and Linc had adopted. A call from Seth provided her another avenue to investigate their father's recent movements so she spent an hour delving into online forums frequented by right-wing militia types, digging deeper when she found reference to both Judge Creed and Frank Bannister.

Her phone buzzing broke her concentration. A glance at the caller ID had her smiling. She swiped the screen to answer the phone. "Sam."

"Ellie." His low voice reverberated in her ear and all the emotions of that morning came crashing back. Tension crackled through the connection. "Can you make a doctor's appointment at one?"

She'd forgotten about the directive Ben had issued the night before. "I don't need to go to the doctor. I don't even have a headache."

"Good, then the doctor will clear you with no problem. She's a friend of Ben's and, as a favor to him, is giving up half of her lunch hour to see you."

"Way to put on the pressure, Judge Creed. I'll call Seth and see if he can give me a ride."

"I'm going with you. I'm done with court, and I cleared my calendar for the rest of the day. I'll be home at noon."

"You know, I can't figure out if you're playing the concerned fiancée role really well, or if you like managing people."

"Let's keep it simple. This is me caring about you, but tangled up with it is that you got hurt because of me."

"You've got to let that go. It wasn't your fault."

"You being cleared by the doctor will help."

"Fine." A question had been niggling at her, so she voiced it. "Tell me, how did Seth convince you not to break up with me, I mean, convince you to keep up the fiancée pretense?"

"I'm not going there."

"Why? Is it a secret?"

"Leave it, Eleanor. I'll see you around noon."

***

Hours later, after an all-clear from Ben's friend, Eleanor sat beside Sam in the Land Cruiser. They'd turned onto the street that led over the river and then home. She shifted to look at him. "Take me to where you were parked when you found the C-four on your car."

He gave her a considering gaze, nodded, and drove to a dead-end road where a couple of cars were parked. He pulled off the pavement and parked the Land Cruiser in a dirt area.

"This is it."

She looked around at what appeared to be an informal parking area. There were no neighboring homes or businesses, and no trees or brush to provide cover for someone attaching explosives to a vehicle. "What day of the week was that?"

"Sunday. I found the explosive when I returned from my run, which was before seven a.m."

"Did you habitually run here weekend mornings?"

"Not always, but frequently."

"Who would be familiar with your routine?"

"Anyone who paid attention." He opened the door. "Let's walk."

They took a worn path, the sound of the river reaching her before she saw it. They came to a paved walkway, and a sign said "River Parkway." It followed the Umatilla as it rushed over boulders, then slowed to form swirling eddies and dark pools. Deciduous trees along the banks showed bright fall colors and the autumn sun reflected off the water.

Ellie took a deep breath as the breeze carried the damp smell of the river. She zipped her jacket and tugged her beanie to cover her ears. The temperature didn't feel like it had warmed above fifty, and a stiff breeze chilled her cheeks. Despite that, she enjoyed the weather. "This is really nice. Cold, but nice."

"Yeah."

His distracted tone had her studying him. She didn't bother fighting the pull of attraction. Faded blue jeans encased his long legs, and he had his hands buried deep in the pockets of his forest green wool coat. His brows were drawn low over smokey gray eyes, and a muscle worked in his jaw. What she had to tell him wasn't going to improve his mood.

"Sam, we're looking at Drew for the threats against you."

He stopped to face her. "We've talked about this. It's not him."

"Why do you think that?"

Emotion crossed his face, then was blanked out. "Drew's writing skills are poor. He struggled all through school with a learning disability. That's not reflected in those emails."

"He could be working with someone. In fact, it's likely there's a conspiracy. We've found evidence that links him with SecAm." She hesitated, then went on. "There was a video posted showing a group of heavily armed people, many with illegal weapons, standing around a bonfire. They'd read pages from books, mostly by liberal historians or politicians, then throw the books into the fire while giving the Nazi salute. Drew was one of the participants."

His scowl deepened the lines on either side of his mouth. "I'll ask him about it, but he didn't send the emails."

"Please don't talk to him yet. We don't want to tip our hand. I'm only telling you because he's your brother."

"What do you mean, tip your hand? What are you doing?"

"We're conducting an investigation. There's no doubt Drew is connected to the militia, but whether he has threatened you is unclear. If he is innocent, as you claim, the best way to prove that is to let us do our job so we can find the true culprit."

He ran a hand through his hair, then gave a curt nod.

"You going to tell me how Seth talked you into keeping up the fiancée pretense?" She asked the question to try to lighten the mood, but Sam gave a frustrated sigh.

"The bastard blackmailed me."

"How'd he do that?"

"By being more perceptive than I gave him credit for. He figured out that my concern was for your safety and inferred that I may be developing a thing for you."

He'd said as much that morning, but that didn't stop her heart from doing a slow somersault in her chest at his admission.

"Oh."

"Yeah, oh. The blackmail was sneaky. He said if you got pulled from your current job that you'd go back to your original assignment, which had been to send you undercover to infiltrate a militia group."

"That's hardly blackmail. That had been the plan before I was assigned to be your girlfriend. I was getting friendly with a biker dude who's a member of SecAm. He has an online dating profile and we'd been flirting back and forth."

"You're my fiancée, not my girlfriend, and I didn't like that plan."

She nodded slowly, frowning. "Sometimes my job involves undercover work."

"It's fucking dangerous."

"It can be, but we mitigate the risk as best we can. Regardless, I think Seth was jerking your chain. We'd already decided not to go forward with that plan. There's too much risk that we could cross paths with Richard Jameson. That would have been dangerous and would've jeopardized our entire mission."

He grunted.

They returned to the car and, by unspoken agreement, checked for explosives. Satisfied there were no bombs, they got in and he started the car and pulled onto the street. He glanced at his watch, then said, "Dalia, the woman who cleans my house, is coming in to clean the library. What do you say we get some takeout for an early dinner? There's a Mediterranean place that has good falafel. We can pick up enough for her, too."

"Sounds good."

They arrived home thirty minutes later, passing an aged Honda SUV on the driveway to park in the garage. They walked into the kitchen carrying loaded bags with the dogs trailing behind them. Ellie wasn't sure what she expected Sam's cleaning lady to look like, maybe someone sturdy and middle-aged, but certainly not the petite twenty-something with a fall of black hair and gorgeous dark eyes that met them with a smile.

"Hi, Sam. Good timing, I just finished." She spotted Ellie and her smile widened. "You must be Rachel. I missed you last week.

I'm Dalia. Ben told me about your engagement. Congratulations to both of you."

Since it appeared that Ben had kept their secret, Ellie said, "Thank you, it's nice to meet you."

Sam held out a bag. "This is for you and the boys."

"You didn't need to do that."

"You made time in your schedule to come out here today, so you earned it."

Dalia took the bag and opened it. "Since you got them gyros, it's hard to say no. Thanks."

Sam's tone changed. "You doing okay?"

Dalia raised shadowed eyes, her smile dimming. "I'm fine. I saw the lawyer you recommended and she's starting the divorce proceedings."

"It's the right thing to do."

"It is. But Rudy is the boys' father, and that makes it hard. But I have to move ahead." She glanced at Ellie. "I apologize for talking about something you wouldn't know about. Sam sentenced my husband to prison and we've been friends ever since."

"That had to be...unusual," Ellie half stuttered.

"For other judges, maybe, but not for Judge Creed. Sam does a lot behind the scenes for people who need help."

He glanced at Ellie. "Dalia is a member of my tribe."

"Did you know each other before the trial?" she asked.

"Not really. I knew who she was, but that was about it."

"But now we're friends." She held up the bag. "Thanks for this. My boys will enjoy their dinner. I'll be in as usual on Thursday. Nice to meet you, Rachel."

Dalia retrieved her belongings from the mudroom and left through the back door.

"I feel like there's an entire episode of *Law and Order* there."

Sam gave his half smile. "Good observation. Rudy was involved in drug trafficking, then upped the stakes when he tried smuggling guns into Canada. Dalia and the boys are better off without him."

"You're looking out for her."

He shrugged. "She's Umatilla."

"You're a good man, Sam Creed."

***

Sam stood at the kitchen window, staring into the gathering darkness beyond the glass. The previous week, a crew had replaced his cameras and installed new ones with infrared as well as recording capability. Every member of the US Marshal team had access to the app and helped monitor his property, and still they hadn't been able to identify the guy who'd thrown the flashbang into his house. The cameras made him feel hemmed in, like his life wasn't his own, but until they caught the person threatening him, both he and Ellie were safer.

Gumbie rubbed against his leg and he reached down to pick up the cat and scratch her head.

He wanted to go for a run or to the gym in town and work out. He needed to do something to ease the restlessness plaguing him. But if he went out he could count on Ellie coming with him, and since he attributed more than half of his restlessness to his insane attraction to her, that wouldn't solve his problem.

He also suffered from frustration on top of the restlessness, and that had to do with his brother. When he'd left the courthouse the night before, Sam had walked to the parking lot to find Drew waiting for him, leaning against the Land Cruiser, his behavior the usual mix of insolence and bitterness.

"I need a loan, Sam."

That same stab of anger and frustration that almost choked him whenever he and Drew talked felt like a red-hot knife in his gut.

"What are we talking about, a few hundred or a few thousand?"

His brother's pale blue eyes had burned with resentment. *"I shouldn't even have to ask. You're holding on to money Dad left for me."*

"You know the terms of the will. Dad worked his ass off for that money, and he didn't want you to waste it. He wanted you to use it for something that would help you get ahead."

"What, like going to college like my big brother? Is that what he wanted?"

"You could go to community college to learn business management so you could take over the ranch."

"You're forgetting one little fact." Drew's face had twisted into a sneer. *"You inherited the ranch, not me. I worked like a slave for years on that place, fucking gave my life to it. In the end the old man didn't see me as his true son. You got the ranch and I got shit."*

"If you gave any indication that you could manage the ranch, I'd deed you half right now. I've told you that."

"I don't want your fucking charity."

"You just asked me for a fucking loan." Sam had forced himself to reel in the anger. Yelling at Drew would hardly solve their problems.

"You won't give me what's rightfully mine? Fine. But I want a loan against that money. You owe me that much."

"No, I don't. I'm not giving you anything."

They'd had variations on that conversation a dozen times and it always ended the same. Last evening had been no different. Drew had stormed off, anger evident in his stomping feet and the slammed door of his truck. He'd sped up the street, the truck fishtailing until he gained control.

Sam had the fleeting thought that he should give Drew the money and be done with it. He'd spend it on whatever it was he'd wanted the loan for, but unless Sam also gave him a share of the ranch, Drew would be back to repeat the same scenario once the cash was gone. Despite Sam's issues with Joss Creed, he knew his dad left his estate the way he had because in his own way he'd loved Drew and wanted what was best for him.

The click of the dogs' toenails on the wood floor had him looking over his shoulder. Cleo and Tony came in the room ahead of Ellie. He swallowed convulsively, then had to rap his fist on his chest as he coughed.

Endless legs were covered by second-skin leggings and fed the constant fantasy of her wrapping those legs around his hips. Naked. They'd both have to be naked for that.

An extra sledgehammer of lust hit him when he took in the white tank top folded up to expose a creamy stretch of skin covering her firm abdominal muscles. The top also showcased toned arms and shoulders, and her deliciously rounded breasts he itched to get his hands on.

All the edginess of living with her coalesced into a powerful desire he could barely control. He grabbed for the counter to keep from acting on his impulses.

"Hey, can you replace the bandages? They got wet in the shower." Ellie's voice was muffled as she craned her neck to look over her shoulder. "I got the one on my hand but can't see to do the ones behind my ear and my back."

"Jesus Christ, Ellie. Why didn't you ask for help? The doctor today told you to keep the bandages dry. Ben told you to keep them dry. You should have listened." Anger was a much safer emotion than lust.

"Desire for a shower surpassed concern over wet bandages."

She turned and pulled the long fall of blonde hair over her shoulder to give him a clear look at the wound behind her ear. That she also exposed the long column of her neck provided yet one more distraction. She smelled like her soap, fresh and faintly citrusy. He raised hands that weren't entirely steady to peel off the wet bandage behind her ear.

"The butterfly strips are holding, so I'm leaving those." He pressed a square of gauze over the strips and applied tape. It took all his willpower not to bury his nose in the warm skin at the nape of her neck and breathe her in.

He motioned her across the room, flipped on the light over the table, and sat in one of the chairs. "Stand in front of me and I'll take care of the cut on your back."

Some of what he was feeling must have been communicated to her because for one hot second their gazes clashed and the temperature in the room spiked. She moved to stand between his knees with her back to him while he peeled off the wet bandage.

He cleared his throat. "Color is healthy, looks like it's healing."

"That's good." Her breathy tone didn't do anything to cool him off.

His hands spanned her waist as he pressed tape around the clean gauze. The wound was covered, the bandage secure, and yet his hands stayed on the warm skin, his thumbs rubbing slowly. She looked over her shoulder and this time when their gazes clashed, neither looked away. Slowly, she turned under his hands and, without breaking eye contact, straddled him to sit on his lap.

He closed his eyes as all the blood drained from his head to pool in his groin.

Her breath was warm against his ear when she whispered, "This is a time-out. I'm declaring myself officially off duty."

Chapter Fifteen

Any hold he had on sanity was slipping away. He opened his eyes to stare into the depthless blue of hers. "There are reasons."

"They don't count during a time-out." She nipped his earlobe and his control snapped with an audible crack.

Her lips hovered over his, and he used his hands on her back to push her closer.

Their lips met with an intensity that told him this time neither of them was holding back. Blood heating to boil, he took what she offered in that kiss. Lust, like, love—whatever had been building between them flared with every touch, every murmured word, every sigh. He pulled on her top, mindful of the injury to her back, reluctantly releasing her lips so he could tug the shirt over her head. Her hand fisted in his hair when he used his nose to push aside the cup of her bra.

"God, you're beautiful." His words were spoken with a hushed reverence as he buried his face in her breasts. He cupped one, then the other, nuzzling with his nose until pressing his lips to the deep valley between them. She threw her head back when he used the flat of his tongue to circle an areola, then her nipple. Her ribs quaked at her sharp intake of breath when he pulled the peak deep into his mouth.

She ground against his erection even as she tugged on the hem of his shirt. He let go of her breast and yanked his shirt over his head, the motion bringing him harder against her. With her heat pressed to his, he swore he could feel warm dampness through the layers of their clothing.

He bit back an oath and rose to his feet, bringing her with him. He wasn't making love with her on a kitchen chair. Deeming the beds upstairs too far away, he headed out of the kitchen. She wrapped her legs around his hips, not naked as in his fantasy, but good enough for now. Once again, her hands were in his hair and she was sliding her fingers through, using the pressure to bring his head up.

With her lips against his, she murmured, "You have the sexiest hair."

"Glad you like it." He boosted her higher, his hands cupping her ass. "Got some weight to you."

"Watch it, buster." She sank her teeth into his neck.

His swore at the jab of pain. "You watch it. I don't do vampires. And I like weight on a woman. Almost as much as I like long legs." He walked them into the shadowy living room, the only light coming from the open door of the kitchen. "Besides, at nearly six foot, you could hardly not have some weight to you."

"You're forgiven," she murmured, running her tongue over what he was sure would be a bite mark. At the moment, he couldn't draw the will to care how that would look on a judge.

He sat on the couch with her still straddling him, and she shimmied down until she was kneeling on the floor between his legs, her hands on the waistband of his workout pants. She rolled down the waistband with an expectant look, like she was unwrapping a birthday present. His erection sprang free and her eyes flashed hungrily.

"Yeah, baby," she murmured.

He'd hardly caught his breath before she'd taken him in her warm, wet mouth, and the incredible surge of pleasure had his eyes rolling straight back in his head. "Oh god."

She worked him with her mouth while her hands cupped and kneaded. He felt like he was charging full tilt to the edge of a cliff. That wonderful mouth of hers continued to tease him until his grip on sanity went slippery.

He reached to pull her up before he plummeted over the edge.

"My turn." He nudged her onto his lap, and with an arm around her waist, shifted so she lay beneath him, pulling a cushion under her head. He rose to shuck his pants, then hers and the sexy little scrap of material that passed for underwear.

He settled between her open legs and took in the glory that was Ellie. She reached for him and he held her off. "Hold still, woman."

"Don't want to hold still. I want you."

"You'll have me. But I get you first."

He started with her toes, nibbling along the arch of her foot, and when she twitched, he grinned. "You're ticklish."

"God, you have a great smile. And to my everlasting shame, yes, I'm ticklish."

He moved to her ankle. "I like ticklish. I'm beginning to think I like everything about you."

"Ticklish is a weakness when one has brothers." Her voice had gone throaty as he slid his tongue along the strong line of her shin and dipped into the hollow at the back of her knees. "Jesus, Creed, you'll bring me to orgasm just licking my knees."

"There's a thought."

While he continued his journey with his mouth, he used his fingers to stroke into the wetness of her, finding what made her moan. He followed his fingers with his lips and tongue.

She clutched his hair tight enough to make him worry that she would leave him with bald patches. He brought her to the brink, heard her breath catch in her throat, then, using tongue and hand, sent her surging over that cliff with a long, keening wail.

He battled back the nearly overwhelming urge to bury himself in her, slowing down to hold her while she came down from the euphoria.

She gave a shivering sigh then reached for him. "Come on, come on. I want you. Now."

Her words fueled his desperation, had it clawing at his throat. He was poised above her when he reared back. "Fuck, fuck, fuck."

"Don't say it, do it."

"I don't have a condom. I mean I do, but not on me. Can you stay like this and I'll be back in thirty seconds? Or twenty, I can make it upstairs and back in twenty seconds."

"You disease free?"

"Yes. You?"

"Yes, and on the pill. You're not going anywhere, big boy."

"Thank god."

She gripped his buttocks and he thrust forward, driving deep. Buried fully, he held himself still, the perfection of the moment coursing through him, etching itself in his mind. She tilted her pelvis and urged him on.

Hands on her breasts, he caught her mouth with his, and they began to move together, slowly at first, then building. The urge was there to let loose and drive blindly into her, but he wanted her with him.

"Again, baby. Again," he coaxed with a whisper in her ear.

He continued to thrust harder, deeper, with more intensity, urging her on, pushing her. Her breath gulped in, then shuddered out, and when once again she was flying apart, he let himself go with her, freefalling over the cliff and not even caring if he crashed.

They lay together, limbs tangled, neither moving. Sam decided breathing was necessary and turned her with him until they lay face-to-face on their sides. She snuggled into him and he wrapped his arms around her to pull her closer. He tugged the throw from the back of the couch to cover them both.

"Much better this time." Her lips moved against his neck as she spoke.

The reminder that this wasn't their first time together had him reaching out an arm to turn on the lamp.

"Why'd you do that?"

"To see you." He brushed hair back from her face. "I was an asshole."

"You were a young hottie and I didn't have anything by way of comparison. Not a good recipe for the perfect sexual encounter."

"You were a virgin?"

She nodded.

"Shit. Did I know that?"

"No. It was a long time ago, and in retrospect, not that big a deal. I shouldn't have said anything."

"Don't let me off so easily. It was a big deal, and I was a self-centered asshole."

She huffed out a breath. "Look, it wasn't for lack of trying on your part. But I was inexperienced, and nervous, and couldn't get there. You were sweet, talked to me. You suggested we could sneak out of the party and walk to a nearby coffee shop."

"But we didn't go to the coffee shop."

"No, I was there with a friend who was more than a little drunk. I didn't want to leave her."

Everything inside him froze, the pleasure from the orgasm evaporating. "You said earlier that you'd been drinking that night."

"I had." Even with the light blocked by the back of the couch, she must have read his expression. "Wait, Sam. Don't go there. I wasn't drunk, and was completely able to give consent."

His shook his head. "I'm sorry. I should have called you."

"I understand why you didn't. It's not an issue anymore."

She made a move to get up and he clicked off the light. "Curtains are open. Let's not give the neighbors a show."

***

Ellie plugged in her phone and crawled into bed. Alone. They'd had phenomenal sex, and things had been good between them after, even including the honest discussion about their first time together. But now the ramifications of what they'd done were beginning to prick her conscience.

Checking in with her team made her feel extra guilty. If Seth knew she and Sam had been together, Seth would yank her from the investigation without a qualm. And rightly so. She'd crossed a line by engaging in a physical relationship with the man it was her job to protect.

Calling a timeout didn't change reality.

Earlier in the evening, still feeling unsettled, she'd sat on one end of the couch with her feet tucked beneath her, absently scanning the news on her iPad. Sam had joined her with his laptop, the horn-rimmed glasses he'd put on to read fanning a hot ember of lust in her belly.

She'd turned blindly to an article on whether the Federal Reserve would raise the prime interest rate and forced herself to read. Dry economic forecasts didn't do a thing to redirect her brain because when she'd looked up again his hair had fallen over his forehead, and she'd had to clench her hands into fists to resist the temptation of running her fingers through that lush thickness.

Determinedly, she'd ducked her head and found another article, this one on Oregon state politics, which was a bit more interesting. Minutes later, she'd glanced up to catch Sam's gaze on her, his expression difficult to interpret. She'd lifted a brow in question, and he'd shaken his head and turned back to his computer. His posture had gone from relaxed to tense, brows low over his eyes, fingers on his keyboard clicking as he typed. Then he'd risen and, taking his laptop, disappeared into his office. Then she'd gone upstairs.

She flopped back on her pillow. She wouldn't analyze his every mood. If he had regrets or some other problem with their relationship, such as it was, well, he wasn't the only one. What concerned her more was the hunch that he wasn't being entirely forthcoming about the case.

A rumble of conversation had her frowning. She sat up, head cocked, trying to locate the sound, and realized Sam's voice was carrying through the heater ducts. While the words were unintelligible, the angry tone was evident. She slipped out of bed and opened the door, not making a sound in her stocking feet. She paused at the top of the stairs, then crept down until she reached the bottom step.

Light spilled from the partially open door of Sam's office. He stood facing the darkened window with the phone to his ear, shoulders rigid. Eavesdropping on Sam's conversation felt wrong, but the chance that he might reveal information he'd kept from the investigation overrode her conscience. She moved silently across the floor.

Fury snapped through his voice. "That's bullshit, you know it is. I told you I'm not giving you anything. If you come near her, if she breaks so much as a fingernail because of you, I'll rip you apart. Leave her out of it." He paused, obviously working to measure his tone. "Stop messing with me. You're making a huge mistake. I'll meet you again tomorrow and we'll talk."

She froze in the shadows when he crossed the room to close the door with a firm click. The expression on his face had been one of cold rage. The rumble of his voice followed her as she retreated up the stairs to her room.

Back in bed, she considered what she'd heard. What had he meant by "stop messing with me?" Had he been referring to the email threats? When he'd said to "leave her out of it," had he been referring to Ellie?

Had a threat been directed at her?

***

The next morning Ellie rose early, changed into her running gear, and went down the back stairs to the kitchen. A light was burning over the sink. Cleo rose from her cushion, stretching before approaching Ellie, tail wagging. She reached down to rub the dog's head, then picked up the note left on the counter next to the coffee maker.

Something came up and I had to leave early. Dogs are fed. Talk to you later. Sam

She stared at the note, her certainty there was something going on with Sam...something he wasn't sharing with her was becoming more than a hunch. What would lead him to betray the trust they'd built? The only answer that seemed to fit was his brother.

Despite their differences, Sam loved Drew and was worried about him. Sam's words from the previous night echoed through her head. Had he been talking to his brother? If so, then he'd lied to her when he'd insisted that Drew couldn't be behind the threats against him.

The light on the coffeemaker was still on, so Ellie poured coffee into a mug, considering her course of action as she sipped the steaming brew. What was Sam willing to sacrifice for the sake of his brother? The sad fact was that nothing in her interactions with Drew, nor what she'd observed between the brothers, made her think Drew shared that family loyalty. Sam had to realize that. God knew she understood what it felt like to be betrayed by someone you loved.

Feeling antsy and already dressed for a run with her holstered gun under her jacket, she retrieved her phone and key and let herself out of the house as the sun was rising. After sending a text to Seth informing him of her intended route, she set out at a steady lope, staying watchful even as an internal debate ping-ponged inside her head.

If she wanted to know what Sam was holding back, she could search his bedroom and office for clues. As a Deputy US Marshal working an investigation that was within her purview. But as a woman in a personal relationship with Sam Creed, searching his personal possessions would be a huge violation of trust.

Which was exactly why there were rules prohibiting that kind of relationship.

Grateful that she'd worn gloves because it was *cold,* she took the same route into town she and Sam had taken their first morning, keeping a wary eye out for anything unusual. Crossing the bridge over the river, a flash of white caught her attention. She paused to look over the swirling tributary.

A beautiful egret waded along the shore with stately elegance, poking its head in the water at studied intervals. She watched the bird until it took flight, then Ellie resumed her run into town.

She passed the parking lot to the courthouse, scanning for but not seeing Sam's Land Cruiser, nor was it at the diner. Transitioning to a cooldown pace, she puffed back up the hill to Sam's house and around the driveway to the back. She opened the back door and let the dogs in ahead of her.

She showered, ate breakfast, texted with Linc, all the while conscious of the time. Once she was sure Sam would be in court, she opened the door to his office. Telling her guilty conscience to shut up, she stepped inside. Desk drawers, filing cabinets, papers stacked on his desk—any of those places might reveal something that would tell her what Sam was hiding.

She sat in the high-backed leather chair behind his desk, running her hands over the smooth armrests, tipping it back with her feet. After ten minutes of procrastinating, she realized she couldn't go any farther. Searching Sam's things was wrong.

Finally, in a decision that made her a good human but not a solid Deputy US Marshal, she rose from the chair and walked out of the room.

Chapter Sixteen

Ellie trudged the few blocks to Sam's house after taking the double long way around from what she thought of as Marshal Central where she'd met with Seth and Bella. Linc hadn't been there as he was on courthouse duty and had a lunch engagement scheduled with Gordon Finster. She, Seth, and Bella had reviewed the evidence they had in Sam's case, including what Ellie had heard Sam saying over the phone. She'd been ready for the order to search Sam's private possessions, but her brother had surprised her. He'd agreed that cooperation and trust between her and Sam was critical for the mission, and whatever she might find by searching his things wasn't worth sacrificing his faith in her if he found out. Which sounded good, except that Sam didn't have faith in her. If he did, he wouldn't be keeping secrets.

The Land Cruiser rumbled down the driveway as she was digging out her key to unlock the back door. She stood on the stoop to wait for Sam as he parked and secured the garage. The dogs greeted him at the gate with their snuffling woofs.

He came up the walkway and stopped in front of her. He looked tired. The grooves on either side of his mouth had deepened, his hair looked like he'd distractedly run his hands through it, and lines she hadn't noticed before bracketed his eyes. She wondered if he'd actually slept the night before. He carried his suit coat and briefcase and had loosened his tie, the top button on his dark blue dress shirt unbuttoned. She checked the impulse to brush the hair from his forehead, instead turning to push open the door.

They stepped into the house where he disarmed the alarm and she walked ahead of him into the kitchen. She lifted the lid on the slow cooker, the smell of chicken and herbs wafting up with a cloud of steam.

"You made dinner? I thought you didn't like to cook." He came up beside her and bent his head to peer into the pot.

"Cooking may not be my passion, but we have to eat." She worked to keep her tone light. "Thanks to this Crock Pot I found in the back of the cupboard we're having rosemary chicken with red potatoes. The only thing left to prepare is the asparagus."

"That sounds perfect." His mood seemed to lift and his eyes warmed, and they focused on her lips and for a brief moment he swayed toward her like he might kiss her, then checked himself. The air between them crackled, and she couldn't blame the warmth stealing up her cheeks on the steaming pot.

He backed up a step. "I'll get changed and be back down in a minute."

Ellie put her hand to her stomach to calm the nerves. She filled the dog dishes, her movements mechanical. Sam was nothing if not potent. One hot look and he had her all wound up.

He returned to the kitchen. While Sam in a suit had a certain appeal, she liked him in faded jeans and the red and black plaid shirt he wore open over a black t-shirt. His five o'clock shadow made him a little rough around the edges, a look that suited him. Or maybe it suited her.

"Want me to do the asparagus?"

"Sure."

Leaving the slow cooker on warm, she took a seat at the table, determined to act normal. She flipped through the newspaper, scanning several articles, then noticed Sam had rolled the sleeves of the plaid shirt above his elbows. She'd never thought about it before but somehow rolling sleeves above the elbows was unbelievably appealing, while below the elbows they were just rolled sleeves. Maybe it was because he had good arms, the corded muscles flexing as he used a knife.

Watching him deal with the asparagus struck her as all kinds of sexy. Where she would have steamed the spears, added a little salt, and called it good, he tossed them with olive oil, used a micro-grater to shred parmesan, sprinkled sea salt and pepper, then arranged them on a baking tray. After sliding the tray into the oven, he washed the dishes he'd used, then worked the cork out of a bottle of Chardonnay.

He brought her a glass and sat across from her. "Are we good?"

She sipped her wine, and then placed the glass carefully on the table. There were things they needed to discuss, but not until after dinner. But that wasn't what he was asking about. "Sure, we're good."

"Regrets about last night?"

She stared into the straw-colored wine. "Last night I said I was off duty, but I still crossed a line between my professional and personal life. I could get fired for that." She frowned. "But at the moment it felt worth it, so no, I have no regrets." She raised her gaze. "You?"

"Your job brought you into my house. I don't like feeling like I took advantage of you."

"Did I act like I was being taken advantage of?"

Gray eyes glinted silver. "No."

"Okay, then let's settle the ethical issues here and now. We both wanted what happened, neither of us was under duress, and we're both unattached, healthy adults."

"I can live with that." A timer chimed. "That's the asparagus."

They worked together to get dinner on the table. Maybe the air had been cleared somewhat, but she couldn't help wondering whether a repeat performance was off the table. Neither of them had mentioned it, but she'd bet Sam was thinking about it as she was.

Ellie gathered plates and utensils, he brought the food, and in minutes they were taking their seats. Sam had dimmed the kitchen lights, giving the room a cozy feel, and she wondered if she was the only one affected by the intimacy of sharing a meal at the small table. By unspoken agreement, they delayed talking about the investigation.

She found Sam easy to talk to. They shared an interest in history and discovered they'd both read the same biography on Eleanor Roosevelt.

"She should have left Franklin when she found out about his affair with Lucy Mercer." Ellie gestured with her fork to emphasize her point. "She should have demanded a divorce and published the love letters she'd found so everyone could see him for the dirty dog he was."

"Easy to say when you're not living under the social constraints of the early 1900s. People then tended to be more scandal averse, and divorce held a social stigma, which is why Franklin's mother pushed him to reject that option. She had political aspirations for her son."

"All true, but I hate that he treated Eleanor so badly, though she certainly came into her own during his presidency." She sampled the baked asparagus. "Mmm, this is really good."

"The entire meal is really good. Thank you."

"You're welcome. You know, I'm named after her."

"You're named after Eleanor Roosevelt?"

"Yeah, my brothers and I were all named for famous historical figures."

"Linc is short for Lincoln?" At her nod he said, "Then that one's not hard to figure out. What about Seth? The only historical Seth I can think of is Seth Bullock of Deadwood. He was a US Marshal, too, wasn't he?"

"That's the guy."

"Did Seth become a marshal to fulfill his historic destiny?"

"No, becoming a marshal was more our stepfather's influence. Being marshals gave us a legal way to pursue Richard Jameson and bring him to justice."

"And when he's behind bars, what then?"

"You think we'll get him?"

"I have no doubt."

His confidence pleased her. "When he's behind bars we'll have removed a threat to our government, and on some level made him pay for his betrayal. I want my mom and Arch to be at the trial."

"And when that's over, what will you do?"

She considered her answer as she carefully sliced her chicken. She knew how her brothers would respond. They would go on being US Marshals, pursuing fugitives, protecting witnesses, and guarding federal judges. They'd never even talked about it because the assumption was that they were marshals. It's what they did.

"I'm thinking about that."

He brows shot up. "As in you're thinking you might not continue your career as a marshal?"

"Let's say I'm considering my options."

"Like what?"

She chewed thoughtfully, swallowing before answering. "I went to law school, so I could take the bar."

"Why? Was bringing your father to justice the only reason you became a marshal?"

He watched her with the intense focus she found so stimulating. As Bella had said, Sam paid attention, and when he looked at you, he made you think you were the only person who mattered to him.

"Bringing Richard Jameson to justice was a big motivating factor, and I've enjoyed the work, but there are things I'd like to have in my life that being a marshal makes more difficult."

"Like what?"

"Like a home that's more than an apartment that I spend less than half my time in."

He nodded. "Understandable. What else?"

Get married, have a couple kids. But there were limits to what she was willing to reveal to him, so she went with what was easy. "A beagle."

"You're kidding."

"Not kidding. I've wanted a beagle since forever. But I'm always getting on a plane and flying somewhere, sometimes for weeks at a time. It wouldn't be fair to the dog if I'm away from home all the time."

He tipped his head to the two dogs sharing a cushion in the corner. "You could always come back here. I've got plenty of beagles, and Cleo follows you around like she's already yours."

A throwaway comment, or was he serious? This was the first time the possibility of seeing each other after the end of her assignment had been broached. But coming back to visit the dogs wasn't quite the same as coming back to see Sam.

She kept her tone nonchalant. "Sure, I'd love to see Cleo and Tony."

Sam pushed his plate aside and sat back in his chair. Ellie did the same, fiddling with the engagement ring on her left hand. He reached out and took her hand, holding it up where the emerald-cut diamond glittered as it caught the light. He brushed a thumb over her knuckles. "Looks good on you."

"Guess we're lucky it fits. Tell me about the previous fiancée, unless the subject is painful."

"Why do you assume there was a previous fiancée?"

"This is an engagement ring, Creed, you happened to have lying around? If it's a sore subject, you don't have to talk about it."

He shrugged. "There was no fiancée. The ring was my aunt's."

"Really? From the young man who died in Vietnam?" She stared at the ring with a new regard, rubbing a finger over its surface, then started working it off her finger. "This is special, Sam. You shouldn't have given it to me."

He took her hand and pushed the ring back in place. "Wear it. My aunt would have liked you. She wore the ring on special occasions, and she'd have been fine with you wearing it now."

She fisted her hand. "Okay, I'll be careful with it."

They took the dishes from the table to the counter. Sam filled the dishwasher while Ellie found containers for the leftover food, then ran hot water in the basin for the hand washing.

The connection with Sam had intensified throughout the meal. They were in a situation that demanded they spend a lot of time together. Add the undeniable attraction that had led to the shared intimacy the night before, and heated tension was bound to keep building. She felt like it was swelling beneath the surface, and that neither of them was as in control of their emotions as they'd like.

They went through their evening routines. Ellie felt they were tiptoeing around the pull. Last night had proven how good they could be together, but going there again was complicated. From her corner of the couch she watched him staring at the screen on his laptop, earbuds in his ears. His lips turned down in a frown, and he drummed his fingers on the arm of the chair.

When he looked up, she caught a look of raw emotion before it was blocked. She motioned to his ears and he pulled out the earbuds, setting his laptop on an end table.

"What happened this morning? Where did you go?"

A simple question, but the filters dropped over his eyes. "Personal issue, sorry." His tone made the boundary clear.

"There's no personal right now." She frowned as a thought occurred, one she didn't care to examine too closely. "If you're more comfortable talking with Seth or Linc, then do it, but you can't hold back with us."

Heat kindled in his gaze. "You think I left here this morning to meet a woman? After last night?"

"How would I know? You're not exactly Mr. Talkative. The night the flashbang was thrown in the house, you were late then, too."

"I'm not seeing anyone in the manner you're thinking."

When she didn't respond, he swore and ran a hand through his hair. "I'm trying to figure something out. I'll tell you when I can."

"That's not how this works, Sam. You have to be honest. Seth made that clear when we decided on this course of action."

"I'll tell you when I can," he repeated.

She couldn't keep the edge out of her tone. "You made a decision to bring us in when you reported the threatening emails to the Marshals Service. That was the right thing to do, because you're a federal judge, and, like it or not, a threat against you is a threat against our system of justice. You don't get to hold back when the information you have isn't convenient to share."

"Convenience has nothing to do with it. I told you it's personal."

"Personal because it's about Drew?"

"Leave him out of it."

"Leave him out of it when I think he's involved?" She shook her head. "I heard you last night."

"Heard what?"

"I heard you on the phone. Your voice carried through the vent to my room. I came downstairs. You were in your office and sounded angry. Was it Drew?"

"Back off, Ellie." His sharp tone told her he was at the edge of his patience.

"I won't back off. This is my job."

His gaze narrowed, eyes turning a flat gray. "How far will you go for your job, Eleanor? You listened in on what was obviously a private conversation, so you crossed that line. Was it your job to get close to me to get more information?"

Everything inside her froze. "What exactly do you mean?"

"I'm talking about you and me last night. Maybe it wasn't as spontaneous as I'd assumed. Maybe the marshals assigning you to be my girlfriend was more calculating than I gave you credit for."

"Calculating in what way?" But the hollow pit in her stomach told her she already knew what he was going to say.

"Did you tell Seth that you and I had been together when we were both at University of Oregon?"

She sat up, closing the cover of her iPad with careful, precise movements. "Let me get this straight. You think Seth and I manipulated you using an encounter you didn't even remember."

"Did you?"

"No. I was too embarrassed to admit to my brother what an idiot I'd been thirteen years ago. But let's get to the more important assumption, the one that I'd use sex as part of my job. You know, fake orgasms, get you off, all to gather information. That's what you're saying?"

"I didn't say the orgasms were fake. Nothing wrong with enjoying your job."

Her hands were shaking as she rose to her feet. "You may be an asshole, but I'm not a whore."

He scrubbed a hand over his face, the rasp of his beard drowning out the ticking clock. "I didn't say you were a whore."

"Really? Because that's what I heard. Except that instead of money, I get paid with information. So if my motivation was information, which I didn't get by the way, what was yours? Another sexual conquest like thirteen years ago?"

"Don't blow this out of proportion."

"You suggested I prostituted myself for the Marshals Service and I'm blowing this out of proportion?" Her voice rose despite trying to stay calm. "I think you said exactly what you meant. I'll talk to Seth about getting reassigned because we obviously can't work together."

The look of relief that flashed across his face was gone so quickly she might have imagined it.

"That might be best."

Hurt cut through her with a lancing pain. She forced herself to think past it. "Is that what this conversation has been about, you want me thrown off the case?" Realization dawned. "You bastard." She picked up a cushion and hurled it at him. "We're back to that, are we? You want me reassigned because you think I might get hurt."

He caught the cushion and tossed it back on the couch. "Cut it out."

"Well, fuck you. You have no respect for my ability to do my job. You want to tuck me someplace safe while others put themselves in danger to protect you."

"I would hardly have gone along with the fake engagement if I didn't think it was a good idea, but it hasn't worked out."

"Maybe I'm assuming you actually care about me when in reality you're worried I'll figure out what's going on with Drew. My bet is that you didn't know he was involved when this first started. Now that you do, you want to stop the investigation. I take it back. I'm not going anywhere. If your plan was to get rid of me so you can cover for your brother, I'm not cooperating. You're stuck with me."

***

The next morning, Ellie stood outside Sam's closed office door. Whatever had been developing between them was dead. Maybe he did care about her, but he was obstructing her ability to do her job.

They hadn't gone on their morning run, and she'd stayed in her room, watching through her bedroom window until he'd left for work. By now he was safely in court, so she put aside whatever misgivings she might have had and turned the knob. He'd locked it.

No matter, Arch Bollinger had taught his stepchildren how to pick locks using whatever tools were at hand. She went up the stairs to her room and returned a minute later with a bobby pin. Seconds later, she had the door open.

She started with the antique rolltop desk set against one wall and determined it was used for things related to the house: manuals for kitchen appliances and electronics, sample books for countertop material and flooring that suggested Sam planned to update the kitchen, and even an architectural drawing of the house dated nearly a hundred years before.

Tucked next to it she found an envelope with a school-project valentine printed in a child's careful hand to "Auntie Nan" and signed "Your nephew, Sam." In the center of the red construction-paper heart was a small school photo of a serious, dark-haired boy. Oh geez. Was there anything that could pull harder at her heartstrings than that lonely little boy who had lost his mother? She returned the valentine to the envelope and tried to put a lid on the emotions the card had pulled up.

She moved and sat in the high-backed leather chair in front of the wide desk Sam regularly used and shut down her apprehension about going through his personal things.

She started with the desk drawers first, pulling each open to examine their contents. The top left drawer was stacked with receipts, mostly from online retailers, while the middle one held bills. The deep bottom drawer held a couple of squeeze-type grip strengtheners.

She picked one up and worked it a few times before replacing it to continue her search. An organizer in the top right-hand drawer held paper clips, Post-its, pens and pencils. How could someone only have boring pale yellow Post-its, plain metal paper clips, and yellow wooden pencils? She wondered what that said about Sam's personality.

It wasn't until she got to the bottom right drawer that she found hanging files, one with a tab that read "Rock Creek Estate." Inside Joss Creed's will, the deed to the ranch, and correspondence with a lawyer were all neatly organized, Sam having written notes on the boring yellow Post-its with his precise script. She leafed through the documents, gaining a clearer picture of the difficult position Sam's father had left him in, and why Drew was so resentful.

She pulled out the last file in the drawer. Inside was an unlabeled manila folder containing a stack of papers. One glance told her these were copies of the threatening emails. She read through them again, reviewing the now familiar messages from the self-described Freedom Defender.

The last sheet contained the most recent email. She frowned as she read. This email had been sent two days ago, and Sam hadn't shared it with her or the team.

Like the others, FD claimed to be preserving the Second Amendment. After the usual diatribe against Judge Creed, accusing him of being part of a conspiracy to subvert the Constitution, the last line read: *Enjoy the time you have left with your girlfriend. When she dies, her blood will be on your hands. We'll keep you alive long enough to witness her death, then you'll follow her to hell.*

"Talk about overly dramatic," Ellie muttered to herself. She took out her phone and snapped a photo of the email and sent it to the rest of the team.

***

The next morning, Ellie steered the Land Cruiser toward the grocery store, reviewing how everything had evolved over the past twenty-four hours. She bit back a sigh. The best way to describe her and Sam's current relationship was as a deep freeze with brief flashes of heat. After work he'd shut himself in his office, and an hour later she'd received an email from him. He'd forwarded the threat she'd found in his drawer to herself and the others.

Good thing, because now the team could talk openly about it in his presence without giving away that she'd snooped through his desk.

Seth had called. She and Sam had driven around for fifteen minutes to throw off anyone watching them before going to Marshal Central for a late evening meeting. Sam had hammered on about the threat to Ellie, but Seth had refused to change her assignment. She was becoming more and more discouraged with the lack of progress. Bella's questioning looks told Ellie that the tension between her and Sam hadn't gone unnoticed.

The friendship they'd seemed to be developing before their argument was a memory. Now they ignored each other. Or at least he ignored her. Her dilemma was that while she was putting on a good act, she couldn't help being hyperaware of everything about him.

His scent triggered a response if he walked too close to her, an aroma she labeled *Hot guy on a crisp fall day*. Maybe she should shorten it to *Sam*. When his hair fell over his forehead, she had to leave the room before she jumped him.

There was that moment in the courthouse parking lot earlier that morning. Sam had driven, so she'd stepped out of the Land Cruiser to switch seats. They were standing behind the vehicle when a pair of women had walked toward them. Sam's expression had turned speculative, then he'd leaned forward to cup the back of her neck and lowered his mouth to hers. The momentary touch of lips had been like flash lightning, scorching in its brief intensity.

He'd stepped back and released her to jam his hands in his pockets, expression unreadable. A moment later she was watching his back as he strode toward the courthouse.

She pulled up in front of the grocery store, her mind on trying to figure out something for dinner. The brooding sky and icy temperature matched her mood perfectly. Sam, who did aloof really well even as he was handing her an umbrella, had informed her of an impending storm. The clouds stacked up in the western sky and the biting wind made her grateful she'd opted for her padded down coat.

With her purse slung over her shoulder, she pulled up her hood, bent her head against a strong gust, and trudged toward the glass doors of the store. A van pulled to a stop, blocking her way, the passenger door opening as she stepped sideways to go around it. It wasn't the man who got out of the vehicle who caught her attention, but the pale face under the dark beanie of the driver. Frowning, she opened her mouth to speak. A movement in her peripheral vision was her only warning before a blow to her head had the world spinning into darkness.

Chapter Seventeen

Ellie's head throbbed. She blinked open her eyes and bit back a groan as she tried to sort out her surroundings. The surface under her cheek vibrated, her clue that she was in the back of a moving vehicle. Her heart pounded heavily. Shit. This was bad.

Voices, loud and angry, carried from the front. Sharp pain radiating from her forehead muddled the words so she couldn't make them out. The smell of cigarette smoke permeated the air. She rolled to her side, fighting back a wave of nausea, and became aware that her hands were uncomfortably secured behind her. She pulled at the restraints and heard a metallic clink. Handcuffs.

A desperate thought had her awkwardly bending her arms and in that split second, her situation kicked up from bad to grim. Her holster was there, but the gun was gone. No doubt, if they'd found her gun, they'd found her phone.

Hoping desperately for a break, she cast around frantically for her purse but didn't see it. Then she remembered shoving her phone into a pocket of her coat. She couldn't get her hands to her front to check for that, but she didn't feel the weight of it. Something wet trickled along her eyebrow and she guessed it was blood. Gritting her teeth, she pushed herself up so she could lean against the sidewall.

Clearly, she'd been kidnapped, which meant whoever had taken her was trying to get to Sam. Linc was at the courthouse today, as were Seth and Bella. They would keep Sam safe.

She was in some sort of work van with a low, flat floor and two bucket seats in the front. Two men in heavy coats and beanies were taking turns snarling at each other. There were no windows in the back, only what looked like a couple of toolboxes and gray plastic bins with lids. A packing blanket wrapped around something bulky lay on the opposite side of the van.

"What the fuck was she doing with a gun?" Ellie jerked as she tuned into the conversation. Then she remembered that brief glimpse of the driver. His voice was pitched high with worry. Drew Martin glanced at the man in the passenger seat, then returned his attention to the road. For Sam's sake she wished her suspicions about his brother had proven unwarranted.

"This is an open carry state, half the people in this county are armed." The man in the passenger seat was heavier than Drew and appeared more relaxed as he sipped from a to-go cup, a cigarette dangling from his fingers.

"I'm telling you, there's something off there. She wouldn't let me come in the house with a gun. Said it made her *uncomfortable.* Why would she say that if she's one of us?"

"I'm not saying she's one of us, dickwad. I'm saying it doesn't prove anything. Creed could have given her the gun to carry for protection because we're threatening him."

"I don't think so. Maybe she's FBI or something."

"Does she look FBI?"

"How the fuck should I know what FBI looks like? Isn't that the point when they go undercover, that you don't know who they are? We need to get rid of her before they come after us. I kept telling you guys taking her is a mistake."

Her stomach knotted when she thought of what he meant by getting rid of her. And who were "you guys"?

"We stick with the plan. We grabbed her to get leverage over Creed. We want him to overturn Bannister's conviction, and we don't want the government taking our guns. If Big Dog wants us to get rid of her, then that's what we do, but not until then."

"We shouldn't have done this. You don't know my brother. You think he's all civilized, but I've seen him lose his shit. Thought he was going to kill a guy once who'd punched Ben for being a fag."

"We'll deal with Creed." The passenger looked over his shoulder, a wide smile splitting his round face. "Well, well, look who's awake. Hello, sweetheart." He frowned and pointed at his head. "Man, that looks painful. Sorry I hit you so hard. Had a job to do, that's all. How you feeling? Got a headache?"

She ignored his questions. "Who are you?"

"You can call me Sarge, everyone does."

"Why are you doing this? Where are you taking me?"

"We're taking you someplace safe, and we're going to hold on to you for a bit. You don't have anything to worry about."

"Shit, shit, shit!" Drew swerved and Ellie braced to keep from being rolled around.

"What the hell's wrong with you? I should never have let you drive."

"Cops are behind us with their lights on." Panic edged Drew's voice, and between the seats she could see his hands, knuckles white, gripping the steering wheel.

A thin, piercing wail sounded over the whine of the engine.

"Don't freak out. They can't be after us."

"Someone must have seen us grab her in the parking lot."

"No way. The van blocked the view from the store. There was no one in the parking lot when we grabbed her, and we had her in the car in less than thirty seconds. No one saw us. Pull over nice and easy like every other idiot out here and we'll be fine."

"The signal turned red. Should we run it? We get pulled over with her in the back and we're done for."

"Fuck no, we don't run it. You're such a dumbass."

Drew stomped on the brakes and Ellie tumbled to her side. The sirens drew closer.

"What the fuck, man? Are you *trying* to get their attention?" Drew wasn't the only one losing his cool.

The sirens passed, the sound fading, taking Ellie's brief hope with it.

"Holy shit, I nearly pissed myself."

Sarge made a sound of disgust. "If you'd listened to me in the first place, you'd save yourself a shitload of grief. Now get going before someone calls the cops to report a reckless driver." He turned in his seat. "How we doing back there?"

Ellie remained slumped on the floor, her shoulders aching from her hands being pulled behind her back. She squeezed her eyes shut. "Not good. My head hurts and I get motion sickness. I feel like throwing up." It didn't take much effort to put a tremor in her voice. "Why have you kidnapped me?"

"We're not planning to hurt you." She didn't believe that for a second. Maybe Sarge didn't realize she'd overheard him and Drew talking about "getting rid" of her.

Drew slowed the vehicle.

"What the fuck are you doing?" From the temper in his voice, Sarge was at the end of his patience.

"She throws up she'll stink up the whole van. I'm stopping. We got to look for a bag or something."

Ellie could feel the vehicle turning. She moaned and gulped in a breath. With the headache and being in the back of the van, her claim of nausea wasn't entirely a fabrication.

"Get back on the damn road. Who cares if she pukes all over herself? We've got to get her stashed before we're pulled over for real."

"She pukes, I puke. Happens every time."

"God, you're an idiot."

The van stopped and Drew threw it into park.

"Could you have picked a worse place to stop? Circle around to the back of the store, dickwad. There'll be dumpsters there and we'll find something for her to spew into so your delicate sensibilities aren't upset."

"Stop calling me that." The van rumbled to life again.

"What, dickwad? You are a dickwad, so that's what you're called."

"Everyone in the militia chooses a code name. Big Dog's is Big Dog. Mine's Lobo. That's what you're supposed to call me."

Sarge barked out a laugh lacking in amusement. "You got to earn your name, dickwad. I earned mine in the Marine Corps. Big Dog's earned his because he's big and he's the top dog. So far all you've earned is dickwad."

The van stopped and Ellie made a retching sound. She lay curled on her side, eyes closed.

"Shit, she's gonna hurl." Drew shoved open the driver's door.

"Jesus Christ on a crutch." Sarge opened his own door, and a second later, the rear doors of the van flew open. "Get out, girl."

Ellie opened her eyes and gave him a suffering look. "I don't feel good." Behind Sarge's silhouetted figure, the sky looked heavy with gray and sullen clouds.

He flicked away a lit cigarette. "We aren't taking you to a garden party so I don't really care if you don't feel good. You need to puke or not?"

"I think so, but I can't sit up with my hands behind my back."

"Well, I'm sure as hell not taking those cuffs off." He tugged her feet to draw her to the opening before grabbing her elbow and pulling her to a sitting position. "Get your feet under you and stand up."

Drew stuck his head around the open door. Ellie stood, bent over at the waist, and made herself dry heave, then breathed heavily through her nostrils.

"You faking it, sweet thing?" Sarge jerked her upright.

"I'm trying *not* to throw up." She groaned and pulled free to sit on the back bumper of the van. She looked at Drew. "Why are you doing this? Why are you trying to hurt Sam?"

Drew's face contorted. "He brought this on himself. He tell you I asked him for a loan against my inheritance, money that's rightfully mine to begin with? He told me to fuck off."

"Sam wouldn't have said that to you."

"Maybe not using those exact words, but the intent was the same. He thinks because he's a big-ass judge he can treat his own brother like shit. Us snatching you will get his attention. Then we'll have ourselves a conversation and he can give me some goddamn respect."

Sarge shoved Drew aside. "You're full of shit. This isn't some petty personal vendetta. We're doing this for the cause. Creed needs to be taught he can't fuck with the Constitution."

Ellie groaned and her legs shook. "Oh god. I have to find a bathroom."

"You have to pee?" Drew sounded nervous.

"I think I have diarrhea."

He reached into the front pocket of his jeans.

"What the hell are you doing?" Incredulity laced Sarge's words.

Drew pulled a ring of keys from his pocket. He fished through them, then held up a small handcuff key. "We can't take her to the bathroom in handcuffs. It'll draw too much attention. We've got to get her to a toilet or she'll shit her pants. I could use the john myself."

"Oh my god, could you be any more stupid? We're not taking her anywhere with blood dripping down her face." Sarge held out his hand. "Give me the goddam keys."

Ellie moaned. Sarge snatched the keys from Drew, then scooped her legs up and pushed her into the back of the van and slammed the doors. Through the closed doors she could hear Sarge telling Drew that if he didn't want to get left behind, he'd get in the van. The driver's door was thrown open and Sarge got behind the wheel, jamming the key into the ignition.

Drew took the passenger seat, slamming his door shut. "I've got to use the john, asshole, didn't I tell you that? And you didn't get a bag for her to puke in."

"She's faking it. We've got to do our job or there'll be hell to pay."

Sarge was more astute than she'd given him credit for. They set out again, turning onto what she thought must be the highway as the first drops of rain spattered against the windshield. She guessed they were traveling south but couldn't be entirely sure.

The rain began falling heavier, the drumming sound loud on the roof. There seemed to be fewer stops at intersections, so she guessed they were heading out of town. Eventually they turned, and then turned again. With the mental map she was trying to keep in her head, she thought they might be in the general area of Rock Creek Ranch. A strong wind was blowing the rain in sheets that the wipers struggled to keep up with. A particularly strong gust sent the van swerving.

"Stay on the road, asshole. We go down the embankment and we'll need a winch to pull us out." Drew's tone turned sullen. "I should be driving."

"I am staying on the road," Sarge growled. His earlier affability had evaporated.

Maybe twenty minutes later, with the rain beating harder, Drew swore. "There's flooding up ahead. You crossing that? We get stuck in the mud, we'll need to get towed out."

"We're going to my house, aren't we? I know what I'm doing. That dip in the road floods a couple times every winter. This van's got all-wheel drive. We won't get stuck."

"If that water's deep enough, unless you're driving a tank, we'll be stuck."

"We won't get stuck." Sarge sounded like he was pushing his words through gritted teeth.

Ellie scooted to the opposite side of the van to lean against the packing blanket. As much as she could with her cuffed hands, she felt along the blanket. Her suspicions were confirmed when her fingers closed around what was probably the barrel of a long gun. She scooted down until she could trace the hard cylinder, then the one next to it. When she sat back again, she was sure she was leaning against at least three rifles, most likely assault-type, rolled in the blanket.

The throbbing pain where she'd been hit on her forehead made her grimace and she had to force herself to think around it. *Focus, Ellie.* She wouldn't let fear paralyze her.

Drawing on her training, she tried to clear her mind and formulate a plan. The engine strained as they steadily climbed in elevation. Through the rain-spattered windscreen, she could make out the tips of pine trees silhouetted against the cloudy sky. They must be in the mountains. Paying attention to details could mean the difference between survival and death. She didn't intend to end up dead.

The road transitioned to an unpaved surface and they bumped along, gravel hitting the underside of the van. After about ten minutes, the road leveled out. Sarge steered around a bend, then applied the brakes, putting the van in park.

"Your place is a dump, as usual."

Sarge swung out an arm and backhanded Drew. A second later, Sarge had a gun out, eyes narrowed as he sighted down the barrel at Drew.

Chapter Eighteen

"Watch what you say, dickwad, because it wouldn't take much to pull this trigger and blow your brains out. The only thing that's holding me back right now is that I'd have a mess to clean up." The expression on his face said Sarge was dead serious. A dog barked outside the van.

"All right! Fuck it. I didn't mean anything."

"You insulted me." Sarge's voice carried over the rain hammering on the roof. He eased back, though continuing to point his gun at Drew. He threw a glance over his shoulder. "Don't worry about this, sweetheart. We're not going to hurt you. This loser needs a reminder of who's in charge and what good manners are." His attention returned to Drew. "Come on, dickwad. We've got to get her settled."

He holstered his weapon and opened the driver's door, animosity evident on Drew's face as he watched Sarge. Sam wasn't the only one to have earned his brother's hatred.

Sarge opened the back of the van and Ellie scooted forward. A large mixed-breed dog sniffed Drew's jeans, then Ellie's. Sarge grabbed Ellie's arm to help her stand, using his knee to push the muddy dog aside. "Out of the way, Rex."

Ellie gazed around, trying to absorb details. They were in a valley between low hills with higher mountains rising behind them. The driveway led past the house to a barn with a sagging roof. She didn't see any sign of close neighbors. Rain pelted down, immediately soaking her and sending a rivulet of icy water under the collar of her coat.

Sarge pulled up her hood over her hair, and Ellie made a point of thanking him. She would exploit any division between her captors she could, even appearing to want to get on Sarge's good side.

He led them toward the house, and she surreptitiously studied Drew. His tight expression and clenched fists indicated seething anger. She wondered if Sarge had pushed him too far.

She stumbled over uneven bricks in the walkway. The area in front of the house couldn't really be called a yard. Weeds grew unchecked around used tires and broken-down machinery, and a large propane tank sat on a concrete pad.

Curls of peeling paint flaked from the window trim and eaves of the house, and the bottom third of the stucco walls looked damp. Ellie detected a faint skunky smell.

The dog followed them into the house, leaving a trail of muddy paw prints as he collapsed onto the carpet in front of a fireplace in need of having its ashes cleaned out. The cramped living room smelled of stale cigarette smoke.

One wall sported a mounted deer head, and a rack over the fireplace held two hunting rifles. An AR-15 leaned against one corner. On a desk shoved in a corner an old-style, bulky computer monitor sat next to a CPU that blinked a red light like a warning.

On the far side of the room a dining table was weighted down with stacks of papers, empty soda bottles, and a couple of overflowing ashtrays. Beyond the table was a sliding glass door that revealed a narrow patio with a rusting barbecue and a muddy backyard. In the middle of the yard was a blackened area that held charred chunks of wood, the remnants of a fire. She wondered if Sarge's backyard had been used for the book-burning bonfire.

He pushed her forward with a hand in the middle of her back. They passed by a wide doorway to the kitchen where a Nazi flag was held on the refrigerator with a magnet like one would keep their child's artwork. She glimpsed a backdoor through the kitchen, which meant there were at least three points of entry to the house.

Sarge stripped off his coat and threw it over the back of a chair and she spotted her gun tucked in the back waistband of his baggy jeans, another in a holster at his hip. With Drew trailing behind them, Sarge took her down a hallway where he opened a door and flipped a switch to light a narrow set of stairs that descended into darkness.

Ellie's stomach churned, the feeling that she was being led into a dungeon doing nothing to ease her apprehension. She hated feeling powerless and at the mercy of these two men. Nothing they had done suggested that they intended sexual assault, but they'd hit her hard enough for her to lose consciousness, and she didn't doubt they would hurt her again if they wanted. She had to come up with a plan to protect herself.

Sarge flipped on more lights at the bottom of the stairs to reveal a minimally furnished basement room. In one corner, a twin-size bed was neatly made, covered with a thick comforter. A table with a couple of folding chairs had been arranged next to a mini-refrigerator and counter with a small sink. A microwave that had to be twenty years old sat on top of the fridge, and a TV and VCR of possibly even older vintage were perched precariously on a small, wheeled cabinet.

"Here we are, sweetheart. Home sweet home, for the time being, anyway." He took out his phone and snapped a picture of her. "I'll be sending that to your boyfriend. Can't use you for leverage if he doesn't know we have you." He dug the keys out of his pocket, and whistling a jaunty tune, proceeded to unlock the handcuffs.

Ellie moved her arms, biting back a groan when pain shot from her shoulders down her arms. She rubbed her wrists as she looked around the room.

Sarge opened the cabinet doors under the sink. Cup O'Noodles, Cheez-Its, and a box of instant oatmeal packets were among the food items on the shelf next to stacked paper plates and napkins. Ellie had a flashback to her college dorm room.

"See? You won't starve. And there's even the VCR for entertainment. It's old school, but it works. TV's not attached to the cable, but there are movies you can choose from in the TV stand." Sarge seemed proud of the furnishings. He waved a hand at a closed door. "The bathroom's in there."

"I want to go home."

His eyes flashed. "Show some respect. We haven't violated you. We haven't harmed you other than that little bump on your head. We won't kill you unless there's no alternative. I've set up a nice place for you to stay where you'll be comfortable. Show some appreciation."

The offhand mention of killing her sent ice straight to her bones. "You *kidnapped* me and are holding me against my will, and I'm expected to show appreciation?" Ellie knew she was walking a fine line.

Sarge seemed to have certain standards for his personal behavior, not that those standards met societal norms. His casually violent treatment of Drew demonstrated how quickly his temper could flare. She would take care, but if she wanted to develop a viable escape plan, getting Sarge to talk might reveal information that could help her.

Still wearing her coat, she crossed her arms against the chill. "This does look comfortable, but I'm scared and confused, and want to go home. I don't understand why you brought me here. When are you going to let me go?"

"I'll tell you." Drew's face twisted in a sneer. "We brought you here to give my privileged brother the message that he can't mess with me and he can't mess with our movement. He hides behind the law to keep for himself what's rightfully mine. He thinks because he's a fucking judge he gets to decide who should be protected by the Constitution and who shouldn't. He's letting illegals overrun our country while throwing good people like Frank Bannister in prison for exercising their rights. The Second Amendment lays it out that we got a right to our guns. No judge can take that away." The words came from his mouth with a spray of spit.

"Shut up, dickwad. She doesn't need to know any of that."

"I can say what I want to say. She should know what kind of man she's engaged to."

"You're more of an idiot than I gave you credit for. Just shut up."

Drew's face flushed angry red. He reached for his holster, fumbled a moment, then raised his arm, gun in hand, and aimed at Sarge. With much cleaner movement, Sarge palmed his own pistol and mirrored Drew's stance. The sudden silence was broken only by the faint thudding of the rain.

"Well, well. Looks like we got ourselves a Mexican standoff." Sarge's sardonic tone indicated a decided lack of concern.

"You think you're so cool. I'm fucking tired of how you treat me, asshole." Drew's gun shook like a fall leaf in a stiff wind.

Ellie stepped toward the stairs, moving slowly.

"Interesting, since I'm fucking tired of you whining like an overgrown toddler. Go ahead and shoot. You're shaking so much I think I can put a hole between your eyes before you could steady yourself enough to pull the trigger. Want to try out that hypothesis, *dickwad*?"

Ellie could see the rage on Drew's face, the desire to pull the trigger as Sarge goaded him. As much as she wanted to bring in both men to face justice, shooting one another would take care of her immediate problem.

Seconds stretched until finally Drew lowered his gun. "I hate your fucking guts."

"You can hate me all you want, but we got a job to do." Sarge turned his own weapon toward Ellie. She froze with her foot on the bottom tread "You don't want to do that, sweetheart, because I won't have any problem shooting you if I have to. You asked when you'll be released. That'll depend on how much Judge Creed wants your freedom." Sarge motioned Drew to the door. The loathing on Drew's face made her determined to use his anger if she had a chance.

"You sure she can't get out of this place?" Drew asked.

"Not unless she's a freaking ghost. There's only one door and it's got a deadbolt. She's not getting out of here."

Drew climbed the stairs without a backward glance.

Sarge gestured to the room. "Make yourself at home. You may be here for a few days."

He turned to the stairs, and Ellie said, "Wait. Can't you give me my purse? I have Tylenol in there, and a hairbrush."

"Should I give you your Glock back, too? Nice try, sweetheart." Sarge shook his head. "Everything you need is here."

The deadbolt slid into place, locking the door to her prison. The quiet intensified, the only sound the faint hush of air through the vents.

With her arms locked over her stomach, Ellie turned slowly to scan the room. The desire to curl up on the bed and bury her head under the blankets nearly overwhelmed her. She was being held prisoner, her head ached relentlessly, and she could feel panic creeping over her skin like the plague.

She absolutely believed Sarge when he'd said he would have no problem shooting her. Practicing a breathing technique to calm herself, she tried to recall her training and what could help her in her current situation.

First things first. She made a beeline to the door Sarge had indicated. The bathroom appeared recently converted. The space was cramped, containing a toilet, a sink and vanity with a postage-stamp-size counter, and a shower stall so narrow she thought she'd likely bruise her elbows if she actually used it. There were still stickers on the glass door of the shower and the mirror over the sink. After using the toilet, she washed her hands, leaning forward to examine her reflection. "Jesus, I look like I'm made up for a Halloween party."

With the tap running to get hot water, she pulled open the drawers of the vanity, searching for a washcloth to clean the dried blood from her face. A top drawer contained a multi-pack of toothbrushes, the tube of toothpaste next to it promising to make her breath minty fresh. The next drawer held a hairbrush and comb, both new. She found a first aid kit and set it on the counter. It wasn't until she reached the bottom drawer that she allowed a tight smile. A metal towel bar and the attachments to fix it to the wall lay inside, along with a long screwdriver. She took out the screwdriver and slid it under the waistband of her jeans and lay the towel rod on the counter. They would be of no use against a gun but might prove worth having in hand-to-hand. She'd take what she could get.

Not finding a washcloth, she dampened the corner of a hand towel and scrubbed the blood. When she rinsed the cloth, red-stained water swirled into the drain. Lifting her hair, she examined the injury high on her forehead, close to the hairline. She hoped it was one of those cases that looked worse than it actually was, because it looked pretty bad.

At the crest of a raised lump, a deep half-inch semicircle cut into her skin, the surrounding area puffy and purple caused by a pipe or the muzzle of Sarge's gun. It probably needed stitches, but that wasn't happening.

She found antibacterial ointment in the first aid kit and swabbed it on, then used Band-Aids as best she could to cover the wound.

Once she was done tending to the wound, she went to the kitchen area and examined the contents of the cupboard. She was right about the food being like college all over again. A jumbo container of cheese balls in neon orange was nestled next to a tray of Oreos and little packets of soft cheese and crackers, but there was nothing that resembled what she considered real food.

She wandered through the room and determined Sarge had been telling the truth. Other than the door with the locked deadbolt (she'd tested it), there was no other way out of the basement.

Finding pain reliever in the cabinet, she downed a couple capsules. Lying on the bed, she pulled the comforter around her shoulders and closed her eyes. Worry churned in her stomach, but for the moment, she was safe.

She only meant to lie on the bed until her headache eased, but it was several hours before she stirred again. When she woke, the time on the VCR told her it was late afternoon. She rose, and keeping the comforter around her shoulders, opened the kitchenette cupboards again.

Cup O'Noodles, she decided. With the Styrofoam cup filled with water and heating in the microwave, she studied her surroundings more carefully. She didn't doubt that Sarge had hidden surveillance cameras. He might have seen her taking the screwdriver and towel rod from the bathroom. Cameras were tiny these days and easily camouflaged. If they were here, searching would tip them off that she knew about such things, and she wanted them to continue to think she was frightened and helpless.

Ellie sat at the small table and used a plastic fork to eat the noodles. The ceiling above made creaking noises as someone walked about on the first floor—or several someones because it sounded like too much creaking for only Sarge and Drew.

There was a rumble of voices, the slamming of a door, and even faint barking that made her think Rex was outside. She refused to give in to the temptation and lay her head on her arms and have a good cry. Deputy US Marshals didn't cry. While her situation was bad, it wasn't dire.

If Sarge had sent that photo to Sam, he was now aware she'd been kidnapped, and regardless of the current problems between them, he'd be worried about her and would notify the team. Her brothers and Bella were no doubt looking for her. She gave a fleeting thought that they might be able to track her phone but guessed her captors had taken out the sim card. Assuring herself that things could be much worse helped, but didn't do much to dispel the feeling that she was on her own without the tools she needed to get herself out of this place.

The soup's warmth radiated from her stomach and made her feel infinitesimally better. She munched on Cheez-Its, washing them down with water, and guessed she'd probably surpassed the recommended sodium consumption for an entire month. More creaking came from above, then voices, followed by thumping on the stairs. She sat up straight as the deadbolt slid back and the door to the stairs was thrust open.

Ellie's heart gave a hard lurch when Sam stumbled into the room, shoved from behind. She let go of the comforter and surged to her feet. The door slammed shut behind him, the deadbolt sliding home. He no longer wore the suit and tie he'd had on when she'd left him at the courthouse. He was dressed in denim jeans and a dark coat over a sweatshirt, shoulders and hair wet from the rain.

She rushed around the table. His face was a battered mess. His left eye was swollen so badly she wondered if he could see from it, and mottled bruising shadowed his jaw. He moved toward her, relief, rage, and something she couldn't identify sweeping across his face as he opened his arms, clutching her to him.

"You okay?" The words were a harsh whisper in her ear.

She nodded. "What happened? How'd they get you?"

"I went looking for them."

Chapter Nineteen

Sam's arms remained tight around Ellie. She was alive. The terror he'd been living with the past several hours eased a fraction. They stood locked together until she huffed out a breath and loosened the grip she had on the back of his shirt. Now that he'd found her, he didn't want to let her go.

She pushed against his chest and forced him to loosen his grip.

"You okay?" he asked. "How did you get captured?"

She raised a hand to cover his mouth and shook her head, then pulled his shoulder down and put her lips to his ear. "There may be hidden video or listening devices."

He nodded. Before she could move away, he lifted the hair from her forehead to reveal the white bandage. She pulled against his hold.

"How bad is it?"

"It probably needed stitches." She shrugged. "I did the best I could with a first aid kit I found."

Fury welled, nearly choking him, a familiar pattern for the day. "And the pain?" He could see it in her eyes.

"It's better than it was. I took some ibuprofen a couple hours ago."

"They'll pay for this." He kept his tone low so only she could hear.

She backed out of his hold. "We should put a cold compress on your eye. How'd that happen?"

"I didn't come without a fight."

He followed her into the bathroom. Sam turned on the taps and the ceiling fan. The noise should drown out their voices if there were any listening devices. He stood on the toilet to examine the vent, then hopped down to search the rest of the bathroom. "We're clean in here."

Ellie leaned against a wall, still wearing her coat.

She nodded, then picked up a towel and moistened it before wringing out the excess water and carefully folding it into a pad.

His left eye had swelled shut and ached like he'd been hit with a hammer, which wasn't far off the truth since Big Dog's fist had felt like one. But it was the injury to Ellie's face that had him wanting to slam a fist through the wall. He closed his eyes and drew in a deep breath. Anger wouldn't help them to escape, and escape was the goal.

Ellie was avoiding looking at him, and he was reminded of the angry words spoken the night before. He'd make things right with her once they were free.

"Sit." She motioned to the closed lid of the toilet. He sat, and when she lay the compress on his eye, he groaned. The coolness felt good and eased the ache, but it was more than that. He'd found her, and, at least for the moment, she was safe. The fear that had lodged like a ball of ice in his belly melted at her touch.

His set his hands on her hips as she stood in front of him, his hand brushing over something under her coat. Lifting the hem and frowned. "What's that?"

She pulled a long screwdriver from under the waistband of her jeans. "I found it in a drawer, along with a metal towel rod. The rod is under the blanket on the bed, I'm carrying this just in case."

"Smart woman."

"Not smart enough to avoid getting caught. Who brought you here?"

"A guy they call Big Dog."

"Did you see Drew upstairs?"

He gave a curt nod. The betrayal cut deep. He'd been deluding himself about his brother. "Yeah, and another guy I don't know."

"That's Sarge. This is his house."

"Okay." He repeated his earlier question. "How'd they get you?"

"I was in the parking lot of the grocery store. A van stopped in front of me and a guy got out. I didn't think anything about it. I don't even remember him hitting me on the head, but the next thing I knew I was waking up in the back of a work van with blood running down my face."

The mental image of Ellie helpless and alone had his gut clenching. "You were knocked unconscious? Do you have headache or nausea?"

She ran water over the pad to cool it, then lay it again over his swollen eye. "Yes to all of that."

Her eyes appeared flat, the spark that always lit her face missing. He wasn't sure if it was due to their current predicament or the screwed-up state of their relationship. Maybe it was a combination of both. "You could have a concussion."

"Blame Sarge, he's the one who hit me. Drew was the driver, at least at first. Those two barely tolerate each other."

"Good to know," he murmured. He reached up to hold the compress and she stepped back. Hard to do in such a small space, but she managed to maximize the distance between them. "With your symptoms a concussion is likely, and we need to be careful with you to minimize damage." He rose to his feet. "You're lying down."

"We need to work on getting out of here."

Creaking came from overhead as someone moved around on the first floor. "I'll figure out a plan, because you're resting your brain."

"We'll both figure out a plan. I tried to keep track of our direction when we were in the van. Are we anywhere near your ranch?"

He nodded. "About three miles from here, as the crow flies."

"Do you know Sarge?"

"No."

"I don't think he or Drew expected you to become their captive. The plan was to use me as leverage to force you to free Frank Bannister and to make a decision on the side of gun rights on a Second Amendment case. Mixed in with all the other nonsense, they also blame you for letting undocumented immigrants overrun the country."

Not for the first time, Sam wished he'd talked with Drew before his ideas had led him down the path he'd ultimately taken. Maybe Sam could have made him see the light. He gave a sigh of frustration as Ellie took the compress from his eye to run under cool water once again, then moved to stand between his knees.

He couldn't tell whether the compress was doing the job, or if it was simply that he was with Ellie. Regardless, the pain around his eye eased and he felt ready to take on every one of their captors. She stood close and he wanted more than anything to wrap her in his arms and simply hold her, but she kept her touch brief and impersonal.

He closed both eyes and allowed himself a moment to be grateful he'd found her. That she'd been hurt because of him only added to his anger. For now, he would hold on to the fact that she was alive, and once she was safe, he'd make sure every one of her captors, including his brother, paid.

"There's ibuprofen in the kitchen area. You should take some for the pain and swelling."

"I need to check for spy equipment, then I will." He rose to his feet, sighing in frustration when she moved to avoid him. "We'll get out of this, Ellie."

She looked away. "Sure we will."

***

Ellie rested her head on the pillow and closed her eyes against the light. She wasn't sure how long she'd been asleep, but it felt like hours. Sam had insisted she lie down and her head hurt so badly she couldn't manage to argue with him. She had a vague recollection of Sam shaking her awake more than once. She pulled up the blanket under her chin as a shiver wracked her body. Even with her coat and under the comforter, she felt cold.

The events of the day played in her mind like a horror movie on endless loop. Her brothers and Bella had to have realized something had happened to her and Sam. The thought that even now they might be closing in on her captors gave her hope. She felt like she should be doing something, helping to search for hidden mics, formulating a plan of escape, fighting back, but her head was bad enough for her to know that she needed to conserve her energy. Add all her symptoms together and she was pretty sure Sam's concussion diagnosis was spot on.

Ellie heard him moving about and unscrewed her eyes enough to see what he was doing. He'd dragged a chair to stand on while looking up at the vent on the ceiling. Her vision blurred and she let her eyelids droop again.

She needed to put aside her personal feelings so they could act like a team to survive whatever lay ahead. She couldn't let the fact that he'd destroyed her heart get in the way. Sure, he probably cared for her in his own way, but that wasn't enough. She wasn't a woman who went to pieces when a man cast her aside or hurt her.

Not that Sam had cast her aside.

Technically, they hadn't even been together. Their entire relationship was built on a false premise, and if she'd lost sight of that, if she'd thought there was something more between them, then that was her mistake. Her heart would heal and she would move on without Sam Creed.

The mattress dipped and she opened her eyes to find Sam on the bed beside her.

"Sit up so you can take these. It's ibuprofen."

She propped herself with her elbow and he dropped the tablets onto her palm. She swallowed the pills with a mouthful of water from a paper cup he held out for her.

"Did you take some?"

"Yeah." He set the cup on the floor. "Look, I'm sorry about last night. I was way off base."

"I don't want to talk about it."

"I need to explain."

"No, you don't." She forced herself to stay alert when all she wanted was to burrow under the blanket and shut out the world. "Tell me how you were captured."

"I tried calling at lunch but you didn't pick up. Went home to see if you were there and not answering your phone because you're pissed at me."

"I wouldn't do that. It's not professional." It was easier to talk with her eyes closed.

"I was getting worried, so I had to check. The rest of your team was at the courthouse. I let them know I was heading home to find out what was going on." He glanced at her. "Then I made arrangements to get myself here."

She was drifting, so it took a minute for his words to sink in. "That doesn't make sense," she mumbled.

The bed dipped farther. "I'll explain later." There was a brief touch on her forehead that made her wonder why he would kiss her, then sleep claimed her.

***

It seemed like only moments later that a hand on Ellie's shoulder was shaking her awake. She opened her eyes to find the room in darkness, only a faint light coming from the bathroom. "What's going on?"

"Shh. I'm making sure you're asleep, not unconscious."

Sam's voice, barely audible, came from immediately behind her, his breath warming the back of her head. She tried to sit up but found that she was cuddled next to him, his arm wrapped around her middle and his head next to hers on the pillow.

"How's the head?" he whispered.

"Not as bad." She matched her voice to his. "How's yours?"

"Swelling is down, so better."

"You're in bed with me."

"Observant, marshal. Feels right, don't you think?"

"God, how come you sound so chipper?"

"Not chipper, but at the moment, I'm right where I want to be."

She turned her head to try to look at him. "Held prisoner in a basement is where you want to be? I don't get you."

"That's because your brain is muddled. You'll figure it out. Until then, getting in bed with you keeps us both warm because it's damn cold down here. Plus, it seemed like the best option for keeping an eye on you, and there's only one bed."

"Oh." She figured she should object but couldn't gather the energy. Sam pulled her tighter against him, the warmth of his body sinking into her bones, and despite their current predicament, his outdoorsy scent and his strong arms wrapped around her made her feel safe.

When Ellie roused again, it was to Sam's low voice rumbling in her ear.

"Time to wake up, love."

Ellie blinked open her eyes and tried to clear the dream from her head, a dream that had included someone chasing her through a pounding rainstorm until she'd been captured, only her captor had turned out to be Sam, and they'd tumbled into wild, no-holds-barred sex. This was not the time to be having sex dreams about the man currently spooned snugly against her. "I'm not your love," she mumbled.

"Heard that, did you? Voices low, remember?"

"Right. What time is it?" She rolled over to face him. Considering the erection nudging her backside, it seemed prudent.

"According to the clock on the ancient VCR, almost five a.m."

"You didn't sleep?"

"No. I needed to wake you every two hours. That, and I had work to do."

Ellie tried to make sense of what Sam was saying. What had happened to the man who'd accused her of prostituting herself for the Marshals Service? His tone, his words, his care for her—none of those matched the cynicism with which he'd lobbed accusations the night before.

She'd like to blame her jumbled mental functioning on the possible concussion, though she suspected that might be better explained by Sam's proximity. It didn't seem to matter that he'd hurt her and she was still angry with him, or that they were in danger. All she could think about was how good it felt when he held her close. She spread her hands that had somehow become lodged against his chest, the steady beat of his heart reassuring.

"I didn't find any surveillance devices," he whispered. "Doesn't mean there aren't any, so we talk quietly. How do you feel about getting out of here?"

"Favorably."

"Good, because they plan to kill us."

A chill raced down her spine. She spoke so quietly she barely breathed the words. "Why would they kill us? It won't get them what they want."

"They screwed up, and they know it. Their original plan may have been to use you to pressure me, but now that they've kidnapped a federal judge they're adjusting. They think killing us will send a warning to others in the justice system, and potentially ignite their movement."

"I still don't get how you got caught."

"I'll tell you about that later."

His response made her wonder why he was stalling, but she let it go. "How do you know their plan?"

He moved his head on their shared pillow until they were nose to nose. "I overheard them. Remember how you said you heard me through the vent in your bedroom? There's a vent in the ceiling that must connect to the living room. I was searching it for a hidden camera and heard voices. They were having a nasty argument. Couldn't make out every word, but I got enough to know they plan to shoot us and bury our bodies somewhere on this property. Drew argued against it, but the fucker was eventually brought around." His breath fanned her cheeks as he whispered. "Big Dog is in charge. He took off a couple hours ago, said he'd be back in the morning so they could deal with us."

She jerked her up to lean on an elbow. "Why'd you let me sleep? We need to do something. Now." She didn't know how, but there had to be a way out of the basement. Sitting and waiting for someone to come through the door with a gun wasn't an option.

He used a hand to her back to pull her against him. "I was waiting for Sarge and Drew to either leave or go to sleep."

"How would you know if they're asleep?"

"I can hear Sarge snoring. He must be on the couch or recliner. Drew doesn't snore so I know it's not him."

"So where's Drew?"

"That's the wild card because I don't know where he is. I heard a door being opened and shut, so maybe he left. His pickup was parked by the barn when Big Dog brought me in, so he could have gone to the ranch."

"And if he didn't, we'll deal with him."

"Exactly."

"Okay, I'll use the bathroom, then we'll have to figure a way out of here. We don't have much time."

"Use the bathroom, but don't flush. We don't want anyone upstairs to know we're awake." He turned on a lamp and when she returned, he'd stripped the pillowcase from the pillow and was filling it with water bottles and a couple of granola bars. He opened the box of Cheez-Its and stuffed a handful in his pocket, putting the rest of the box in the pillowcase.

"Hungry?" she whispered.

He shoved some in his mouth. "Yes, but these?" He indicated his pocket as he crunched. "They're for Fido up there."

"His name is Rex. What's your plan?"

He pointed to the door. "See that?"

Her brows flew up. The door was still firmly shut, but the pins had been pried out. She winced at the throbbing pain reminding her that the wound on her forehead was nowhere near healed. "How'd you get the pins out of the hinges?" she whispered.

He pulled the screwdriver from his waistband, tipping his head next to hers when he handed it to her. With their heads together they talked in low tones. "Here's your weapon back. Took time to work the pins out with that and not make a lot of noise, but the door's only recently been installed so the hinges are well oiled. They slipped out fairly easily, considering. We should be able to slide the door out, even with the deadbolt."

Ellie nodded, mind leaping ahead. "So our plan is to get out of the house as quickly and quietly as possible and not engage. If we have to overpower Sarge, we do it, but with Drew's location unknown, there's a risk of alerting him. Problem for us is Sarge likely has guns stashed around the house. I saw an AR in a corner of the living room, and two rifles on a rack over the fireplace. There were weapons in the van. He has at least two handguns, one of them mine. He could have guns under the couch, in drawers, under the cushions. He could sleep wearing his holster. There's no telling."

Sam nodded. "It'll help if the dog is outside. If he's inside, he could sound the alarm as soon as we go up those stairs. I hope he likes Cheez-Its."

"There's the front door and a sliding glass door by the table, plus the kitchen door. If Sarge is in the front room, the kitchen door will be the best option."

"Okay. Did you see where the barn is when you came in?" At her nod, he continued. "There's a big oak behind it. We get out and if we get separated, we meet there. From there, we're heading to Rock Creek Ranch."

"Can you get there from here in the dark?"

"It's a hike, but yeah, I can get us there. And dawn isn't far off."

He grasped the front of her coat and tugged her toward him.

"Sam, I can't—"

"Shh, I know. We need to talk, but later." He dipped his head and then his lips were on hers in a kiss that warmed her all the way through. They were both breathing more heavily when he stepped back. "We stick together and we'll get through this."

Chapter Twenty

Ellie crept up the stairs, Sam behind her. The door to the basement now leaned against a wall. It had been surprisingly easy to remove, and since it was an internal, hollow-core door, it hadn't been all that heavy. The door at the top of the stairs was closed. The knob turned easily in her hand and she pushed the door open a half foot. The sound of snoring, much like a sputtering engine, filled the air. Sam's hand at her waist tightened and she turned her head as he reached the top step beside her.

"I'll go first." Even with his mouth close to her ear, the words were barely audible.

She shook her head. "I'm the marshal, I go first."

After a long pause, he gave a brief nod.

Pushing the door wider, she stepped into the room, standing frozen as she took in details. Dim light emanated from the kitchen, enough that she could see that Sarge lay in a fully extended recliner. From what she could tell, he didn't have a gun on his lap. That was something.

She didn't see Drew. Given the animosity between the two men, she didn't think he'd stayed the night in Sarge's home. A movement on the rug in front of Sarge's chair had her stomach sinking. Rex raised his head, dark eyes gleaming. He stood, head lowered, and padded toward her across the carpeted floor. Ellie took it as a win that he wasn't growling.

She reached out a hand to Sam. "Cheez-Its."

He filled her hand and she bent forward to hold one out. Rex's gaze moved from the Cheez-It to her face, then back.

Sam whispered in her ear. "We go for the kitchen door."

She nodded and tossed a couple Cheez-Its in front of the dog. He stared at them, seeming to weigh his options, then gobbled them up.

She angled herself so she was facing the dog, backed a few steps toward the kitchen, and threw down more crackers. Sam must have figured out her plan because he moved behind her, hand gripping the back of her coat as he guided her backward toward the kitchen. Every couple feet she tossed crackers. And so they went, the dog following them as they moved toward the kitchen and escape.

Grateful for the single low-wattage bulb over the stove that offered enough light to see where they were going, she stepped inside the kitchen. Though her nerves were stretched tight, she thought they might make it. Then the snoring stopped. They both froze.

Sarge gave a phlegmy cough, and his chair creaked. She controlled her breathing, willing back the panic that urged her to bolt for the door. From where she was, she couldn't see into the living room.

An electric whirr sounded overly loud and Sam's grip tightened on her coat. She knew that sound. The footrest of the recliner was being lowered as the back was brought up. Rex's gaze remained fixed on the crackers in her hand. The floor creaked and she straightened, waiting for the moment when Sarge would come around the corner and find them. But then another light came on, this one in the hall, followed by a shuffling of feet, and then the unmistakable sound of pee hitting water in the toilet. A minute later there was a flush and more shuffling footsteps. The chair creaked again, followed by the whirring sound. Giving a mental *ew* because Sarge hadn't washed his hands, Ellie reached back for more Cheez-Its. So quietly she could hardly make out the words, Sam whispered, "That's the last from my pocket."

Several agonizing minutes later while she was dropping crackers one at a time, the snoring restarted. Ellie was never so happy to hear someone snoring in her life. She and Sam continued their painstaking trek across the kitchen. After swallowing the last cracker, Rex turned his head, ears perked, with an expression that said *Where's the Cheez-Its?* his gaze shifting to Sam when he slid back the deadbolt and turned the knob. A cold breeze came through the opening as Sam stepped outside. He kept his hand on her coat and Ellie eased out after him. Sudden furious barking erupted as Rex launched himself against the door. Ellie reeled backward to be caught by strong arms. Rex had done them a favor by slamming shut the door so he couldn't come after them.

Sam released her and grabbed her hand, yanking her after him. "Run!"

They raced around the house. A door slammed and Rex's barking shot up in volume, and that told her he was outside.

"Go! I'm dumping the Cheez-Its from the bag to distract the dog." Sam must have detected her hesitation because he snapped out, "Run, I'll be right behind you."

She ran. It was near impossible to see more than shadows overlaying shadows, the only light coming from a fixture attached to one corner of the barn and the pale glow of a crescent moon.

The storm had cleared leaving a star-strewn sky. The grass underfoot was wet and the patches of bare ground muddy. Ellie moved as swiftly as she could. The front yard was an obstacle course that would be a challenge in daylight. In the dark it was a nightmare.

She hit mud and her feet slid from under her. She regained her footing only to trip over something half buried in the dirt. She bit back a howl of pain when what felt like a knife sliced through her jeans and into her knee. Forcing herself to block out the pain, she struggled to her feet. She couldn't hear Sam and could only trust that he was behind her. She pressed ahead, limping, her goal the tree on the far side of the barn. Even if the crackers slowed him down, if Rex wasn't leashed he'd be after them in seconds and the meetup spot wouldn't be safe.

Straining to hear over the thundering of her heart, she raced through the night, the pain in her knee excruciating. The barn lay up ahead. She'd circle the structure to the left to stay out of the light, hoping that as her eyes adjusted she'd be able to see well enough not to run into a fence or tractor or whatever else could be around.

In the pitch-black darkness at the side of the barn, she moved as quickly as she could, keeping her hands in front of her. She stumbled into a fence built against the corner. With a hand on the metal railing, she loped along as it turned back toward the barn and she realized it was some sort of corral. She paused, listening. A noise, like clothing rustling, had her reaching for the screwdriver. She patted her hip where it should have been, heart sinking when she realized she must have lost it when she'd tripped.

She kept still, waiting for Sam. She didn't dare call out to him. Then a distinctive sound had her blood turning to ice—the metal on metal clank of a round being chambered into the barrel of a gun.

"Well, well, isn't this a surprise. No sudden moves, now. I wouldn't want to shoot you before it's time."

Drew. Ellie swallowed. She thought she heard the faint thudding of someone running, maybe Sam trying to reach their rendezvous point. Rex continued barking, but nearer the house. She prayed Drew hadn't heard the running footfalls. Using the darkness, she shifted into the shadows.

"Hold it right there." A light flared and she blinked as Drew shined a flashlight in her eyes.

"Let me go. Don't make what you've done worse than it already is." Drew was a dark form in front of an outline of what must be a back door to the barn.

"You think you can talk your way out of this, sister? Not going to work. We'll take a little walk back up to the house so Sarge can see who takes care of things when he fucks up. The asshole thought there was no way anyone could break out of that room, but now it's up to me to catch the escaped prisoner."

Ellie's knee throbbed and she could feel blood soaking into her jeans. At least if Sam had escaped he'd be safe, and she'd only have to worry about getting herself free. The thought of Sam came with a strong yearning. When she was with him, she felt like somehow they'd come out of this mess alive. Without him beside her that optimism faded, but she refused to give in to the despair.

Drew's tone changed. "It'd be even better if I bring you back with Sam. Where's that brother of mine?"

"I don't know."

"Bullshit. Tell me where he is, sister. Do that and I'll try to get them to go easy on you." His attention caught on her leg and he lit it with the flashlight. "Fuck, you're bleeding pretty bad. Come on up to the house and we'll take care of it, but first tell me where Sam is."

"I really don't know. I tripped and we got separated."

He prodded her with the muzzle of his gun into walking in front of him. "Ha. He wouldn't leave you behind. Maybe Sarge caught him." The beam of his light shone on the ground in front of her.

"Who's the 'them' you mentioned? I only know Sarge."

"Asshole Sarge and Big Dog. Not going to lie, they're planning on killing you both. I don't much like that, but I get why they want it done. It'll send a message to the courts not to try to take our guns, plus show that we'll fight for our rights. We'll be heroes like Jesse and Frank James. Bet we'll have people falling over themselves to join our cause."

Ellie never got what made the robber and murderer Jesse James heroic but wasn't going to argue the point. "Murder is a lot more serious than simple kidnapping, Drew. You know all hell will break loose if you kill a federal judge or his girlfriend. Anything happens to us, this entire state will be crawling with law enforcement looking for you. And you will get caught. Things will be better for you if you let me go."

He shook his head. "You should never have gotten with my brother. He never heeded the warnings and pulled you into his mess, so this is on him. If he'd reversed his ruling and let Bannister out of jail, none of this would have happened. But fucking Judge Creed has no problem trampling all over folks' Constitutional rights."

They paused under the light at the barn. Drew's truck was in the shadows. Rex was still barking, but near the house. Sarge shouted something. Walking slower to stall, anything to give herself more time, she said, "He loves you, you know. Sam told me about you and your mom. He loved her, too."

"Don't you talk about my mother."

"I'm not talking about her, I'm talking about Sam. He believes in you, believes you can be the man your mother hoped you would be."

"Don't you fucking talk about my mother." His voice cracked and he shoved her forward.

"Sam said she made the ranch a home. That she loved you, and she even loved him. Would she be proud of you now, Drew?"

An explosion of barking and wild shouts erupted from behind the house, followed by the sharp crack of a gunshot splitting the air. Ellie slapped a hand over her mouth to stifle a scream.

Sam!

Blood drained from her head and her vision grayed. Had he been caught? She'd thought he'd run past the barn, but then what had Sarge shot at? Drew grabbed her arm and pulled her up the driveway to where light from the house illuminated the front yard. Rex bulleted from the back, racing past them at the same moment a repulsive, sulfurous odor assailed her nostrils.

"Goddamned dog!"

Drew clicked off the flashlight and pulled his coat over his nose. "He can't ever leave a skunk alone. You'd think he'd learn after he's been sprayed a couple times. Hope Sarge killed the damn thing."

Sarge charged around the side of the house, bringing the smell with him. Rex rolled on the ground, rubbing his face in the grass.

Drew took a hasty step back when Sarge stopped beside him, pistol in hand. "God, you reek as bad as the dog."

Sarge scowled. "Damned dog can't leave the fucking skunk alone. Thought he'd found our prisoners, but no, he had a skunk cornered by the woodpile. Sprayed him right between his eyes, then he tried to rub it off on me."

Seeing the men and dog occupied, Ellie again moved back a step to the edge of the light.

"You shoot the skunk?"

"Missed it. Damn thing got away, but now I've got a dog that stinks to high heaven and I'll have to burn these jeans. Damn dog can stay outside until he stops stinking. I can't be giving him a tomato juice bath every time he gets stupid."

The sound of a car engine coming up the road rumbled in the distance. She eased back one more step. Drew spotted her and she could have growled in frustration when he motioned her forward with a wave of the gun.

"I caught one of the prisoners you let escape. Good thing I stayed in the barn or she'd be gone. Guess your basement wasn't as secure as you made out it was."

"How was I to know they'd pry the door off its hinges? Now where's Creed, or did you let him get away, too?"

"Let him get away? You let him get away, asshole, not me. I got her, didn't I? You're the dumbass who let them escape."

"You think you're all that? Then go ahead and put a bullet through her head, dickwad. Those are our orders. Once she's dead, we'll go after Creed."

"You think I won't do it? You think you're the only one who can do the real business? After this, you'll give me some goddamn respect and call me Lobo."

"You'll always be dickwad."

Drew raised his arm, the barrel of the gun leveled at Ellie's head.

Ellie couldn't take her eyes off the dark hole in the muzzle of the pistol. She heard a vehicle roar around the bend and Drew lowered the gun. "We'll see what Big Dog says."

Ellie wheezed out a pent-up breath as a white truck with dual wheels in the back came to a hard stop under the circle of light by the barn. It struck her that the night wasn't quite as dark. A faint pink glow was lightening the eastern sky.

She breathed deep to slow her racing heart. Both men holstered their weapons, making her wonder who had arrived that elicited that kind of response.

There was a scuffle by the newcomer's truck.

"What the hell's going on over there?" Drew craned his head to see.

"It's got to be Creed," Sarge groused. "Big Dog will get him. We'll get our asses chewed that we let them escape."

"*You* let them get away, not me."

"All Big Dog will care about is that they escaped."

"Shit." Drew started shifting back and forth like he was nervous. "You think he needs help?"

Sarge gestured. "Does it look like he needs help?" Sam was walking toward them, a tall man behind him looming large.

As they neared the light, Ellie could see that the man following Sam wore an old-fashioned holster slung low on his thigh, the pearl grip of a revolver gleaming in the light from the house, a black cowboy hat tipped forward over his brow. He shoved Sam ahead of him.

Sam approached where she was standing, his gaze traveling over her, eyes blazing. He stopped in front of her. "You okay?"

At her nod, he mouthed the word "fight."

Fight? Against three men with guns? The odds weren't good, but they were worse if they did nothing. And taking the offensive would be unexpected and could catch their captors off guard. She gave an imperceptible nod.

Their adversaries clearly didn't expect the attack. Sam rotated on the balls of his feet, swinging up and landing a punch that caught Drew square in the face. He went down like a puppet with its strings cut.

The big man reached for his weapon, but Sam went in low, tackling him to the ground in a tangle of limbs that sent the cowboy hat flying. Ellie turned on Sarge, leading with a roundhouse kick as he went for his gun. The force of her kick spun him around, but when he came up, he had his gun in his hand. For the second time in only minutes, she found herself staring into the muzzle of a gun pointed at her head.

"Good choice," he said as she froze. "Creed," he barked, "give it up."

Sam gave no indication of having heard. Straddling the other man, he used an elbow to crack him across his cheekbone, ducked to avoid a swinging fist, and gave a short jab to the nose.

Sarge raised the gun and shot a bullet into the air, then brought it back down again to level on Ellie. Sam leapt to his feet, fists clenched.

"Time to decide if your girlfriend lives another ten seconds, Creed."

Sam's gaze whipped from Ellie to Sarge.

"Easy. No need to be any more stupid than you've already been." Sarge's voice was utterly cool as the other men breathed heavily. Drew rolled onto to all fours and slowly pushed himself to standing.

"You fucking assholes." The big man had gained his feet, wiping blood from his nose with his sleeve. He spoke with a deep voice rife with disdain. "Lower the gun, Sarge."

Sarge hesitated, then did as he was told. The man picked up his hat, swatting it against his leg. When he locked his gaze on hers, Ellie felt like a trapdoor had dropped from beneath her.

Chapter Twenty-One

"You fucking assholes," Richard Jameson repeated. "You kidnapped a Deputy US Marshal."

"What the hell are you talking about?" Sarge snapped. "This is Creed's fiancée."

"I doubt that. This woman is a Deputy US Marshal."

"A marshal?"

Sarge turned to her but Ellie couldn't take her gaze off her father. Sam moved to her side.

She'd imagined this moment so many times. Would he know her? Would she recognize him? Would she feel anger? Betrayal? Love? Now she knew.

Resentment boiled over and her vision hazed red. She lunged forward, pulled back her fist, and rammed it into his belly. His breath wheezed as he doubled over. "That's for Mom, you bastard," she snarled. She pulled back a leg to kick him, but Sam grabbed her arms and yanked her back.

"What is she talking about?" Sarge's gaze tracked from Ellie to her father.

Jameson straightened. There was a stoop to his shoulders that reminded her he was close to seventy years old. "Sarge, meet my daughter, Deputy US Marshal Eleanor Jameson."

"Your daughter? What the hell is this about?"

"God damnit." Drew turned on Sarge. "I told you she was undercover, but you wouldn't listen."

Sarge ignored Drew. "How the fuck were we supposed to know your daughter is Creed's girlfriend, and that she's a US Marshal?"

Sarge's voice sounded tinny in her ears as Ellie wrapped her arms around her middle to quiet the sharp tremors shaking her body. Memories of her mother's strength in the face of Richard Jameson's abandonment and betrayal had her bearing down on the emotional pain. This was not the time to sort out the destructive feelings her father elicited. Survival for her and Sam was paramount.

Jameson's gaze finally left Ellie as he replied to Sarge. "By using your fucking brains, that's how you know. And if she's here, you can bet her brothers aren't far off."

"Her brothers?"

"Both US Marshals."

"Shit. We're fucked. Do you think you could have shared this with us before we grabbed your kid?"

Jameson disregarded Sarge's irritation, flicking a glance at Sam, who had positioned himself beside her before Jameson returned his attention to Ellie. "Well, daughter, it's been a long time."

This man was not the father she remembered. She'd studied images of him taken by security cameras, but in those he'd been conscious of surveillance and had taken care to obscure his identity.

They'd never been clear enough for her to make out the details she observed now. A mane of white had replaced his once-dark hair, and his face held deep grooves on either side of his mouth. Despite the years that had aged him, he was still striking, though the warm blue eyes of her memory were no longer full of light. Instead, they looked glacially cold.

Nothing of the man of towering strength who would hold his daughter high above his head so she could pretend to fly was evident in the old man who stood before her now.

"A long time since you abandoned your family."

He shrugged. "Regrettable, but it had to be done." Time had changed his voice, making it gravelly and coarse. "Your mother would never have followed me in the life I wanted, and I didn't want to disrupt the lives of my children."

"You're a coward and a liar. You didn't care about Mom, and you didn't care about us kids. Let's get something straight, you're not my father. Archer Bollinger is my father."

"God, I can't believe Margaret married that asshole. He hounded me for years." Disdain laced his words. "But understand this, daughter, I was there when you were born and I raised you until you were nearly grown. It's my blood that's running through your veins. That makes me your father."

Ellie shook her head and let contempt ring from her voice. "That makes you a sperm donor who hung around too long."

Jameson's fists clenched, and Ellie thought he'd strike her. Then his face closed and he settled his hat on his head.

"Doesn't matter. These guys made a monumental screwup and now I've got to deal with it." He turned to Sarge. "You ready?"

"We're going through with it?" Sarge raised his brows.

"Why wouldn't we? We've got to take care of these two and get out of here. I told you she's a marshal. Her brothers are marshals. They won't be far behind her."

Any thought that her father would let her and Sam live evaporated. Richard Jameson had participated in courthouse bombings, but he'd never been involved in cold-blooded murder. But now he was ordering an execution. Hers and Sam's.

Sam wrapped an arm around her and pulled her back against his body, pressing a kiss against her temple. "I'll create a diversion. You run," he murmured the words against her skin.

"No, we stay together."

"No more chances, Creed," Sarge said. "You deserve this."

There was no time for any diversion. Sarge raised his pistol, and Sam shoved Ellie to the ground as a shot ripped through the air.

As she went down, Ellie caught a brief glimpse of Sarge reeling back, the top of his head a bloody mess. Sam landed on her, his hands covering her head. Another shot rang out. Ellie's only thought was to get Sam to safety. She pushed against his weight, pulling on his arm.

They scrambled to their feet, Ellie grasping his hand as she pulled him toward the back of the house. A rapid spate of gunfire erupted behind them. At any moment a bullet could cut either one of them down.

They rounded the corner of the building as a loud blast rent the air and the ground shook. She looked over her shoulder even as she ran. A huge orange fireball erupted into the early morning sky with a roar like thunder.

The gunfire stopped.

They ran past trees bordering the yard, Ellie refusing to let her injured knee slow her down. The next thing she knew she was being pulled behind a wide trunk. Sam backed her against the tree and wrapped his arms around her. With his face bent next to hers, he said, "I don't know what the hell happened other than the propane tank exploded."

190

She nodded and held on to him. They were alive. Beyond everything else that had happened, they'd survived. She tried to sort out the impressions of the past few minutes.

"Sarge is dead," she told Sam. "The first shot took him out."

"Who shot him?"

"I'm not sure. I think the team is here, so it could have been Bella as she's the trained sharpshooter." She paused. "I didn't see what happened to Drew, but with gunfire and an explosion, I don't think it's good."

She pushed against Sam and he loosened his hold. "The shooting's stopped. We wait here until the team comes for us when the scene is clear."

Sam frowned when Ellie stepped away from him, her arms crossed tightly in front of her.

***

She'd called it. Sam figured they waited no more than ten minutes before Seth came around the house. Ellie stepped from behind the tree and called his name. Her brother jogged toward them, not stopping until he'd scooped his sister up in a fierce hug.

"You're safe," he murmured as he held her, eyes closed. After a long minute he released her.

"We're good," Ellie assured him. "Linc, Bella?"

"Fine."

"Seth, Dad was there."

Seth nodded. "We'd gotten into position when he drove up and Sam allowed himself to get taken."

Ellie turned on Sam. "You let yourself get taken?"

"I couldn't protect you if I wasn't with you."

"It was *my* job to protect *you*. You should have stayed safe."

Sam kept his mouth shut.

Seth gave him a speculative look, then asked his sister, "He recognize you?"

She faced her brother. "He did. He knows we're all marshals, and that Mom and Arch are married." Her voice tightened. "He told Sarge to kill Sam and me."

"The fucker. He's beyond redemption, Ellie."

"I know. Any doubts I had are gone."

Seth put an arm across Ellie's shoulders like he still needed reassurance that she was in one piece. Sam wondered how Seth dealt with his sister being in danger on a regular basis. "You can hope he's better than he is, but he'll always disappoint you. He got away."

"What? How?"

"All hell broke loose and he slipped past us, that's how. First shot took out Petrie, the guy who owned this place."

"Sarge. The members of this militia give themselves code names. Dad's is Big Dog." To Sam's ears, Ellie sounded exhausted. He felt tapped out himself. His priority now was to get her checked at a hospital, then he'd be happy if they could go home and shut the door to the world for a week or so. That he saw her with him after her assignment was completed no longer surprised him.

Seth motioned them to follow him. "Let's go. That burning tank makes it too dangerous and too hot to go that way, so we'll go around." Seth led them in a wide circle, avoiding the house. They tramped along until they came to a fence and followed it to the barn. The propane tank continued to burn.

Through the trees Sam saw that fire had spread to a van parked next to the tank. He figured Seth was leading him away from the scene of carnage. He was pretty sure the fire would keep the team from getting to bodies. He asked the question that was at the front of his mind. "Is my brother dead?"

Seth turned to Sam, gaze steady. "I'm sorry, he is."

Sam waited for the wave of emotion. Nothing came except a feeling of numbness.

"Funny thing, though," Seth continued. "That first shot? Bella was sighting through her scope and saw what happened. Drew shot the guy you call Sarge before she could."

"Drew shot Sarge?"

Ellie grasped his hand. "He saved our lives, Sam."

"Or maybe he hated Sarge enough to kill him."

"He saved our lives," Ellie repeated. She turned to her brother. "How did Dad get away?"

"We think Drew was planning to shoot him, too, but Dad shot Drew first." He shook his head. "We were going to take Dad out if we had to, but you and Sam blocked our shot. Once you were out of the way, we waited to see how it played out. Dad started running, shooting at the propane tank. Damn thing went up like a fucking pyrotechnic show. He got to his truck and got away."

"We saw the fireball. There must have been a leak for it to explode like that. I thought I caught the skunky smell of propane when they first brought me here. Hard to know for sure, because Sarge was having trouble with skunks." She paused. "What happened to the dog?"

Seth shrugged. "Don't know. We'll keep an eye out for him."

They arrived at the barn. Richard Jameson's white truck was gone.

"How'd you know we were here?" Ellie's fingers were cold so Sam brought them to his mouth to blow warm air across them. His gaze stayed steady on Seth's when he saw the man give him a considering look.

"Got a call from Ben Montoya. Sam would know more about this than me. His father's the foreman of your ranch?"

Sam nodded. "That's Pete Montoya."

"When you two went missing, Ben went out to your ranch and he and Pete searched Drew's things. They came across evidence pointing to Drew's involvement in the SecAm militia movement and tying him to Petrie as well as to a plan to kidnap Ellie. Lucky for us you'd told Ben that Ellie is a marshal and that he'd met Linc. He contacted us." Seth spared Sam a glance. "You've got some explaining to do about how you ended up their captive as well."

Bella approached them, a rifle with a scope in her hand. She gave Ellie a one-armed hug. "Glad you and Sam are safe, friend."

"Me too," Ellie said.

Sam spoke quietly to Seth. "She's hurt. She's got a head wound, probable concussion, and her leg's bleeding."

Ellie shot him a look of exasperation.

"We've got aid coming," Seth assured him.

The deep wail of a fire truck in the distance and a whumping sound cutting through the air were welcome. In minutes a windstorm kicked up as a helicopter with an official insignia set down like an ungainly insect in a wide section of the driveway.

There was a flurry of activity as officers in law enforcement gear disembarked. Seth took a phone call, pressing a finger in one ear to hear. Sam saw a woman with a red cross stitched as part of her shoulder patch and waved her over. She introduced herself and followed him to where Ellie had hobbled to an upturned log to sit with her injured leg straight out in front of her.

"Ellie, this is Sue Delgado, she's a paramedic with the county."

He had to give Ellie credit because she didn't automatically claim to be fine, as was her usual response. "She has a head injury and possible concussion."

"We'll check that out," Delgado assured him, not taking her eyes off her patient.

"Her leg is bleeding."

Delgado nodded.

"She needs to go to the hospital."

"That's why she's being checked out." The paramedic grinned at Ellie. "Does he always hover like this?"

"Pretty much," Ellie grumbled.

"Aw. He cares."

Delgado opened her medical kit and took out a stethoscope. Linc came over to check on his sister, so when Seth beckoned, Sam figured Ellie was taken care of for the moment and went to see what Seth wanted.

The following hour passed in a blur. More official vehicles arrived. An APB was issued for Richard Jameson, though Seth said the effort would likely be fruitless because the fugitive was a ghost adept at disappearing.

Sam glanced in Ellie's direction and found that Delgado had cut off the leg of her jeans and was wrapping her knee. The propane fire finally burnt itself out, and the coroner took possession of the bodies, both charred beyond recognition. Sam watched as they were placed in black bags and thought of Drew's wasted life. His brother had made his choices, but that didn't make Sam feel any less guilty.

The goal that had been driving him for the past twenty-four hours of keeping Ellie alive had been achieved. Exhaustion was biting at his heels, but he needed to push through until he got Ellie home. Remembering the moment Sarge had raised his gun caused him to break out in a cold sweat.

He borrowed Bella's phone to call Pete and let him know about Drew, and that Pete should expect a team of US Marshals at the ranch later that afternoon to take possession of anything belonging to Drew they thought was relevant.

Sam stepped out of the house with Ellie's brothers. He'd shown the marshals the basement where he and Ellie had been held captive.

Seth studied Sam, brows pulled low over his eyes. "Want to explain how you found Richard Jameson and got him to bring you here? We've been after him for years."

"First, understand that I didn't know who he was. He introduced himself as Big Dog. Then I did what I thought I had to do to protect Ellie."

"Given that she's my sister, I appreciate that. But her job was to protect you, Judge, and what you did put your life in danger."

Sam responded, gaze steady on Seth's. "I won't have her sacrificed to keep me safe. Ever."

"Why don't you tell us what happened?" Bella asked. Sam figured she was trying to defuse the tension.

They were owed an explanation so he tried to organize what had happened in his head, wishing he had a quart-size mug of coffee.

"Okay. Yesterday morning I went home because I couldn't reach Ellie. I'd barely gotten in the house when a text came in of Ellie in cuffs." He remembered how a jagged hole had opened in his gut when he'd seen that image. "There was a warning not to call law enforcement if I wanted to keep her alive. I got a call from a different number belonging to a man calling himself Big Dog. He arranged a meeting, said if I didn't come alone, my fiancée was as good as dead. I met him in the parking lot of a closed business. He told me if their captive was going to survive—I don't think he knew her name—I had to reverse the ruling on Frank Bannister so he would be released, and make other statements from the bench that would help his cause. I refused."

Sam rolled his shoulders. "We, ah, ended up fighting. That made him mad enough that he decided to go for a bigger impact by killing a federal judge. I got the feeling he didn't really care about Bannister. I was counting on him bringing me to where they were holding Ellie. It was a risk, but it worked out."

Seth shook his head. "You should have called us. We could have done this without jeopardizing your life, or Ellie's."

"Your primary goal is to protect me, the federal judge. My primary goal was to protect Ellie any way I could. If I'd called you, you could have fucked it up and she'd have ended up hurt worse than she already was. Or dead. I wasn't willing to risk that."

"Your way almost ended up with both of you dead."

"Luckily, it didn't."

After a long, considering look, Seth finally nodded.

"What my brother means is thanks for helping keep our sister alive." Linc clamped a hand on Sam's shoulder.

"Yeah, that." Seth's expression didn't change. "Do we need to talk?"

Though he guessed what the Chief Deputy was getting at, Sam wouldn't make it easy on him. "About?"

"About you and my sister and your fake engagement."

Bella rolled her eyes. "If you value your life you won't do this. You know Ellie will be unhappy."

"I'm responsible for her."

Sam figured it was a good time to keep his mouth shut. Maybe Seth would forget about "the talk," but somehow Sam knew he'd come back to it. The rotors of the helicopter began spinning, picking up speed.

"As a marshal, maybe," Bella insisted, "but definitely not as a bossy big brother."

"You saw what kind of a dad we have, so it falls to me."

The noise from the helicopter increased until it took off with a roar of sound. Sam looked around and felt a clutch of panic.

"Where's Ellie?"

"On the chopper," Bella said. "That's what I came to tell you. The paramedic thinks Ellie has a concussion, and wants her knee stitched at the hospital."

"What the fuck? She can't go by herself. She needs me with her." Sam stared at the retreating helicopter and felt like half of him had gone with it.

Linc clamped a hand on his shoulder and grinned at the others. "See those little hearts circling his head? I think that's a definite yes to 'the talk.' This boy's got it bad."

Chapter Twenty-Two

Ellie stirred, pain from her throbbing knee pulling her out of sleep. She blinked several times as awareness returned. She'd been flown to the hospital in Pendleton, lost the argument about being admitted overnight, and had finally been able to fall asleep sometime around midnight.

The muted glow of early morning shone around the blinds over the window, casting enough light to allow her to see the man sprawled in a chair beside her bed. Sam had arrived late in the evening and she had to admit that when she'd heard his voice, her anxiety dissipated. It was like she knew on a subconscious level that if Sam was there, she was safe.

Though she'd been ready to kick him out when he'd insisted that the doctor admit her after he'd diagnosed her concussion. The doctor had agreed with Sam's point that since the blow to her head wasn't the first incident affecting her brain in a matter of weeks, she needed observation.

Now, with long legs stretched in front of him and wrapped in a too-thin, too-short blanket, he hardly looked comfortable. Dark lashes resting against high cheekbones made her wonder why guys always scored long, thick eyelashes.

Tousled hair falling over his forehead would've given him a boyish look but for the bruising around his eye and the dark whiskers shadowing his jaw.

He had to be exhausted to be able to sleep in that position.

There were so many things about him she admired—his sharp intelligence, his sly humor, his basic decency—things that she would commend in many people, but in Sam they were on top of something more, something that had her feeling like she was dangling over a cliff by her fingertips. If she loosened that grip by even one finger, she'd free-fall into love with him, and that scared her as nothing in the past few days had.

Her feelings for him weren't exactly straightforward, because thrown into the mix was the knowledge that while he might care for her, caring was a long way from love. Their fake engagement had led to forced proximity, which by its nature amplified feelings that would wane as life got back to normal.

She wished Sam didn't feel responsible for her. And she wished even more that he respected her ability to do her job.

She shifted onto her back, trying to stifle a groan at the soreness in her knee. She wanted to use the toilet, brush her teeth, and, most importantly of all, take a shower and wash her hair.

Sam stirred and sat up. "Hey, you're awake. What time is it?"

She glanced at the clock on the wall. "Just after seven."

He tossed off the blanket and rose to his feet to stand at the side of the bed.

"How are you feeling?"

"Better. Headache is gone." She used a button to raise the head of the bed. "Would you help me get up?"

"I'll call the nurse."

"Fine, but while we're waiting, I want you to help me to the bathroom."

He pressed the call button as she pushed herself upright. "Hang on," he said. He lowered the side rail. "I'll carry you."

"No, you won't carry me. It's not like I have a joint injury and have to keep weight off my knee." He offered his hand and, holding on to him, she tested her weight on her leg. "See, I'm good. There's no additional pain."

"You're being stubborn. Let me carry you."

"No, I can make it." She walked with him to the bathroom, and when she got there, shut the door firmly lest he decide she needed even more help.

She returned to the room as Bella walked in carrying several bags.

"You found my purse? Thank you."

"And your phone, so you're welcome." Bella handed it to her, plus a plastic bag, before shrugging a daypack off her shoulder. She dug in her pocket to hand Sam his phone.

"Cool, thanks." Sam immediately began thumbing through messages.

"I brought a change of clothes and some toiletries you might need." Bella emptied rolled clothes from the daypack. "The pants and shirt are Seth's. They'll be too big but will fit better than mine or Linc's would."

"Whatever you brought is better than a hospital gown, so thank you again." Ellie opened the plastic bag to find a toothbrush and toothpaste, hair products in small bottles, and hand lotion. "This is wonderful. You're a lifesaver."

"How are you feeling?"

"Head's good, knee hurts." She picked up the bags. "I'll feel even better after a shower." Ignoring Sam's scowl, she made her way back to the bathroom.

When she got out, Bella had gone. Sam had pulled up the window blind to allow in the morning light, and stood with his back to the room, staring through the glass.

He turned when he heard her. "Bella said she'll be back later with your brothers and food."

"Okay." She studied Sam's expression, wondering if there was something going on with him.

"The nurse said he'd be back to change the bandages on your knee and forehead. He didn't sound happy that you were getting them wet."

She shrugged. "I hadn't had a shower in two days. Feeling clean will help me to get better."

She'd rolled the waistband on Seth's flannel pants, and the sweatshirt came well past her hips, but she felt infinitely better out of the hospital gown. She started to ease onto the bed when Sam strode over.

"Jesus, will you wait a minute? I'll help you."

"I'm fine, Sam. I'm not an invalid."

"Not unless being pigheaded makes you an invalid." He watched her with an eagle eye, clearly unhappy that he couldn't pick her up and arrange her on the bed himself. Once she was settled, he took her hand in both of his, rubbing his thumb over the engagement ring she still wore.

She stared at their joined hands. "Thanks for being here. You must have spent a miserable night on that chair."

"I couldn't leave you."

Her heart seemed to grow in her chest. "I'm glad you didn't."

He brushed a kiss over her knuckles. "Ellie, I want—"

Whatever Sam had been about to say was cut off when the door swished open. Ben came into the room, his white lab coat stitched with "Benjamin Montoya, MD." He grinned as Sam let go of her hand. "You're doing the engaged act really well."

Sam ignored the comment. "Thanks for coming."

"Glad you're both okay, brother." Ben stood at the foot of the bed, his dark gaze traveling over her. "How's the pain, Ellie?"

"The headache is better, but my knee hurts. A lot."

He consulted his iPad before saying, "Mind if I have a look?"

She shook her head, and he pulled back the sheet. "Didn't like the hospital duds, I see."

"Yup."

Sam stood on the other side of the bed. "She took a shower and got the bandages wet."

"Then we'll take those off." Ben pushed up her pant leg to reveal the damp bandage and peeled the tape from around her knee. "Someone got in their sewing practice, I see. Twelve stitches is impressive. It looks healthy."

"Is there permanent damage?" Sam asked.

Ben shook his head. "No. It should heal pretty quickly."

He followed the same process with the wound on her forehead and the old injuries on her back and behind her ear. "Everything looks good, you're healing well."

"Great, when will I be released?"

"Soon. You'll need to let the nurse replace the bandages and give you care instructions. Your chart says you're due for your pain meds. Once that's done, release will be dependent on what your convalescence arrangements are."

"She's coming home with me."

Ellie frowned at Sam. "Why? Sarge was sending the threats and he's dead. My assignment is done."

"Your assignment is done because that concussion has bought you a two-week off-work order, with full rest for at least one. That means no screen time, phone included," Ben warned. "We're not releasing you until we know you'll be looked after."

"She's coming home with me," Sam repeated. "I'll look after her."

"You don't need to do that. They'll make room for me at Marshal Central."

Sam was already shaking his head. "You're coming home with me."

Ben grinned at his friend. "You two work it out. Staff will check back to see what you decide." He turned to go, saying to Ellie, "I'll let your nurse know you're ready for the pain meds."

Sam walked out with Ben, returning minutes later with the nurse, who introduced himself as Kai. He reapplied the bandages and handed Ellie pain pills to swallow. Once he'd left, Sam dragged the chair he'd slept in closer to the bed and collapsed onto it. Dark circles shadowed his eyes.

"You should go home and get some sleep. You look exhausted."

"I am exhausted."

He picked up her hand through the bed rails, his thumb once again rubbing the engagement ring. "We need to talk, Ellie."

"That sounds ominous."

"Not ominous, but we need to talk."

It suddenly hit her, his restlessness, the way he kept touching the ring.

"Oh, right, the ring." She pulled her hand from his and began working it off her finger.

"What are you doing?"

"Giving you back your ring."

"Why? You don't need to do that."

"Of course I do. You must want it back. It was a prop. A beautiful prop, but not mine." She ignored the hollow feeling in the pit of her stomach and held the ring out to him.

His gaze locked on hers but she couldn't read his expression. With a scowl, he took the ring. "Right."

He tucked it into his pocket as the door swished open, this time admitting three US Marshals carrying Styrofoam take-out containers and a caddy with hot drinks. Sam stood and moved to lean against a wall, arms crossed over his chest. He took a coffee Bella handed him, closing his eyes as he took a sip. Linc commandeered chairs from somewhere, bringing them in to arrange around her bed as food was passed out.

The next time she looked, Sam was gone.

A shower, food, coffee, pain meds, Ellie should be feeling better, but instead her mood deflated like a popped balloon. So that was that. Her assignment was done, her ring finger bare. And somehow she'd ended up with a broken heart.

She thought she was hiding her feelings well enough until Bella raised a brow that Ellie read as *What's wrong?* She shook her head, swallowing against the lump in her throat, and forced herself to pay attention. She was a Deputy US Marshal, and she would do her job.

After answering the general questions about her welfare and eating most of her breakfast burrito, she asked Seth, "What happened? Did you get Dad?"

Seth dumped the container from his breakfast in the trash before answering, anger tightening his features. "No sign of him. Marshals from Portland are fanning out, visiting all known contacts in the area. If he's still here, they'll find him."

"Except he won't be anywhere around here."

Seth nodded. "Agreed. He'll be long gone."

"On the positive side, we've broken SecAm," Linc said. "We have possession of Sarge's computers and Drew's. If any members of the group are involved in the crimes Sarge committed, we'll have the evidence to prosecute them."

Linc shook his head. "Drew was using his last name as his password. We've already accessed his email account and have proof Sarge was sending the threats to Sam. Sarge was Freedom Defender. There were also details of the plan to target Sam while he was out running. Sarge wanted Drew to drive the truck, but when he refused, Sarge did it himself. Lucky for all of us, he failed."

Linc sipped his coffee. "Oh, one more thing. We found the dog. Smelled godawful, but we took him over to Rock Creek Ranch. The old guy, Pete Montoya, said they'd get him cleaned up and keep him."

"Oh, that's good." Ellie was glad the dog hadn't been left to fend for itself. "Thanks."

"We also discovered that problems at Rock Creek Ranch were Drew's doing," Seth added. "We found an email where Drew said ranches being harassed, particularly by environmentalists, would bring calls from the community for stronger protections of gun rights."

"And our father is part of all this, including being a member of SecAm." Ellie didn't pose it as a question.

Seth rubbed a hand over the scruff of his beard. "He is. From what we can see so far, he doesn't get his hands dirty. He posts ideological diatribes online that get their followers stirred up, then he leaves them to take illegal actions that might get them thrown in jail."

"We found C-four in Sarge's barn," Bella added. "Turns out he had explosives training in the military. It appears he's the one who planted it on Sam's car."

"To what degree was Drew involved?" Ellie asked. Whatever Drew had done, hopefully knowing that in the end he'd acted to protect his brother would soften Sam's feelings of betrayal.

"Only peripherally until he kidnapped you," Seth said.

"What about the flashbang thrown into Sam's house, and whoever drove through the backyard?"

"Linc's been working on that." Seth motioned to his brother. "Want to explain?"

"We're waiting on a warrant to search the vehicle and electronic equipment of nineteen-year-old Jeremy Finster."

"*Jeremy* Finster? Gordon's son?"

"Yeah. We've questioned both father and son. Gordon says his son doesn't belong to any militia groups because he knows it would jeopardize dad's job. But while he may not have joined any militia groups, we have evidence Jeremy participated in online forums advocating anti-government action to protect gun rights. We think he took it a step farther when he targeted you."

"How'd you figure out it was the son?"

"Gordon was having car trouble and borrowed his son's truck to drive to work. Same make, model, and color as in the video. We took it from there."

Kai opened the door, entering the room carrying a sheaf of papers. "I've got your discharge orders. We'll process them once I know where you'll go for convalescence." He raised his eyebrows in question.

Bella answered the Ellie. "She'll either be with us or with her fiancé, Sam. She will be looked after."

"Great. Here's a copy of her care instructions."

"Sam's not my fiancé," Ellie muttered after Kai left.

Linc was busy texting on his phone but looked up. "Tell him that. Are we ready to pack up?"

Feeling miserable, Ellie kept her unhappiness to herself as she took her seat in a wheelchair. Linc set her purse on her lap, slinging the other bags over his shoulder. "Seth and I will get the car."

The female attendant took the push handles with a sigh as the men walked out the door. "Those two? They're what my grandma would call a long, cool drink of water."

"Ha," Ellie said. "Don't let them hear you say that. It'll go to their heads."

Bella walked beside the wheelchair as they made their way through the maze of hallways. Once outside in the bright midday sunshine, Bella sat on a bench next to Ellie's wheelchair to wait for her brothers.

"I noticed you aren't wearing your engagement ring," her friend said. "Want to tell me about it?"

"It wasn't my engagement ring, and Sam broke up with me." Ellie knew that didn't make a lot of sense.

"He asked for the ring back?"

"Well, no. But he acted like he wanted it back. And we're not engaged, so of course he should have it back."

"Did you ask him? Never mind," Bella said. "I wish I'd taken a picture of that look on his face when you were flying off in the helicopter without him."

Ellie glanced at the attendant, then at Bella. "It was all fake, you know that."

"It may have started out that way, friend, but things changed for him."

The Land Cruiser pulled into the patient loading area and Sam stepped out.

"See what I mean? He's not done with you," Bella murmured with a grin.

The attendant fluttered a hand over her chest as Sam strode over. "Another one? You're one lucky lady, let me tell you."

Chapter Twenty-Three

"Ready to go?" Sam's gaze traveled over her.

"Why'd you leave?"

"I had to get my car. Ready?" he repeated.

"My brothers are taking me to Marshal Central."

"Bella can come with us. I texted Linc that I was on my way to get you. Something came up they need to take care of, so this works out."

Bella was busy texting as Ellie settled in the front passenger seat and Sam put her bags in the back. Bella stepped away from the vehicle as Ellie waved good-bye to the attendant.

Ellie narrowed her gaze. "Aren't you getting in?"

Bella shook her head, smiling brightly. "Linc says they'll pick me up, so you two can go ahead."

"We've been set up," Ellie said as Sam drove away from the hospital.

"How so?"

"You're kidding, right?"

He gave her a quizzical look.

"Never mind." They drove through town, and Ellie thought Sam was steering more carefully than usual.

"What are you doing?"

His brow furrowed. "Driving."

"You're driving like a bump in the road will make me break."

He increased the speed by maybe five miles per hour.

"You missed the street to Marshal Central."

He turned onto his own street. "No, I didn't. It makes more sense for you to stay with me. There's plenty of room, and your things are there."

She crossed her arms in front of her. "But you no longer need marshal protection."

"True." He turned into his driveway.

Sam's house looked tidy and welcoming, the sun reflecting off the front window and chrysanthemum blooms waving in the breeze. This was what she'd been worried about. She loved Sam's home, and coming back made her yearn for something that couldn't be. The garage door rolled up, and Sam parked inside. Ellie slid from the vehicle with only a twinge from her knee while Sam retrieved her bags and purse from the back.

She walked through the yard littered with bright orange and brown leaves shed by the giant Oregon white oak. Her entire world had changed in the few weeks since she'd first come home with Sam.

The dogs were barking from inside. Sam opened the door and they scrambled out, tails wagging.

"Hey, beautiful babies." Her gaze rose to Sam's in alarm. "Are they starving? Have they been fed?"

"They're not starving. Before I went after you, I called Dalia. She took care of them and I swung by earlier this morning to feed them."

She looked at him sharply. "Before you went after me means you planned to get taken."

"We'll talk about it. Let's go in."

She followed Sam into the house, the dogs remaining outside. He took her bags up the back staircase and Ellie wandered around. The flowers she'd put in a vase on the window ledge had faded, the bananas in the fruit basket were now spotted. In the living room, Gumbie lay curled on the couch.

She scooped up the cat to hold on her lap as she sat. Gumbie began kneading her paws and purring. Water ran through the pipes upstairs and she guessed Sam was taking a shower. She should begin gathering her things together and pack her suitcase. As much as Sam said he wanted her to stay, she couldn't hang around. Two weeks of being off work was a long time. Maybe she'd fly to San Diego and spend that time with her mom and stepdad.

She'd gotten over Sam once before, she could do it again.

The other option was to simply talk to Sam and tell him how she felt. What if his feelings for her ran deeper than responsibility? The thought of opening herself, of being vulnerable, scared her like nothing else. But what did she have to lose? She could ditch her pride and lay herself open.

She closed her eyes and cuddled Gumbie, grateful for the cat's warm comfort.

***

Feeling a little more human after his shower, Sam stepped into the living room, his gaze immediately drawn to the woman sitting on the couch with the cat on her lap. The pensive expression on her face pulled at his heart.

"You okay?"

He sat next to her, shoulders touching. Gumbie jumped to the floor with her tail swishing.

Ellie turned her head to face him, eyes sober. "Sure, I'm fine."

He didn't believe that. He reached out a finger to loop a lock of hair behind her ear. "I've got to be careful where I touch. You have so many injuries I could hurt you."

They killed him, every one of the cuts and bruises she'd received because of her assignment to protect him.

"The only one that still hurts is my knee." She plucked at a thread on the rolled cuff of the sweatshirt she still wore. Without looking at him, she said, "You let Richard Jameson kidnap you."

"Heard that, did you?"

"No, guessed it." She met his gaze. "You didn't trust me to get myself out of that situation."

"They sent me a photo of you in handcuffs. I had no idea what they were doing to you or how badly you were hurt. I felt you'd have a better chance if I was with you."

"I was supposed to be protecting *you,* that was my job."

He chose his words carefully. "You're good at your job, but you're not invincible."

"I was working on a plan." She tugged harder on the thread. "I think the problem is that I'm a woman. Since I started this assignment, you've been resistant to me doing my job. You think you have to protect women, so therefore a woman can't protect you. Maybe it has something to do with losing your mom and stepmom the way you did. You think women need saving."

He shook his head. "Interesting, but not accurate. You're more than capable, and you were doing a fine job on your assignment. I'm still in one piece, aren't I? But it's not women in general protecting me that I have a problem with, it's you."

"Wow. At least you're honest."

He grasped the hand worrying the thread. He used his thumb to stroke her palm, then raised it to press a kiss in its center. "Try this for honest: I'm in love with you."

She went perfectly still, so still that he didn't think she was breathing. Not a good reaction.

"What did you say?"

He turned to face her. "I'm in love with you, Eleanor." He brought her hand to cover his heart. "You grabbed me right here and I haven't been the same since. I don't want to be the same." He huffed out a breath. "There's a part of me that's you, Ellie. Maybe it's corny, but I was only half alive until you came into my life."

She didn't move. He was sure he'd misjudged, that he'd laid himself bare and she would politely tell him to fuck off.

But in the next moment she beamed a beautiful smile and launched herself into his arms to rain kisses over his face. "It's not corny, it's beautiful. You're beautiful."

His heart swelled until he thought it would explode. He gathered her close for a long moment where he felt everything inside him settle, then, hands framing her cheeks, he held her back so he could see her eyes. "No matter how good a marshal you are, and you're damn good, I'll always try to protect you. It's impossible for me not to."

Her arms went around his neck and she buried her face in his shoulder. He heard a telltale sniffle and his heart clutched. "Are those bad tears or good tears?"

She shook her head. "They're happy tears."

He tugged her back again. A tear slid down her cheek and he wiped it with his thumb. "Happy tears are good, right?"

"Yeah, they're good. Better than good."

She shifted so she was sitting on his lap. He closed his eyes as she ran a hand through his hair and pressed her lips to his like she couldn't keep from touching him. That was okay because he pretty much felt the same.

His eyes opened when she took his hand and mimicked his move, laying it over her heart. "I had a thing for you thirteen years ago. It never entirely went away. When I met you again it slammed back into me like a tidal wave, and it hasn't let up since." A brief flash of vulnerability crossed her face, then disappeared. "I love you, Sam Creed."

He felt the grin splitting his face. "We should say that a lot, make up for lost time." He leaned forward and their lips met. "I love you."

She kissed him. "I love you."

With a nip to her bottom lip he held her away from him, trying to reach the pocket of his jeans. "Move it, woman. I need something."

Her eyes danced as she rubbed against the bulge in his jeans. "Maybe I need something, too."

"Ha ha. Don't distract me."

He pulled the small box from his pocket. Her gaze locked on it like it was a magnet and she did the frozen thing again. He was beginning to suspect that it was her shocked speechless reaction. He opened the box and held the ring between them. He was probably moving too fast, but with his love so huge this was the only possible course.

"A young man gave my aunt this ring when he asked her to marry him. She cherished it for the rest of her life." He steadied himself with a deep breath. "Will you wear it, Eleanor? Will you marry me? Will you love me forever?"

The blue of her eyes looked deep enough to drown in. "Yes, Sam. I'll marry you. I'll love you forever."

He slid the ring back on her finger where it belonged. She held out her hand so the emerald-cut diamond caught the light. "I thought we were done when you took back the ring."

"You insisted I take it back. Worried the hell out of me because our fake engagement felt real to me. But I needed to propose properly."

She leaned forward and their mouths met as they clung to each other.

When she moved against the erection nudging her thigh, he shook his head. "It kills me, but we can't."

"We can, and we should."

"No."

"Why not?"

"Concussion, remember?" She wiggled again and he groaned, then set her away from him. "I asked Ben. He said you have to limit your physical activity for a couple of weeks, and that includes sexual activity."

"You're joking."

"I would not joke about that."

"It's going to be a long two weeks."

***

Ellie and Bella sat next to each other at the small kitchen table while the men did the after-dinner cleanup. Ellie wasn't allowed to carry a dish or even fill the dishwasher, they said, for an entire week. For the moment, she was okay with that. Cleo and Tony lay on their bed, Cleo's soft eyes steady on Ellie. The little dog had remained close all afternoon.

Bella tapped Ellie with the toe of her suede boot. "I'm happy for you, El."

Ellie tipped her head on her friend's shoulder. "I'm happy for me, too." She held out her hand so the diamond caught the light. "See my ring? It's the most beautiful engagement ring ever."

"Agreed, it is the most beautiful engagement ring ever." Bella pulled out her phone and began scrolling. "I want to show you something." She tapped, then angled the screen.

Ellie peered at the image. Bella had caught the moment after Sam had first put the ring on Ellie's finger all those weeks ago. The emotion evident as they looked into each other's eyes jolted her. "It looks like we're already in love."

"It does. You were. I'm framing this photo as an engagement gift."

"Aw, thanks."

A knock sounded. Ellie stood and crossed to the front door to look through the peephole. A young man stood under the porch light, head bowed.

"Hold on." Sam came behind her and bent forward to look through the peephole. "I don't recognize him." Seth and Linc joined them. Sam draped his arm around Ellie's shoulder as he opened the door. The young man took a step back, his Adam's apple bobbing. He probably had a reason to be nervous, because two of the tall men looking at him were armed and wore badges.

The resemblance struck her, and Ellie guessed his identity.

"Jeremy Finster?"

A nervous gaze darted to her. "Yes, ma'am."

Linc stepped onto the porch. "Jeremy, I'm Deputy US Marshal Lincoln Jameson. I want you to turn around, spread your feet with your toes pointed outward, and lace your fingers behind your head."

He complied. Linc gripped his hands and did the pat down. "He's clean."

Linc allowed him to turn around and face them. "Why are you here?"

He cleared his throat. "I want to apologize to Judge Creed."

His hand still on Ellie's shoulder, Sam nodded to the others. "I've got this." After a long look, Linc returned to the house and closed the door.

Gaze direct, Sam said, "Well?"

Jeremy cleared his throat. "I'm sorry, sir. I screwed up. I should never have messed up your yard or thrown that flashbang."

"This is my fiancée, Ellie. If it had been only the yard, I wouldn't be so pissed. But Ellie's everything to me, and she got hurt with the flashbang. We're lucky the injuries weren't more serious."

Jeremy's Adam's apple bobbed again and he shifted his gaze to Ellie. "I'm sorry, ma'am." She couldn't see anything other than remorse on his face. "I was reading stuff online. It messed up my thinking. My dad talked to me, made me look at things different." He looked at Sam. "I know Dad has some other trouble at the courthouse, but he didn't know what I did until the cops came. I knew it was wrong when I did it, but I was dumb, and I know I'm still in trouble with the law. No matter what happens, I'm sorry."

Ellie nodded. "Apology accepted."

Sam extended his hand. "Apology accepted."

Jeremy looked relieved and shook Sam's hand. "Thanks."

They watched the young man walk up the driveway. Sam pulled Ellie into him, his chin resting on top of her head,

"That was hard for him," Ellie murmured.

"It should be hard. I'm glad he had the guts to do it."

"Me too."

Contentment seeped through her as they stood, arms around each other. Ellie tipped back her head. "I really like your house. Am I going to move in with you?"

"Is the house all you really like?"

"No. I really like you, too, Sam Creed."

"Hell yeah, you're moving in with me. Then we've got a wedding to plan."

He leaned forward and Ellie felt the promise of his kiss burst through her like a bright shining star.

ABOUT THE AUTHOR

National Readers' Choice Award winner for her novel, *Solitary Man*, Diane Benefiel has been an avid reader all her life. She enjoys a wide range of genres, from westerns to fantasy to mysteries, but romance has always been a favorite. She writes what she loves best to read – emotional, heart-gripping romantic suspense novels. She likes writing romantic suspense because she can put the hero and heroine in all sorts of predicaments that they have to work together to overcome.

A native Southern Californian, Diane enjoys nothing better than summer. For a high school history teacher, summer means a break from teenagers, and summer allows her to spend her early mornings immersed in her current writing project. With both kids living out of the house, in addition to writing, she enjoys camping and gardening with her husband.

Diane loves hearing from her readers.

Website: dianebenefiel.com
Twitter: twitter.com/dianebenefiel
Instagram: diane_benefiel
Pinterest: diane_benefiel
Facebook: facebook.com/DianeBenefielRomance
BookBub: bookbub.com/authors/diane-benefiel
Goodreads: goodreads.com/author/show/8075321.Diane_Benefiel
Newsletter: https://landing.mailerlite.com/webforms/landing/n1i2u8

www.BOROUGHSPUBLISHINGGROUP.com

If you enjoyed this book, please write a review. Our authors appreciate the feedback, and it helps future readers find books they love. We welcome your comments and invite you to send them to info@boroughspublishinggroup.com. Follow us on Facebook, Twitter and Instagram, and be sure to sign up for our newsletter for surprises and new releases from your favorite authors.

Are you an aspiring writer? Check out www.boroughspublishinggroup.com/submit and see if we can help you make your dreams come true.